ALIEN CAPTIVE

A SCI FI WARRIOR ROMANCE

LEE SAVINO
GOLDEN ANGEL

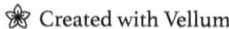

DISCLAIMER:

The authors are not responsible for any actual alien abductions that may result as a consequence of your purchase of this book.

1

D awn

IT WAS a dark and stormy night.

I know, such a cliché, but it is. Dark and rainy with rumbles of thunder in the distance like the sky is growling. I curl up under an old quilt my grandma made and hope the weather quiets soon so I can sleep. The power went out earlier, so the only light is from my e-reader propped up on my knees.

I swipe and read the next page in my current book obsession: *Tsenturion Tales: The Captive Bride.*

The Tribute takes her first step out of the Jabolian capsule onto the Tsenturion deck.

Lines of soldiers in full battle dress line her route to the bridge. They stand at attention to honor their High Commander as he accepts the human female as his Tribute and bride.

As the Tribute approaches the great High Commander, the Bride Trainer around her waist comes to life. Activated in the presence of her new master, the Trainer ensures she bonds to him right away. A low vibration begins between her legs, stimulating her sex. The Trainer continues to brew her pleasure as she comes onto the bridge and kneels to greet the High Commander. It will stimulate her as long as her master desires. Only he holds the key.

The wind howls in the eaves as I reach "The End." *Damn.* I was hoping these books would get me through the night.

Thunder crashes overhead, and I shudder, taking deep, even breaths, the way I instruct my students to do when I'm teaching one of my yoga classes. My e-reader is still at half - power, and though I just finished the Tsenturion Trilogy, I already want to read them again. I press my thighs together against the ache the last book created, my mind drifting back to some of my favorite scenes. What can I say? These books are so hot.

There are three books in this story, all of them about a human woman who gets sucked through a portal to an alien galaxy, where she's married off to a "Tsenturion Master," a huge, muscular warrior who sees to her every—*ahem*—sexual need. The Tsenturions are a space-faring race without a home, without a planet, and without enough females, so women are taken from other planets and given to them as mates. The story's kinda kinky and a little unclear on some things—like who fetches the women to be the Tsenturions' mates and who the Tsenturions are fighting. It's pretty much focused on the mating aspect, which is how I ended up getting sucked into the story. Women are so scarce, they're treated with extra care but also trained to be responsive to their Masters' needs. It's pretty awesome. Most of the training comes through rewards of multiple orgasms.

A flood of light blinds me as my e-reader begins to glow...

Dammit. I shake the device. It better not break. It's the only thing that will get me through this bad weather.

I hate storms. I never met my dad; he was killed in a tornado before I was born. My mom died in a storm when I was four—she ran off the wet road in bad weather. My grandma raised me, until she passed from brain cancer last year—again, during a bad storm.

Storms are bad luck.

Another rumble of thunder shakes the house like deep, evil laughter. The storm is getting louder, and the wind picks up, the rain battering my windows with a loud clatter. I snuggle deeper into my blankets, ignoring the tightness in my chest. Ignoring the little voice inside my head which always gets louder during storms, insisting something terrible is going to happen. I'm safe in my bed. Nothing can happen to me. The worst thing that can happen is my e-reader breaking. Right?

I shake my device, willing it to turn back on. The glow from the stupid thing is growing brighter, the color changing somehow, as if the screen is a crystal reflecting back a hundred million rainbows into my eyes. I can't figure out what's wrong with it, but I can't look away.

The storm grows louder, the thunder roaring in my ears, and the glow from my e-reader has turned into a ball of light in my hands. There's a tugging sensation on my body, as if I'm in a wind tunnel and the wind is so roughly fast that it's tearing the skin from my body.

I open my mouth to scream, but there's no air.

Rings of light and color burst ahead of me, and darkness is all around. I start to panic, but I don't have much time because the pain is excruciating, as if I'm being crushed, flayed, and pulled in twenty different directions all at the same time. Then...nothing.

I DON'T HURT.

Thank God. Not only do I not hurt anymore, but gone is the patter of rain, the howl of the wind, and the loud rumbles of thunder. It's almost blissfully silent. Although... there is a strange hum. Very quiet, very subtle.

Frowning, I open my eyes.

My heart stops.

This is not my bed.

"Greetings, Dawn Cahill."

A face looms over mine, but, like the bed and the salutation, it's wrong. Eyes, nose, mouth, they look *almost* right, the way CGI looks almost human, but there's something wrong enough that the more human a CGI creation looks, the more wrong it feels because it's not quite right. The skin doesn't help either; it's flesh colored but almost translucent looking, shiny in a way no human would ever be.

I scream, trying to jerk back against the bed that's not mine, and the being—whatever it is—flinches, losing its shape so the face and head melt away, the body turning into a large, amorphous blob. The only thing that doesn't change is the color. I scream louder, not only because watching a humanoid-looking thing turn into a non-human thing is freaking terrifying, but because when I try to scuttle away, I find I'm secured to the bed around my waist. I'm also completely naked and completely panicking.

"Dawn Cahill! Dawn Cahill! Stop! Calm down!" It's the same voice, although I can't tell how the creature is speaking without a mouth, but I'm freaking out way too much to listen to it.

Calm down? Seriously?

I'm naked, tied to a bed that's not mine, and there's a *thing* speaking to me. If there was ever a time to panic, it's now.

The thing makes a sound like it's irritated, and the next thing I know, there's a puff of some kind of smelly air in my face and—

Blackness.

~

"SECOND ATTEMPT at communication with the Hu-man." The voice says 'human' in a weird way, like it's never said 'human' before. "Dawn Cahill?"

"Mmm?" I feel calm. Rested. Maybe a little loopy. I open my eyes. There's...well, it's not a human looking down at me, even if it vaguely looks like one. I remember that now, but the memory and my panic seem very far away. "What *are* you?"

The thing's expression doesn't change. The facial features might be vaguely human, but they apparently only have one setting. Kinda constipated looking, actually.

"I am Frllil, a Jabols Luminary."

I blink. "I know you spoke words, but none of them made sense."

The thing makes a weird trilling noise. "I believe the closest thing to my profession in your vocabulary would be a scientist."

"And you're an alien?"

"I believe that is the correct terminology you would assign me."

"Holy crap. Um...why aren't I freaking out more?" Because I should be, and logically I knew that, but I couldn't quite work up the energy. I was definitely becoming a little agitated, but nothing like how I'd been before.

"After your poor reaction to me earlier, I concluded we would be able to communicate more effectively if you were given a sedative." The complete lack of expression and intonation in the thing's voice was starting to creep me out. Well, sort of. As creeped out as I could be while whatever he'd given me was influencing my reactions. Whatever the sedative was, it was powerful.

"Oh." I did have to admit, in a lot of ways this was much preferable to my earlier freak out. Information was good, panic was bad.

Okay Dawn, you've been hijacked by an alien—that can melt into a blob, I wasn't questioning that at all—and he's a scientist and he has you tied down to a bed in what is, presumably, his spaceship. He's also made it so you can't panic. That's good, right? Because if I was panicking, I wouldn't be able to figure out how to escape, but since I'm calm, I should definitely be able to. So really, he's already started working against himself and for me...right?

"Congratulations, Dawn Cahill, your interest in and completion of the Tsenturion trilogy made you eligible to be a Tsenturion Tribute. You have been chosen from your people as the first Tribute in the Tsenturion's mating program."

I blink. "Um...what? You stopped making sense again."

Or to put it another way, he was making too much sense, but my brain didn't want to believe what he was saying. Because I'm pretty sure that sentence was *directly* from the incredibly exciting, sexy, and *terrifying in reality* books I'd just finished reading on my e-reader right before it had started glowing, and then I'd started to hurt, and then I'd passed out and woken up here…

"Dawn Cahill, you will calm down," Frllil said. He isn't commanding though, he sounds almost nervous and whiny.

"I'm not mating with you!" I squeak, trying to shrink away from him and only then remembering that I was secured to the bed. My heart is starting to beat faster again. My fear feels strangely distant, but it's rising. The thought of mating with freaky Frllil is overriding my artificial calm.

"I am a Jabols," Frllil reminds me impatiently. "Jabols do not have mates. Our procreation is much more sensible and less messy and requires no outside partner. You will be the mate of a Tsenturion, High Commander Gavrill."

Okay, I'm not mating freaky Frllil, I'm mating a Tsenturion warrior. An alien species I'd thought was entirely fictional. An alien species which, according to the trilogy I'd read, was made up of huge, hulking warrior mercenaries with metallic golden skin, huge cocks, and a penchant for spanking their mates.

"Nope. Nope, nope, nope, nope, nope. Whatever trippy drug ride this is, I want off! Do you hear me?! I want *off*! I'm not doing this! This is fucked up! I don't care what you spray me—"

The gas gets me right in the face again.

I BLINK. Yawn. Try to figure out why the lights are so bright.

Oh right. Captured. Alien spaceship.

This is the third time I've woken up on it.

Any hope that I'm on some loopy drug trip or that this is

all a terrible dream is fading away. I wait for the rise of inevitable hopelessness, but all I feel is numb.

"Dawn Cahill, you will be calm."

Is it my imagination, or is Frlil starting to sound really petulant?

"Yeah, yeah," I yawn. Not super interested in being knocked out again. "I'm calm. Look, I know I read the books and—okay, they were pretty hot—but I'm not really interested in being an alien bride. I have a life on Earth, you know. I have..." My voice trails off. I was about to say *people who care about me,* but that's not as true as I would like to be. I definitely used to have people who cared about me. Now... well, my yoga students would be upset when I didn't show up to teach the classes. Maybe.

"I have personally examined your life-profile, Dawn Cahill," says Frlil. Either I'm projecting, or I'm getting better at interpreting his emotions, but to me he sounds kind of smug now. "You are what your race defines as a 'loner.' You have no strong emotional attachments or connections. You have no family, your friendships are shallow, and no one in your life will notice that you have gone missing. The only attachment you currently display is to the residence you inhabited. There is no reason you could not easily begin a life elsewhere with little adversity."

Wow.

"Brutal, Frlil," I mutter under my breath.

"I do not understand this comment."

"Don't worry about it," I say dryly, a little louder. Even heavily sedated and mostly numb, it's still not exactly easy to hear how lonely and sad my life sounds. My deepest attachment is to my house? Yeah...that's probably true. But it's my gran's house. That's a real connection. Still...his summation of my friendships is pretty on point, sadly. Lots of acquaintances, no true friends. My truest friend in years had been my e-book reader.

And now it has betrayed me.

With friends like that, who needs enemies?

"Okay, so what now?" I ask tiredly, trying to prod my tired brain into remembering exactly what came next in the Tsenturion books. Something to do with an examination and changing...

HORROR SLIDES THROUGH ME. Distant horror. Like my emotions are on the other side of the glass wall. But I know I should be horrified.

"What have you done to me?" I whisper, looking down my body. It didn't look any different. But would I know? "In the book, the women, they went through...changes."

"Yes," Frllil says. "I have implanted a translator and made other improvements. Your cellular regeneration rate has been increased considerably, resulting in an extended lifespan equivalent to that of a Tsenturion warrior."

"What does that *mean?*" I can't help but feel a little dizzy. Should I be excited? Horrified? Longer life, that's desirable... but the circumstances and quality of life are important to exactly how desirable. "How much longer?"

Frllil sighs. "You will remain calm."

"If you don't tell me how much longer I'm going to live, I can't make any promises," I snap, though I don't want to get zapped again.

"Approximately eleven hundred Earth years." Frllil eyes me as I grab the edges of the bed I'm lying on, my chest tight with shock. Horror definitely seems to be winning out.

Approximately eleven hundred years as an alien's mate, his Tribute. And I still don't know what that means, except the descriptions from the book which I'm now hoping were greatly exaggerated. "Breathe, Dawn Cahill."

Frllil makes a trilling sound again and moves closer. I look down and realize he's on some sort of platform that holds his blob-like body off the floor. A floating platform. An alien modifying my body. If I wasn't sedated, I'd be out of my mind with panic.

I let my head fall back and suck in lungfuls of air. Frllil hovers close. If I didn't know any better, I'd say the amorphous blob looks vaguely displeased.

"According to my records, breathing is an innate function your body performs automatically. I should not have to instruct you."

"Oh, so you're the expert?"

Another trilling sound, this one pleased. "I am. I based my studies on the Tsenturion form and finding a compatible race to supply females. I received a commendation. My superiors put me in charge of the Tribute program."

"Okay, Frllil," I try his name out, mimicking the rolling trill that the alien makes. "I'm new to all this. This Tribute thing—walk me through it."

"But you know of the Tribute mating program. You accepted our communication and have read the manual."

"Manual?" Light dawns. "The e-reader and the books, you mean? You sent it?"

"Yes. After basic monitoring, you were selected for further study."

I remember the day the e-reader showed up in my mailbox. I was so pleased, I didn't stop to wonder where it came from. I figured I'd won a contest I'd forgotten I'd entered.

"It was calibrated to unlock only for you. Then it monitored your responses."

"My responses... to the stories?" I blush so hard, I'm afraid my face will catch fire. The Tsenturion stories were so hot; by page three, I was reading them one-handed. "The stories about the Tsenturions—that's the manual?"

"Yes. The manual served a dual purpose: to test you and start your training as Tribute. You'll be pleased to know you are the first to pass the test, Dawn Cahill. Your eagerness to study the manual and responses to it made it clear you were perfect for the mating program."

"Oh," I say weakly.

"You are welcome. I am pleased the process went so well. It was my design." Frllil floats away. It's a good thing I'm strapped to this table, otherwise I would fall off. The e-reader. The stupid e-reader. If only I hadn't read the stories so many times... if only they hadn't turned me on so much... but that isn't exactly knowing consent either.

Before I can start to get angry, Frllil is talking to me again.

"Dawn Cahill, you will give attention," Frllil instructs. He's down at the foot of my bed, beside a floating piece of what looks like glass. As I watch, an image appears on the glass—it's a screen playing a movie. "It is time for you to learn your duties as a Tribute." The image comes into focus, showing the nose of a huge silver spaceship.

"This is a Tsenturion ship. The Tsenturions are a warrior race, sworn to protect the galaxy. They live on a fleet of spacecrafts, as they have no home planet."

"They used to though," I say, reciting what I know from the books. "It was destroyed by an enemy race. Only a few warrior males survived, which is why they needed Earth brides."

"Very good, Dawn Cahill. You remember." Frllil makes a movement, and the image on the screen changes. He reminds me of an adjunct professor I once had, a nerdy guy who barely looked at the class, preferring to simply recite his lessons from a slide deck.

The image on screen changes, and I gasp.

2

D awn

"THESE ARE TSENTURIONS," Frllil says. Three huge figures fill the screen. They're huge, with Arnold Schwarzenegger-sized muscles under skin that shimmers like it's made of metal. Their faces are covered by some sort of helmet. At least I hope it's a helmet.

"Are they wearing... armor?"

"Yes. The suits are Jabol-design. The suits are protective and enhance the Tsenturions' physiology. In addition to being strong enough to withstand most weapons, the suits regulate their bodily functions for optimum lifespan."

"Will I get one of them?"

This time, Frllil's trilling sounds amused. "No, Dawn Cahill. You are a Tribute. You have no need to withstand weapons. Your Tsenturion master requires you to be accessible." He turns back to the screen, and the image zooms in on the central figure. "Besides, Jabol technology has advanced. Your body has been modified without need of a suit. You will receive a training belt before the presentation ceremony. During the ceremony, it will imprint to the High Commander. He will use it to modify your responses and prime you for him."

I barely take in all of this. I'm too busy studying the sharp, helmet clad face and massive body of the figure on screen. After a second, parts of the helmet retract, revealing a hard-boned face with a strong jaw and glittering eyes. His facial features are pretty humanoid; two eyes, one mouth, one nose. His nose is broad, and his jaw is squarer than most humans I've seen, but other than the golden sheen of his skin, he could blend in with the human race. The shiny gold of his skin contrasts with the silver-grey of the armor, making him look incredibly exotic.

Unfortunately, the armor doesn't pull back anymore, so I have no idea what he looks like elsewhere. My eyes instinctively drop to his groin, and I can't help but think about the Tsenturion books I was reading and wonder exactly how accurate they were...

FRLLIL MAKES a sound to catch my attention, and I pretend I wasn't checking out the Tsenturion's crotch.

"This is High Commander Gavrill. He commands the entire Tsenturion fleet."

I shift in my bonds, feeling both frightened and a little aroused, but I don't look away. I memorize the rest of his body. Forewarned is forearmed after all. A row of short spines protrudes from his forearms, but maybe that's the suit. The 'manual' definitely didn't mention any death-spikes. As I watch, the suit color darkens from silvery-gray to deep copper.

"The suit responds to changes in mood. You will want to pay attention and modify your behavior when the suit darkens. A lighter color means he is pleased. You should feel honored to be chosen as the first Tribute to the Tsenturions, as you have been paired with The High Commander Gavrill."

"Hang on," I begin when something pricks my neck. "Ow!" I writhe in my bonds. A machine stands beside my bed, a needle extended on one of its mechanical arms. "What the hell was that?"

"A stimulant," Frllil says matter-of-factly. "It encourages the correct response to your Tsenturion master."

"My what?" I'm still jerking as much as the restraints allow. A prick of pain is supposed to encourage my response? I'm not reassured by that or Frllil's use of the word "master." My brain is starting to send all sorts of warning signals to me. Frllil and the picture of the High Commander have distracted me so much that I'd forgotten exactly how, um... demanding the Tsenturions were in the books. That had to be embellishment though... right?

"Your master. Tsenturions have strict protocol when it comes to their Tributes. Do not worry, the High Commander will train you. It is part of the bonding process.

Train me!? I'd scream, but my mouth is too busy hanging open. Then again, I know exactly what Frllil is referring to. The books on the e-reader made it pretty clear—the Tsenturions treated their women like a BDSM-practicing dom would treat a hardcore submissive. Maybe even a sexual slave. In the books, it was super-hot. I loved the thought of an alien dom training his bride, rewarding her with orgasms and punishing her with spankings. Not to put too fine a point on it, the stories... uh... got me off. Big time. Apparently, I'd responded *too* well while an alien life form was watching.

How mortifying.

"In the future, your training belt will prime you. We must use primitive methods for now." Frllil motions to the needle.

"What did you stick me with?"

"Pay attention," Frllil instructs. The screen images change to a long angle view of the ship. Two rows of armored Tsenturions line a path right up to a gangplank. At the top stand four figures. The High Commander is in the front, with two hulking giants on either side. A smaller figure stands behind him. As the image zooms in on Gavrill, I notice my body heating up. Not naturally like it had before when I'd been checking him out and wondering what was behind the groin armor... no, this is more intense. More frightening.

I'd press my legs together if they weren't held down as my lower body comes to life, a tingle starting between my thighs. When Gavrill fills the screen again, arousal blooms like a mushroom cloud, filling my head with screaming pressure, stealing my breath. My nipples pucker, and I can feel my pussy spasm emptily, the tingle turning to a full-on throbbing ache to be filled. It's the horniest I've ever been in my life, and it scares the heck out of me.

"What's happening?"

"You are being primed," Frllil says. "This is the proper response to your master."

"No," I grit out, clenching my fists. It's no use. The ache between my legs intensifies. Wet trickles down my leg. I moan, shuddering and trying to reject the feelings stirring inside of me, the need that's growing... looking at the High

Commander again, I whimper as my pussy quivers. I feel like I could orgasm just from looking at him long enough, which is crazy, but... fuck me if I don't want to.

The image zooms out, and the pressure lessens. I come down from the heights, panting.

"*No.*" Despite myself, I moan. I'm not used to being denied.

"Only your master can trigger climax. Until you meet him, you can only be primed."

My pussy throbs, angry at being denied.

"This is messed up," I mutter. My fingers twitch. If I wasn't tied down, I'd show him just how well I can trigger my own damn climax, thank you very much. I glare at Frllil, who completely ignores my reaction. He's way too pleased to let something as *insignificant* as my ire affect him. I'm really starting to hate Frllil.

"That was most excellent, first Tribute. I knew I'd chosen well. The Commander will be pleased."

Something pricks my neck again. Frllil moves away, and the lights start to dim, his voice sounding like it's coming from a distance. I struggle to keep my eyes open, but it's useless. "You will sleep now. In a few cycles, you will be fitted for your training belt. After that, the Tsenturions will arrive for the mating ceremony, and you will meet your new master."

∾

GAVRILL

THE BORAL NEBULAE is a thing of beauty, cloudy rings interspersed with patches of glittering dust, like gems in space.

Our ship hovers on the edge of the outermost ring. Waiting. Watching.

Preliminary scan complete, the bridge screen flashes. We're all silent as my warriors study the data collected from three days of analysis. Looking for the proof of our enemy. The reason we're here. If we can find them, and if we can get to them once we do.

"There." I tap the screen, and it zooms in on a dark patch behind a particularly thick cloud of dust. "The Vgotha ship."

The ship's shield hid any heat signature but couldn't escape a density scan. Triumph surges.

Anticipation hums through the deck as our armor darkens, a display of our high emotion and readiness for battle. There is not one of us who would not die to see our mission through, though it has already been a long mission and the years stretch endlessly before us before it is complete. The Vgothas destroyed our entire planet, the whole population, in one day. No survivors... except for us. It was their only mistake.

They couldn't have known that our ship was late returning home for the festival. Everyone knew that Tsenturions returned to Tsentur for the Mating Festival. It should have been a complete genocide. Instead, we came home to a planet of rubble, of melted slag... there were no bodies to bury, the surface had been scoured clean. We still didn't know what weapon they had used or how they had done it, but it didn't matter.

We carried the only knowledge we needed with us—their identity.

"Carrion scum," my second, Bogdan, mutters. "They cannot hide, not even behind a cloud of their own mercenary stench. Commander, we must engage." His rage is greater than mine, for he'd not only had a very large family of siblings, all of which were now gone, but he'd been ready to attend the Festival and find a mate.

But our people were dead, and we were alone. The Jabols had promised to find us new mates, but none of us are all that hopeful.

We concentrate on our vengeance instead.

I keep studying the scan readings. I will not rush into battle, as my second wishes. I am the High Commander, and I will not be reckless, even if it is to wipe out our enemies. Not if it means the destruction of my ships, and with them, the last of my race. The Boral Nebulae is dangerous, and we cannot rush in. Somehow the Vgothas made it through the rings, evading the debris and moving belt of rocks and radiation, but I cannot immediately see the path they used, though we have now located them.

As they remain completely stationary, I can only assume they only know one route in and out of the minefield the nebula creates. They will wait for us to leave... unless we can outwait them or outwit them.

"Commander," Arkdhem, commander of our scout ships, appears on a lesser screen. His armor glitters bright, a reflection of his mood. Surprisingly, his usual stoic expression is not in place, he looks almost excited. "I received a hail from Frllil. They have payment ready for us."

"Tell them to leave it at the waystation, as usual." Every twenty semicycles, the Jabols reimburse our people for protecting them. They provide weapons, foodstuffs, ship supplies and technology while we guard their planets from the thieving Vgothas and fulfill our need for justice at the same time. A symbiotic relationship that has lasted over a thousand years.

"It's not the usual payment." Arkdhem's suit shimmers with excitement. Curiosity lightens my armor.

"Then what is it? Make your report," Bogdan snaps, his suit flashing red streaks of annoyance through the black. He is completely focused on our mission, as always. His determination to wipe out the Vgothas nears obsession. I am nearly as eager, but I sometimes think Bogdan would be willing to throw our lives away if it meant taking out *one* Vgotha ship.

That is why he is second and I am the High Commander. Cool logic rules me, rather than emotion.

"We have found a Vgotha ship," I inform my third, because Bogdan is correct—our priority is the enemy. Whatever the new shipment of supplies is, it can wait. "I am determining if we will engage."

"Apologies, Commander. I would not have interrupted, but you ordered me to report as soon as I heard the Tribute was ready."

My suit flashes from black to bronze to silver, reacting to my surprise. I am not prone to such displays of emotion, but this is a momentous occasion. Hope claws its way up my chest.

"The Jabols have found a suitable match?" I keep my voice even, but I cannot stop my suit from reacting, a shimmering silver that was echoed around the bridge by the listening crew. I am not the only one affected by Arkdhem's announcement. Only Bogdan's armor remains firmly black, and he glances at me, grimacing with annoyance at the interruption.

"Indeed, Commander. A far-off system, accessible only through a *direth* wormhole." Arkdhem uses the Jabol word for 'small and almost unstable.' A journey through such a wormhole is very dangerous, causing immediate ire—not just in myself, but in many of those who look the most hopeful. That was not good news.

"They risked the Tribute?"

"It was the only way. Apparently, this life form is the only one suitable to our race. The Jabols report that the initial training is proceeding nicely, and she will be ready soon."

Bogdan snorts derisively. "No matter how they train her, she still won't be Tsenturion."

Arkdhem says nothing. His glowing skinsuit relays his happiness. The good-natured warrior won't be baited, no matter how much Bogdan tries to pick a fight. The two of them often clash, their natural competition often creating the best ideas for me to use.

"Commander," Bogdan says in a voice that drips both annoyance and disgust. "Surely you are not thinking of abandoning our post just to dally with... the *Tribute*." From the tone of his voice, he might as well have said 'animal.' A mate does not figure into his priorities at all. "The lead Vgotha ship is almost in our hands. We do not have time for distractions."

A thousand tsencycles of need.

No obvious route to the Vgotha ship.

The promise of a future for my crew.

It is an easy choice.

"Preserving the continuance of our race is not a 'distraction,'" I observe. Arkdhem's suit beams, and there are more silver flashes around the bridge. Bogdan's teeth are practically grinding together. "Besides, entering the nebula is too dangerous at this juncture. Rather than sitting and waiting to see whether we or the Vgothas have more supplies, we will see to our future. Third, inform the Jabols that we are on our way to collect the Tribute. She should be made ready for the imprinting ceremony."

Bogdan grimaces but doesn't argue. Once I have made a

decision, he knows to fall in line. With a flourish, Arkdhem salutes and flashes off screen.

"Second, set a course for the Jabol's ex-planetary lab. The third moon, I believe, of the eighth planet in the Jabolian System."

"Aye, Commander," Bogdan grunts, even as his suit darkens blacker than the deep space around us.

~

Dawn

CLAD in the ceremonial mating robes, the Tribute awaits her master. Her quarters are lush, decorated in the pale colors of Earth's sunrise. She lays down on the sleeping platform, letting the robe open to display her body for her master's delight. As she waits, she breathes deeply, letting her body start to prime.

The door opens. The High Commander enters, his armor shimmering gold, growing brighter when he sees her. The Tribute doesn't move but watches him approach. When he steps onto the sleeping platform, the Bride Trainer fitted around her hips and between her legs hums to life...

"Dawn Cahill, you will wake up." Cool air caresses my face. I open my eyes as the travel pod opens, letting in the light. I recognize Frllil's voice.

That fucker.

The Bride Trainer is a device like a chastity belt, wrapping around my pelvis, fitted tightly to my skin around my hips and between my legs. It's made from the same material that makes up the Tsenturion suits—soft as cloth, tough as metal, pliable as rubber. From what I understand, there's some nanotechnology involved that binds the belt to my skin. It's self-cleaning. It's also smart enough to thwart my attempts to pretend I'm going to the bathroom so that I can touch myself. When I need to go, it opens *just enough* for me to do so and not a millimeter more.

According to Frllil, only my new alien master can unlock it, although he might choose to keep it on indefinitely.

I've already been through some 'training.' Every cycle—the alien equivalent of a day—Frllil plays a new movie for me, usually clips of the Tsenturions. Whenever the High Commander walks onscreen, the Trainer buzzes to life. It vibrates in all the right places, stimulating me to the point of orgasm and holding me there. No amount of whining, wailing or begging will push me over the edge.

And, like a chastity belt, it keeps my fingers from my aching pussy.

"Your pleasure is no longer yours," Frllil scolds me as I writhe and beg for release. "It belongs to the Commander."

I don't think I've ever hated anyone as much as I hate Frllil. Life on Earth seems distant. I can't even concentrate on missing it, no matter how much I hate what's happening to me. It's like my brain has been hijacked by the unfulfilled needs of my body. There is no future, there is no past, there is only the ever-aching awful need of the present. The early days, when I'd tried to use my yoga training to calm my body, seem like a distant memory.

Earth is even farther away. According to Frllil, it's not like I have much to miss anyway. Sadly, he seems to be right. Other than my love for my grandmother's house, there was nothing holding me there, nothing to cling to other than my anger at how I've been picked up and what I'm being trained for. Even that's hard to hold onto though, when the demands of my body have become far more urgent than anything else.

I know I'm being brainwashed by Frllil's training, but I can't seem to stop it. Self-awareness will only get you so far.

So as the pod opens and a cool computer voice instructs me to stand and exit, I'm a hot mess. Nervous, distracted and frustrated with the never-ending loop of arousal.

Not to mention excited because, for the first time in days —maybe even weeks, I've kind of lost track—I might finally find completion. According to Frllil, the High Commander is the only one who can give me the climax I'm so desperate for, and that's who I'm here to meet. There's some tiny bit of self-preservation in me telling me to run, to look for an escape...but it's miniscule compared to the part of me practically sobbing for completion.

As I step away from the Jabolian capsule, onto the vast platform in front of the Tsenturion ship, my legs shaking with both nerves and need, I catch sight of my reflection in the silvery pod. The new and improved Dawn Cahill looks stunningly beautiful. In the past few cycles, I've been groomed, plucked and prodded until every inch of me is perfect. My blonde hair is a shining cape that hangs past my shoulders, and my skin looks like it's glowing next to the golden color of the filmy robe I was dressed in. Even my hazel eyes seem larger, brighter.

The door on the side of the Tsenturion ship opens, and out march rows of soldiers in two straight lines. They're intimidating as hell—their suits molded to their powerful forms, shining silver in the sunlight. Their shoulders are as broad as a doorway, and they're all at least half a foot taller than me. As I wait to see Gavrill in the flesh, my body quivers like it's been trained to do. Just seeing his soldiers has my pussy creaming and nipples puckering under the thin robe.

My mouth is dry. Fear? Anticipation? Excitement? An unholy combination of all three?

In a murmur beside me, the Jabolian capsule orders me to walk between the two lines of soldiers and present myself to my master.

My pussy clenches at the word 'master' without any prompting from the damn belt. I'm the kinky version of Pavlov's dog, but knowing that doesn't help me.

My filmy robes dance around my legs as I move forward, feeling almost like I'm sleep-walking. This whole situation is surreal. I don't look left or right but keep my eyes on the dark entrance to the ship. I'm afraid if I look directly at a soldier, I'll faint dead away. I would never have considered myself the fainting type, but I know that looking at them will be too much for me. Make it too real, too soon.

The movies Frllil showed me explained why there were no Tsenturion women. Long ago, a thousand years as Earth would calculate it, an enemy race called the Vgothas were persecuting the Jabols. Decimating them, determined to wipe them from existence. No one knew precisely why. They'd come out of nowhere and begun hunting Jabols like it was sport.

The peaceful scientist race, desperate to survive, created an alliance with the Tsenturions. While the Tsenturions weren't as technologically advanced as the Jabols, they had military might that the Jabols could never hope to achieve. It was a good alliance... but as soon as the Vgothas realized they were outmatched by the Tsenturions, they'd done something no one could have expected. Something so heinous, so brutal, it defied imagination.

They'd targeted Tsentur, the entire planet, and blown it up during a Tsenturion mating festival, a week dedicated to their future as a species. It was utterly horrific, and I hadn't been able to keep from feeling sorry for the Tsenturions. The few hundred remaining soldiers were alone in the universe now—no families, no mates, no home. They were even more alone than I was.

That didn't make any of what was happening to me less anxiety-inducing.

I swallow hard. The commander is waiting for me, his warriors on either side—none of them have even seen a woman compatible with their species in over a thousand years. That's why the Jabols changed their alliance slightly and began looking for Tributes instead of giving the Tsenturions more technology.

That's why Frllil searched for, and found, me.

I might be projecting when I think I see hope in all of their nearly-blank expressions, but it would make sense. The air seems to be hanging heavy with expectation. I've been over this so many times with Frllil that it seems almost like déjà vu to actually be doing it, like I've already done it a million times before... like this is the moment my entire life has been moving towards. It's like the book I was reading when I was taken, although that seems very long ago and very far away.

My present is my overwhelming need to orgasm, and the knowledge that I will finally—*finally*—get satisfaction draws me onwards. To the ship, to my future... to *him*.

The words from my book—*the manual*—flit through my mind.

The Tribute takes her first step out of the Jabolian capsule onto the Tsenturion deck.

Lines of soldiers in full battle dress line her route to the bridge. They stand at attention to honor their High Commander as he accepts the human female as his Tribute and bride.

It's just like the stories on the mysterious e-reader I read over and over in my attic bedroom... and now I'm here, living them in real life, about to meet my new alien 'master.' My legs wobble a little as I step forward and start climbing the ramp to the Tsenturion ship.

I'm halfway up when he appears. Gavrill, Tsenturion High Commander, the leader of an entire alien race. The male I've been trained to respond to, and the sight of him in the flesh takes my breath away in an automatic response. My legs tremble, and my knees go weak. I'm on the verge of orgasm just from seeing him. My breath is coming more shallowly and more rapidly, making me feel almost light-headed. I can feel my clit actually swelling against the unmoving trainer. It would take the lightest touch, the brush of a feather to make me actually come.

His armored suit shimmers in the light, a gun-metal grey. I try to remember what that color means. Not happy, but not sad or angry either. I get close enough to see the set of his jaw under the helmet, the obsidian eyes. He looks stern, expectant. A Commander, through and through.

There are others standing around him, but I barely see them, because my eyes are locked on him. It's like the entire world has narrowed to one small point, and he stands at the center of it. The closer I walk to him, the faster my breathing accelerates, the higher my pleasure rises, yearning for the peak that has been denied me for so long. It's like nothing else in the universe exists except for the two of us.

When I finally reach the top of the ramp, I feel like I can't breathe. He's so close to me, a head taller, larger than life, and it's like my entire body is aflame, pulsing and throbbing. Frllil had told me not to look him in the eyes, but I can't look away. His gaze is almost hypnotic, drawing me closer to him, step by step... and closer to orgasm the same way.

He does not look displeased as his gaze sweeps over me, from the top of my head down to the bottom of my feet and back up.

When he speaks, his voice is deep but strong, ringing out loudly enough for everyone assembled to hear.

"I, High Commander Gavrill, accept my Tribute."

The receiving deck rings with the gathered Tsenturions' shouted salute. Beneath my robes, the trainer comes to life. It turns off almost immediately, as if the nanotech is smart enough to realize I'm already too close... but it's too late.

A faint sense of triumph is threaded through the crashing waves of ecstasy that roll through me. *Fuck you, Jabol technology.* I'm drowning in my orgasm, and nothing can stop it. Nothing except the blackness that rises up over me from the very intensity of my climax, and even as my rapture is rising, I am falling.

The last sensation I feel before everything goes dark is strong arms folding around me, and my utter erotic bliss is complete.

3

G avrill

ALARM SURGES through me as my Tribute shakes and begins to collapse, her eyes rolling upwards before they close.

She's beautiful. So different from a Tsenturion female and yet so similar. Her hair is like a galass plant, bright and soft, waving gently in the wind as I catch her up in my arms and hold her against my chest.

"Dismissed!" I bellow to the assembled warriors. Many wear startled expressions on their faces, their suits reflecting worry, but I cannot take the time to address that now. I turn to Medik, feeling helpless.

"What's wrong with her? What happened?"

He's already stepping forward, scanner in hand, and he runs it over her body, ignoring my questions. Impatience seethes, but I relax slightly as he looks at the output of the scan and his tension releases. He would not have such a reaction if something were seriously wrong.

A small smile plays on his face, something that makes me stare for a moment. He hasn't smiled since our planet, and his mate and family, were lost.

"She is fine. A simple loss of consciousness as a result of overwhelming sensations."

"The Tribute is weak," Bogdan mutters. He's at my back, hovering in the door as if he can't stand to be near her, but I hadn't missed the way he moved when she fell, just as ready to catch her as I had been. His retreat had been just as swift. Which was just as well. After all, she is *my* Tribute.

The amount of possessiveness and protectiveness I feel is a little startling, and definitely unexpected. But I am used to being a protector, and she is very small. Her skin is soft, completely vulnerable, unlike my own. The nanotech of her training belt protects those areas, but its influence is limited.

"She is actually quite resilient," Medik corrects. "Dense bone structure, decent musculature, healthy tissue..."

He holds the scanner over her leg, and her foot twitches. I hold her a little tighter.

My body is primed to her already, my *seela* writhing and my cock pulsing with anxiousness to be buried inside her softness. I stroke her hip as Medik continues to examine the readout. Then he presses the scanner to her knee, releasing a small injection of nanos into her. I recognize the process, which he uses on minor injuries not needing much intervention.

"Some scar tissue," he mutters to himself. "The Jabol made enhancements to her physiology but missed this. An old injury..."

"Is that why she fell?" I ask.

"No, no." Medik doesn't look up from his scanner as he

taps the screen, directing the nanos working on her. "She, ah... was overwhelmed with pleasure." His lips twitch, almost smiling. "Her body's responses overrode the trainer... that, or Frllil was overly industrious with using it to prime her for you."

"When will she regain consciousness?"

"Any minute now. I have her in stasis sleep while the nano repairs her knee injury. She will awaken as soon as it is done. When that happens, you should be alone with her." Medik turns to face me, an almost fatherly look on his weathered face. Our nanosuits preserve all of our organs, including our skin, so that we do not age, but by the time Jabols gave Medik nanotechnology, he was already old. In many ways, he has become a kind of patriarchal mentor for the rest of us, as we are without our fathers. "After all, you will need to seal the bond between you in order for this mating to be successful. That is done best alone. If you are pleased with her as your Tribute, that is."

"I am satisfied," I say carefully. My words match the steady grey of my suit.

The doctor snorts. He is more expressive than the rest of the Tsenturion legion combined. Before the destruction of Tsentur, he had been retired from the fleet for many, many years, and he still retains many of the habits from civilian life. We all rather enjoy it; a taste of the life we never got to lead.

Except, perhaps now we'll have a chance to. I look down at the female in my arms. The *compatible* female. A miracle, even if she is soft, defenseless, and a different species.

"You do not believe me?" I ask. The doctor is the only one who would dare challenge me.

"I think being calm is just a sign you have no idea what you're in for."

Instead of being insulted, I am curious. "How would you be feeling?"

"Excited. Nervous." The doctor rattles off emotions I have not felt—have not allowed myself to feel—for a millennium. "I remember when I met my Sulli." His smile warms his suit to a glittering blush—a color no Tsenturion soldier would ever allow. Not until they had retired and had a family of their own. "She was the most beautiful creature in the Nine Galaxies. In her presence, I could not even speak."

"A rare event," Bogdan says under his breath. Both of us ignore him.

"If you could not speak, how did you win her bond?" I ask curiously. When our world was destroyed, I had not yet felt an interest in attending the mating festival and so had never given the process much thought. I'd assumed that I had years before I needed to consider how to win a mate, and after Tsentur was gone, there had seemed no point, especially as the years had stretched on without the Jabols finding any compatible females.

Now that I had a female of my own, real and in the flesh, I couldn't help but wonder how others had proceeded when they'd bonded. Their experience would be different, because Dawn is a Tribute and not a Tsenturion, but perhaps some of the general ideas would be similar. I had read the books on the courtship rituals of my Tribute's race and found them to be titillating. Certainly, the differences from my own culture had not seemed too great from what I remembered... but it had been a very long time, and my knowledge had never been complete.

Medik's smile grew nostalgic, his gaze unfocusing as if he saw something very far away. The glittering blush of his armor dimmed, the hue deepening. "I gave a lecture at a medical clinic near her home. She was in the audience, in the back. She chose to approach me. That's the thing about bonding. Both partners can choose. They are equal."

Bogdan snorts. "Not anymore. This Tribute is nothing like us. No Tsenturion woman would have been weak enough to faint from mere pleasure."

He was not wrong. But I was not displeased either. We were similar enough. Frllil had started her training, and I would complete it, and then she would be a perfect companion for me. My Tribute.

"You should write a manual," I tell Medik.

"Perhaps I will." His suit dulls further, turning blue-grey as his grief for his lost mate and family return. Sometimes I think he wishes he had been on-planet when it was destroyed, where he should have been—where he would have been if our usual physician had not been killed in action. Medik had agreed to one expedition with us, while a replacement completed training and instead had ended up with us for a lifetime.

He returns his attention to his scanner.

"The repair to her knee is complete, she should wake any moment." He glances at Bogdan, who is staring at my Tribute again. I repress the urge to growl, unsure of why I don't like him looking at her. He does not appear hostile... although perhaps if he was, I would not mind so much. As derogatory as he has been about my Tribute, I cannot help but remember that he had been about to retire and claim his own mate when we lost our people.

But he cannot have her. She is mine.

"I will take her to my quarters," I say, holding her a little tighter. "To complete the bonding. Bogdan, you have the bridge. Get us back to the nebula. We will pick up the Vgotha's trail."

He nods, and I swiftly turn and walk back into the ship

as she makes a small noise. I pick up my pace, nodding to my soldiers as I pass by them. They watch me go with varying expressions of worry and hope, although they seem reassured that there is nothing wrong with my Tribute when they see I am focused on my path but unconcerned—and since Medik is no longer by my side, they know she is well enough.

She shifts slightly in my arms as I enter my quarters, and I look down to see her eyelashes fluttering. Anticipation rises in me, my cock swelling with interest as my excitement begins to grow again. Bogdan is right, she is not Tsenturion, but my body responds to her regardless.

Opening her robe, I look her over with interest. Her skin is slightly patched, slightly darker on her limbs, face and belly in comparison to the light cream of her breasts. Pink nipples harden on her chest under my gaze. Her coloring is interesting and not unattractive.

I stroke my fingers over the trainer belt, and sensing my intentions, it retreats into a thin band about her hips, uncovering her lower body completely. There too she is lighter. It is as if her body coloring is arranged to attract the most attention to those parts of her which can bring her the most pleasure. I decide I like it.

Pulling her legs open, I inspect her more closely, intrigued by the pink of her inner folds, which is darker than the pink of her nipples. All the color variation on her body fascinates me. The pink is shiny because she is wet; a sign of arousal according to the texts of her people. There is a small bud at the apex of her folds. I cannot tell if it is swollen or not, it looks very innocuous and unimportant, but according to the texts the Jabol provided, it is one of the keys to her pleasure. I take careful note of all of her parts, including the darker, wrinkled entrance to her body that is below her puffy pink lips. The texts indicate that it can be used for enjoyment or punishment, although she may initially be resistant to the idea, even for pleasure. The area was taboo in their culture, although that apparently contributed to the appeal.

Tsenturion rituals demand that we claim our mates in every way possible, so in that manner it seems we are alike. Although I say we will bond, I do not know if we will be able to complete it fully, the way Tsenturion couples do so that they may completely share their lives and emotions with each other. It seems unlikely. Even knowing this, there is a part of me which yearns to see my claiming mark on her skin, announcing to the universe that she is mine irrevocably.

I am determined to be a good mate, so I will bring her great pleasure and she will pleasure me, and we shall lead the way for the future of the Tsenturions. Although bringing more Tributes through an unstable wormhole is a risk, it may be one we have to take if we are to survive as a race.

Even more so if we are to survive as ourselves. Just the announcement that one Tribute has been retrieved has sent morale surging higher than I can ever remember it being. There are a few males, like Bogdan, who remain unconvinced, but the majority are just as hopeful as I feel now.

As her eyelashes flutter again, she stirs, her arms and legs moving slightly. Feeling strangely nervous, I pull my armor back into my spine, so its pale-yellow hue does not betray my unruly emotions. I cannot remember the last time it was that color and am thankful we are alone and no one can witness my uncertainty.

$\sim$

Dawn

I MOAN as I open my eyes and try to jerk back as a golden-hued face fills my vision. I recognize his harsh features immediately, and my pussy flutters... but the trainer doesn't immediately vibrate. My body has been primed to respond all on its own, but it's still odd not to feel the vibrations of the trainer.

Even more odd—I can actually think clearly for the first time in days.

LANDING on this planet and presenting myself to the commander feels like a dream that I just awoke from, and though I feel arousal at the sight of him, the orgasm I had has helped clear my mind. I'm no longer a complete slave to the impulses of my body, because the urgency has subsided, having found recent satisfaction.

Chalk up one for the home team. Take that, alien tech!

I purposefully don't think about how often the alien tech had defeated me prior to that moment. A win is a win, darn it.

"Greetings, my Tribute," he says, that low voice doing all sorts of things to my lower anatomy. I ignore my reaction as best I can.

"Dawn," I say, my voice croaking slightly, the word coming out slightly fuzzy and slurred.

He frowns at me. "What?"

"Dawn," I repeat firmly, getting a better grip on myself. I enunciate carefully, determined not to slur again. "My name is Dawn."

I purposefully leave off my last name, because after so

many days of Frllil's insistence on calling me by my full name, I kind of never want to hear it again.

After taking a moment to consider my statement, he nods formally. "Very well. Dawn."

The English word sounds strange when he says it. It's a common word, as well as a name, but somehow the translator knows the difference and leaves my name alone, which is a relief. He meets my eyes.

"I am your Master."

Dammit, that shouldn't be so hot, but the muscles of my pussy flutter again.

"Gavrill," I reply firmly. "High Commander of the Tsenturion fleet. But *not* my master. I don't have a master." No matter what he, Frllil, or my training has told me.

He frowns, which is intimidating as heck, especially when I'm flat on my back in what I can only assume is his bed, but after a moment his expression clears. To my annoyance, he actually looks kind of smug.

"Ah, yes, your courtship rituals," he says seriously. "I will earn my place as your master by dominating and pleasuring you until your resistance is broken and you submit to me fully."

I blink, nonplussed. "Excuse me? What courtship rituals are you talking about exactly? That is definitely not my how-to advice on dating."

The little smile that plays on his lips is both hot and frustrating, like he thinks I'm lying to him or something.

"The Jabol provided me with manuals on your planet's courtship rituals, they are copies from something they called your 'reader.'" Turning his head, he nods at the table next to his bed. I try to wriggle away from him to get some space and look to see where he's looking at the same time.

But as soon as the small pile of books on the little table beside his bed catches my eye, I freeze in horror.

Oh, fuck a duck.

They went through my freaking e-reader and gave those books to this massively large, already dominant, far too eager alien?! I recognize those names. Lee Savino. Golden Angel. Tracy St. John. Renee Rose. Aubrey Cara. Sara Fields.

Oh, this is bad. This is so, so bad.

"Those are *not* manuals," I say, now scooting away from him in earnest. Unfortunately, the bed is big and he's on the edge closest to me, so all I end up doing is scooting into the middle of the bed, which prompts him to follow, his eyes gleaming with interest. Crap! This is a serious Catch-22... I can either resist him, in which case he'll think I'm following the stupid "courting rituals" of my dirty romances, or I can stop resisting him... in which case I'll get fucked sooner rather than later.

My traitorous body votes for the latter, as if it hadn't already had an orgasm not that long ago.

"They were quite descriptive. Very similar to how a Tsenturion conducts himself with his bonded mate," he says, moving after me, which is when I finally catch sight of what he's got going on between his legs.

"Wha- wha- wha-" I can't even get the word out or look away from his groin and the freakiest looking cock I think I've ever seen. Way, way freakier than any I ever imagined.

It's golden, like his body, but it's got *way* too many parts. The tip of it looks almost like a cobra's mane; there's no mushroom head here, instead it flares out slightly and there's a ridge along the top of it that looks like it would feel really freaking interesting. The actual shaft is almost normal looking, long and straight, although it grows incrementally wider from the head down to where the really freaky stuff is going on.

Waving in a fringe around it is not pubic hair, unless pubic hair moves on its own and is flesh rather than hair. Less than half an inch long, the tiny tentacles writhe and my pussy pulses as I can't help but wonder what that would feel like against my vulva... even more intriguing is the extra-large one, the only one that's about an inch long, writhing above his cock. My clit pulses in response, because surely that kind of appendage is there for one reason and one reason only, and no matter how freaky looking it is, I'm still turned on.

I blame the training.

I point, managing to choke out the words. "What... is... that?!"

He looks down to where I'm pointing. "Ah, yes, I saw no mention of *seela* in the descriptions of your courtship. Perhaps Tsenturions are unique. They are to facilitate pleasure and breeding, as well as our bonding process."

Okay, the bonding process I knew about thanks to Frllil. The armor the Tsenturions wore was nanotech that had become so much a part of them that it was nearly biological. By having sex, some of the High Commander's tech would transfer to me and he would be able to fully control my training belt with just a thought after that—definitely not something on my to-do list—and theoretically they would also help me achieve the biological bond that Tsenturions had with their mates. If it did so, a mark would appear somewhere on my body that would actually help me sense and share his emotions as he would be able to sense and share mine.

But no one had mentioned a freaky alien cock. My perverted brain immediately wonders how all those little tendrils would feel moving against my most sensitive parts. Especially the big one that looks like it would line right up with my clit.

I'm so distracted that the High Commander manages to grab my ankle, and I squeak in dismay as I'm quickly dragged across the bed toward him.

4

G avrill

MY TRIBUTE'S skin is soft against my hand, and the squeaking noise she makes as I pull her towards me is very appealing. There is no need for armor like mine to display her emotions—they are telegraphed across her expressive face. Surprise. Dismay. Arousal.

I can see that her nipples are tightly budded, the cleft between her legs shiny with moisture, and the pupils of her blue eyes dilate, filling the color with black. All signs of her interest.

"Wait! Stop!" She slaps her palms against my chest as I loom over her, planting a hand on either side of her body and caging her in, pushing at me to my amusement. She is much weaker than I am. Having her in this position arouses me further, my *seela* writhing and trying to stretch towards her. But I am unsure whether or not to immediately complete the bonding or if I should assert myself first.

Tsenturion males are naturally dominant when it comes to pleasure. I have dim memories of my mother smiling as my father swatted her bottom when she passed by. Perhaps there will be similar moments with my Tribute? She certainly is not smiling now, although she is highly aroused.

The ways of our people, once mated and no longer military, have passed on with our planet. But my Tribute would not know them anyway. I studied the rituals and training outlined in her people's manuscripts closely. There were even some on interspecies relations, all with similar instructions. They mostly align with my distant memories of our people, and they certainly appeal to my sense of order.

I will be in charge. She will submit. Thwarting the traditions of my people, I shall continue in command on my ship rather than becoming a civilian after my mating, but it's not as if ours will be a full bonding, so there should be no objections. I will pleasure her often, as a good mate should, and she will ease my physical needs and lonely nights. Eventually, if the Jabols are correct about our compatibility, the Tributes will assure the continuation of our race and we can find a new planet to settle on once the Vgotha threat is eradicated. It all begins with Dawn.

I am also aware of how important this will be to all of my men. Although she is only one Tribute, I am determined she will not be the last, for their sakes. Travel through an unstable wormhole is not ideal, and the Jabol will want reassurances that the energy expenditure is worthwhile before they begin to provide us with Tributes in number.

Staring down at her, I sigh inwardly. Although I yearn to bury myself inside of her immediately and attach my *seela* to her flesh, I realize I have not completed the most basic of her courtship rituals. I nod.

"You are correct," I say, though my body aches with need. "We should not skip steps."

Confusion, relief, and then disappointment flit across her face as I pull away.

When I pull her with me, easily flipping her face down across my lap, she shrieks with surprise. I like the noise. I also find the position to be quite enjoyable. My *seela* begin to explore the side of her body, where they can reach as my hard cock throbs against her soft flesh. Her bottom is tilted upward, vulnerable and pale. I look forward to seeing the change in color her manuals spoke of.

Dawn

WHEN I SAID "WAIT—STOP," this was definitely not what I had in mind.

Talk about out of the frying pan and into the fire. There was no mistaking what his intentions were, and yet the words came spilling out of my mouth anyway.

"What are you doing?" My voice quavers, my brain still trying to deny the obvious... the inevitable. I can feel something writhing against my side, exploring me with soft little touches that caress and pull at my skin. It's incredibly distracting, especially because I can feel a certain area of my body perking up with interest—*what would that feel like there?*

"I am establishing my position as your Master, in the manner of your people," he says sternly.

Part of me wants to laugh hysterically, because his formal pronouncement is so over-the-top... and yet I can't because he is entirely serious. My mind goes frantic, trying to think of a protest that will work, a way to talk him out of his obvious intention, but it's like my brain has gone entirely blank in the face of danger, and then -

Smack!

"Ow!" I kick my legs. That really freaking hurt!

"Ah. That is very nice," he says, sounding pleased.

"No, it's—"

Smack!

I howl, more in outrage than pain as his hand comes down on the other cheek.

I haven't been spanked since I was a young child, and then it was never more than a swat or two. I've read about it. Fantasized about it. Masturbated to the idea.

But nothing could have ever prepared me for the reality.

It fucking *hurts*.

The initial sting is followed by a flaring of pain that burns much deeper than the surface, and then *throbs*. Especially as he lays down more hard swats atop already spanked flesh. There's no chance of squirming away as his left hand holds me firmly in place on his lap and he shifts his legs so that my upper body is tilted forward even more, lifting my bottom higher in the air.

Smack! Smack! Smack!

"Please! Stop," I babble, begging and clinging to his tree trunk of a leg, tears already sliding down my cheeks. It feels like my entire ass is on fire.

To my surprise and relief, the spanking stops and his hand rests on my hot flesh. In my mind, I imagine his golden skin against the flaming red that my skin feels like. "You are ready to acknowledge me as your Master already?"

I hesitate, everything inside of me rebelling at his words even as my pussy clenches. I tell myself that's just from the Pavlov dog training that Frllil put me through, that's not *me*.

Unfortunately, *me* is not what he wants. He wants my submission, he wants a sex toy, he wants a submissive female... but he only wants it from me because I'm the only female here.

"Ah," he says when I don't answer.

"Wait—*no!*" I let out a wail as his hand comes crashing down again, but this time he doesn't stop immediately, apparently determined to make an impression on my poor ass before he gives me another chance.

I writhe, bucking. Maybe it's because he paused and gave me a short break, but it feels like he's spanking even harder now. I kick my legs frantically, trying even harder to get away now, despite how useless it is. It feels like my bottom is swollen and thoroughly roasted, from the crest down to the delicate sit-spots just underneath the curve of my mounds. Every time his hand comes down on that tender area, I howl.

And I know that the next time he asks, I will call him 'Master' just to make this stop...

∼

GAVRILL

MY TRIBUTE's reactions are very much in line with the manuals, pleasing me greatly. Although Tsenturions might mete out physical discipline to their mates when it was required, I find that I am quite enamored of her people's penchant for using such measures for both pain and pleasure. Despite her pleas and howls, it is apparent she is not ready for this first step to our courtship to be over, as she chose not to end it when I offered. Although my arousal is becoming painful, I find I am not averse to continuing it either.

The pale flesh of her bottom is now a bright pink, her skin hot to the touch. Whenever she kicks, the swollen lips of her sex become even glossier and wetter with her arousal. The musky-sweet scent is pleasing, and I wonder how she will taste.

I am using a harder hand than I will for pleasurable spankings later. The manuals make it clear that there should be a difference. As this is my first time spanking a female, I am not entirely sure I am doing it correctly. Fortunately, it is obvious that her reaction is one of erotic excitement, despite her pained cries. The Jabol had done *very* well, I decide. My Tribute is more than I could have hoped for.

When I stop, she hangs over my lap, crying. I trace patterns on her pink bottom, fascinated by the heat rising from her flesh.

"Will you call me Master, now?" I ask, hoping that she will say yes. As enjoyable as I am finding this interlude, I am eager to move onward and find more personal pleasure for myself. My *seela* that can reach her are rubbing almost frantically against her body, and my *prime seela* is thrashing with the desire to touch her as well.

"Yes..." She gulps. "Yes, Master."

Satisfaction washes through me at the sound of her tearful voice acknowledging me as her Master. Not just because it fulfills the rituals of both of our races, but I feel a sense of personal pleasure as well. It surprises me how much I enjoy hearing her acknowledge me and the possessive gratification that fills me. The emotion is unexpected.

"Good girl," I say, sliding my fingers to the swollen, wet flesh between her legs. She moans as I begin to explore that area with the pads of my fingers, searching for the little bud that was described as the penultimate point of pleasure for her species.

Moving my other hand from the small of her back to her hot bottom, I gently squeeze her punished flesh as I circle the small, swollen bud of pleasure with my fingers. She bucks, shuddering slightly as she cries out. There is some unhappiness in her voice, but as wetness coats my fingertips, I know that she is enjoying this. The texts warned that human females tend to feel a sense of shame at being aroused when they are mastered; it is a sign that I am proceeding correctly.

"Oh no..." She shudders again as I pinch the pleasure bud, rubbing it experimentally between my fingers.

Later I know I will enjoy using the training belt to discover exactly what affects her most, but for now I am too impatient to be inside of her, too eager for my own release. Pulling my fingers from her body, I inspect the glossy sheen she's coated them with before touching the tips to my tongue.

She tastes like sweetness and flowers, and my body immediately hungers for more. I've heard that the bonding process triggers intense physical reactions and an overwhelming need to claim one's mate, but I hadn't expected the force of it. Feeling more bestial than logical, completely unlike myself, I toss her onto her back on the bed. She shrieks, trying to roll off her bottom, but I am already prying her legs apart to reach the source of her nectar.

My vaunted self-control is gone as the taste of her juices

on my tongue has sparked a craving that thunders through my body. She looks up at me, dazed, but my focus is on the sweetness calling to me between her thighs.

I fall upon her, my tongue sliding up the sweet center, groaning as my body recognizes its mate. Perhaps we are more compatible than even the Jabol realized. I have no experience that compares to this, nothing to help me control the urges raging through my body.

She cries out, writhing against my hands as I hold her legs spread wide open, making her vulnerable to the lashing of my tongue as I lick every crevice of her sweet folds. The flavor intensifies, growing sweeter as my body chemistry adjusts to hers, beginning to align with hers.

Mine.

All mine. Instinctively, I know that from this point forward no other female will ever taste this sweet, will ever satisfy my craving or bring me as much satisfaction as my Tribute. I suck and lick voraciously, and I can feel my armor buzzing along my spine, the nanotech beginning to respond to the addition of her cells within me.

"Please," she begs, her fingers sliding over my scalp, trying to find purchase. "Oh, please..."

I do not know if she is asking me to stop or if she is asking for more, but for her sake I hope it is the latter... I could not stop if I wanted to.

And I *don't* want to.

~

Dawn

. . .

MY ASS IS THROBBING from the spanking, but the way he's licking me—like he's starving and I'm the first food he's had in days—is making me throb and pulse in an entirely new way. I don't know if alien tongues are different, but I know it *feels* different. My entire pussy is tingling, burning almost hot and then cold, and instinctively I know that something is happening that is different from anything else I've ever experienced before. It'd be terrifying if I weren't so aroused.

He has no hair for me to grab, and I can't tell if I'm trying to push him away or pull him closer. My body is a maelstrom of sensation, my emotions conflicting with the greedy, needy ache that's burgeoning inside of me. I want to be furious, I want to hate him, but either the Stockholmian training or the fact that he's so focused on giving me pleasure is making it hard for me to feel either emotion right now.

It's like the orgasm I had out on the ramp never happened, and I whimper and sob, writhing for him like I'm in heat... which is exactly how I feel. I'm burning up inside, not just the surface of my ass, but from the inside out. I can feel the heat spreading outward from my pussy, making me shake and gasp at the unusual feeling.

When he sucks on my clit, hard, I cum almost immediately with a high, loud cry that is nearly a scream. I'd always thought that 'screaming in orgasm' was just exaggeration, but it's like the intensity of the ecstasy is too great for my body to contain and the only way to release it is vocally. It pulses through me in waves, filling me, and yet not quite satisfying me, even as I am wracked with hot bliss.

Then he looms over me and I spread my legs further, reaching for him. Maybe it's my training, maybe there's just something in the animal part of my brain that's running on instinct, but I *need* him inside me. Somehow, I know he's the only one that can make this burning cease, the only one who can give me the satisfaction that my body is demanding. Even the long days of training, of being primed for him without ever being allowed to orgasm, hadn't created this kind of desperate compulsion within me.

I honestly feel like I might die if we don't finish this.

Tears rise in my eyes, and I choke on a scream as he thrusts into me, hard and fast, with one purposeful stroke. He's big and oddly shaped, and, even aroused as I am, the hot pleasure is mixed with some pain as my muscles contract around him, adjusting to the stretch that his proportions require. The little fringe of tentacles around his cock stroke my pussy lips, an incredibly odd and yet pleasurable sensation.

My back arches upwards as the long one slides around my clit, stroking and pulling at the tiny nubbin in much the same way his fingers had. His guttural groan as he shudders against me tell me that he's feeling the same inexpressible pleasure at being joined together. My hands cling to his biceps, fingers attempting to dig into the steely flesh, as I pant for breath.

With one hand planted on either side of me, his large body feels like it's caging me in, trapping me, and yet I feel oddly protected. He holds himself still, as if he realizes I need a moment. It's not until I wriggle beneath him, in reaction to the insistent stroking of the little things he called his *seela*, that he begins to move.

The initial thrusts are deep, long strokes as he moves slowly, making me arch and pant at the hot sensation. He leans down and takes one of my nipples in his mouth, sucking and laving the sensitive bud with his tongue. It tingles with the same growing heat that my pussy had when he'd been licking it, and when he switches his attention to the other nipple, the same thing happens.

It isn't until he's trailed his tongue up to my neck before claiming my mouth in a searing kiss that I realize I'm now tingling and burning everywhere that his tongue has touched. When he kisses me, I automatically kiss him back, our tongues rubbing together as my passion intensifies. He tastes like chocolate and fine red wine, igniting a craving that I don't understand, and I become almost wild beneath him.

Strong hands pin my wrists to the bed as he begins to fuck me harder, his kisses swallowing my cries, my nipples rubbing against his hard chest as my sore ass bounces off the sheets. Heat and pain and pleasure clash and mix, and I begin to feel lightheaded as the ache inside of me grows, my rising ecstasy climbing higher and higher. Being held helpless beneath him only increases my passion as he dominates me with nothing more than his weight holding me down.

I can cry out, I can writhe, I can take his cock... and that's it. The kiss ends as his strokes become more wild, leaving my lips burning.

His strange cock rubs along the inside of my walls, and I swear I can feel the head flaring, moving separately from the thrusting, stimulating the sensitive flesh of my pussy. I can feel every bump, every unexpected ridge, as he moves inside of me, his thrusts becoming harder and faster. Every time he fills me, his *seela* make a sweeping stroke through my sensitive folds and around my clit, making me thrash beneath him.

It's too much.

It's not enough.

The burning inside of me intensifies almost painfully even as ecstasy swirls.

He lunges, filling me completely. The *seela* don't stroke this time—it feels like they surround my sensitive flesh and *pull*. Something squeezes my clit.

Everything *pulses*.

His mouth comes down on mine again, swallowing my scream as I writhe for him, shuddering in utter erotic rapture. The *seela* pulse and pull, sending wave after wave of sweet ecstasy through me, massaging my pussy lips and clit and adding an entirely new level of sensation to my orgasm.

I'm drowning, and I don't even care.

GAVRILL

SOMEWHERE IN THE back of my mind, I am aware of my armor sliding around my hips to join with her belt, artificially locking us together the same way my *seela* suction to her skin. From this point on, her belt will only respond to me and I will be able to control it, and her, completely.

What is more unexpected is how my *seela* have fully latched onto her, triggering my bonding sequence. Whether or not it will ever be complete, I have no idea, but the sensations are even more intense than I could have predicted, and my ecstasy is explosive. I can feel her contracting around me, her muscles rippling over my length and practically sucking my seed out of me.

The sensation is more amazing than I could have ever anticipated.

Panting for breath, I let my arms fold so I can rest my weight on my forearms, laying them alongside hers. She is soft and lax beneath me, still moaning softly as my *seela* detach and begin to soothe and caress her now swollen sex. Little shudders wrack her body, and at first I am concerned, but as they are giving her pleasure, I decide they must not be harmful. They seem almost like tiny echoes of her climax, and I am fascinated.

My Tribute is *highly* satisfactory. Bogdan is wrong; the Tributes will be a blessing for all of us.

As if my thoughts have summoned him, my nanotech pulses with an alert from the bridge.

I barely manage to suppress my growl as I hunch around my Tribute, unhappy with the interruption. Logic asserts itself—they would not bother me now if it were not important.

Drakk, I curse in my head.

My armor slides up my spine to extend a communication tendril into my ear.

"I'm sorry for interrupting, Commander," says Bogdan, his voice neutrally crisp and not at all apologetic. "We have a situation that requires your attention on the bridge."

"I am coming," I respond, my voice low and threatening. If the situation is not urgent, I will have Bogdan cleaning out the most foul area of the ship I can locate.

Beneath me, my Tribute blinks. The almost peacefully satisfied expression on her face clears, and I am sorry to see it go. Her lips tip up in amusement.

"I thought you already did that," she says, her voice teasing.

No one has teased me in so long that I almost don't recognize it. Even so, I don't understand her words. I frown down at her in confusion.

She sighs, her small smile slipping away. "Never mind."

When she turns her head away from me, the moment is over. I can feel a strange sense of unhappiness and regret—

both foreign to me, and they do not feel like my own. It takes me a moment to realize my tech is transmitting her emotions to me.

Scowling, I pull away. Obviously, the bond is not working as well as it should if those are her current feelings. Still, I can see from the flush of her body, the small round red marks my *seela* have left on her swollen flesh, and the looseness of her muscles that she was been well-pleasured. The language barrier between us is not vast, thanks to the translators.

If I were not needed on the bridge, I would have her explain her words, but the demands of my crew and my ship must come first.

Still...

I find I am loath to let her out of my sight so soon. She will accompany me to the bridge.

Standing, I pull away from her and walk over to the closet, where suitable garments have been stored for her. I had them made in the replicator on the way here, based off the garments Tsenturion females would wear during the Mating Festival and their courtship. The filmy material seems out of place on the ship, but I am already looking forward to seeing my Tribute in them.

"Here," I say, picking up a blue one that will closely match her eyes and turning to hold it out for her. "You will put this on."

5

D awn

I DON'T KNOW what day or hour or cycle or whatever alien time unit these guys use it is. I do know that I feel both drained and very awake. My legs are wobbly as I follow the High Commander—my *Master*—down the hallway. I don't want to call him that, and yet somehow it feels easy and right.

Can Stockholm Syndrome be trained into someone? Because I feel like that's what's happened to me.

It's as if I've been split down the middle into two Dawns; Dawn #1 is appalled and horrified, not to mention seriously pissed off, and Dawn #2 wants nothing more than her Master's attention and approval—and another orgasm. I'm not even sure which one feels more real right now.

I catch my reflection in the shiny metal lining the hall

and quickly avert my eyes from the image, gritting my teeth. *Will. Not. Blush.*

Part of me is furious about being dressed in nothing but a filmy, practically see through gown, collar and leash. Another part of me likes the way the fabric swishes around my legs. I peek at my reflection again and see the front and back slit opening and revealing the stupid Trainer, which my *Master* has me wearing like a chastity belt again. I'm actually relieved for the coverage it gives me, as much as I hate it.

I also keep telling myself that as long as I'm sarcastic when I call him 'Master' in my head, then it's okay.

"Where are we going?" I ask as he turns down another hall, my steps slowing as I realize it looks exactly the same as the last one. All the halls look the same. How does he know where to turn? And how am I ever going to find my way around?

"The bridge. There is a situation I must deal with. Come." He tugs the leash, and I pick up my pace again. It's that or fall over, because he's definitely not stopping just for me. The collar and leash make me feel both more submissive and more infuriated. I'd resisted when he'd first attempted to place the collar around my neck. It had taken just two hard swats to my already sore bottom to convince me that wasn't a fight worth having—at least not right now.

Especially since I didn't currently know of a way off this ship. I'm his prisoner, and I can't forget that, no matter that he's currently treating me as some kind of sex toy or exotic pet. We're somewhere in space, and the ship is filled with his crew. If I'm going to escape, I'm going to need to be sneaky about it.

Those "training manuals" he's been reading—they aren't

just about sex. They're about women being abducted by alien males intent on dominating them; women who always get into a lot of trouble when they fight. So I'm going to pretend to be the perfect little Tribute that he wants. I'm going to pretend that my training worked completely, and once I learn all about his ship and the best way off it, I'm out of here.

I am also going to ignore the little voice inside my head that says I'm not pretending quite as much as I like to think I am.

I *will* escape.

With as few spankings as possible.

I walk with my eyes downcast, avoiding meeting the eyes of any of the warriors gawking at the sight of their Commander and his Tribute, and also because Frllil told me that I'm not supposed to meet any of the warriors' eyes. At the time I'd thought it was bullshit, but now I'm almost grateful. It's bad enough that I can feel their gazes on me, and I know they can make out the outline of my nipples under the almost see through gown. I don't want to see them actually staring at me.

Especially not if it gets me punished again.

My resolve lasts until we enter the bridge where a few other alien warriors are waiting. It's my first glimpse of space, and I lift my head to look outside of the windows. The glittering stars against the blackness are stunningly beautiful, like something out of a movie. It almost doesn't seem real.

Movement catches my eye, and then a giant Tsenturion with angry dark armor meets my gaze. He scowls fiercely at me. *Shit*. I've broken protocol. Immediately, I return my gaze to the floor like a good little Tribute. Make it look like I'm thoroughly cowed. Although, if I'm being totally honest, the angry warrior is definitely scaring me a little. I shift closer to *my* warrior. Even if he spanked me, fucked me silly, and then put me on a leash, I still feel safe next to him. It seems crazy to me, but I can't deny it.

Just as I think that, he makes an odd clicking noise and pulls me forward by the leash. *Jerk.* I can feel my cheeks heat with embarrassment. Now I *am* blushing. He sits in a large chair at the head of the bridge. When I hesitate, wondering where to sit, he points to a spot next to his chair. There's some sort of cushion on the ground, and I realize I'm supposed to sit on it like a freaking dog or something.

Oh, hell no.

"I can't sit there," I say, pulling back against my collar to show how serious I am. "I have a knee injury, I can't sit on the ground for long periods of time." I'm stretching the truth a little—years of yoga practice made me more resilient, though my knee does get sore after a time.

He gives me a look, every inch the High Commander who is unhappy to be questioned. Especially in front of his men. My knees feel a little weak, but I refuse to drop down. I'm not lying after all.

"Medik has repaired your knee, you need not worry about it." The calm way he states the impossible has my mouth popping open in surprise. I've been doing physical therapy and yoga for years to keep my knee working properly, because it was the only option. I narrow my eyes at him, crossing my arms over my chest, and jut out my chin, ignoring the stares of the warriors on deck. I don't believe him.

Sighing and shaking his head, he begins to wind the leash around his hand, drawing me closer by my throat. I'm uncomfortably reminded of Jabba and Princess Leia, except that this is actually really freaking sexy, even if I don't want it to be.

"You know what happens when you disobey."

I dig in my heels as I realize his intention, but it's too late. The leash pulls me down and over his lap, ass in the air, and I squeal as I feel the training belt receding, uncovering my already reddened cheeks.

"What?" I kick out, feeling frantic as I try to push myself up. "You can't spank me here. Please! You didn't even give me a chance to sit down!"

"Didn't I?" He sounds amused, and my anger surges. My intention to be sneaky, to be meek, goes flying out the window in the face of his freaking amusement when he's about to spank me with a *freaking audience*!

"No! Not here, dammit," I grit out, kicking my legs as I try to roll off his lap. I'm aware all the warriors are watching. I'm even more aware of the High Commander's cock, growing long and hard under my belly, the *seela* beginning to writhe. The ridges strain the front of his suit.

It gives me an idea.

He pins me down, but I keep wriggling, rocking side to side a little in an effort to... er... stimulate things in my favor.

It has no discernible effect on him. At least not one which is helpful to me in any way.

My wrists are caught in his large hand, my legs weighted by his heavy one. I gyrate like a belly dancer but am caught fast. My ass is still burning from the spanking he gave me in his cabin, and I want to wail in denial.

He pulls aside the flimsy garment I'm wearing and bares my ass to the entire deck. I freeze, my whole body flushing with humiliation. There's no way they can miss the signs of the spanking he already gave me, and now they're going to see me receive another one.

Even worse, I can feel my lower body pulsing in anticipation. My vagina has committed the ultimate betrayal. I'm getting wet. Considering the books I read and the training Frllil put me through, maybe I shouldn't be so surprised. Considering how much my ass already hurts and how embarrassed I am, I am pretty shocked that I'm turned on at all. But there's something about being vulnerable and exposed that is just flat out doing it for me, no matter my other emotions.

"If you did not want to be punished here, you should not have misbehaved here," Gavrill murmurs. Defiantly, I think of him by his name rather than as the High Commander or my Master—even sarcastically. His free hand smooths over my skin, leaving goosebumps rising in its wake. My mortification and arousal grow in equal measure.

"Please don't," I beg, now with a much more proper tone than I'd used before. Large fingers caress my bottom, soothing the sore spots but also readying me for the punishment to come.

"This is mine to do with as I please," he reminds me, sounding way too satisfied with himself. The possessiveness in his voice triggers something inside of me, even though intellectually I know he'd be this way about any woman presented to him. This has nothing to do with *me*, so I can't let myself react too much to it. "Mine to punish, mine to reward. And I must set an example for my men."

I shouldn't have pushed him in front of the others. *Stupid, Dawn.* That was just common sense. Although I hadn't meant to exactly... or had I? Had some part of my brain wanted to see what he would do? How he would react? Had I been trying to find the line?

If I had been, I definitely found it. He's the head honcho, he *has* to be in control of his Tribute in front of the others.

Maybe I can talk back a little bit when it's just the two of us, but not when there's an audience.

His palm cracks down once on both cheeks, quick as a whip, reigniting the burn from my previous spanking. I cry out, my legs automatically kicking. The way I'm propped over his leg, my entire backside is on display except for the narrow strip covered by the belt... something he could rescind at any moment. If any warrior on the deck looks closely, they'll be able to see *everything*.

Including how excited this spanking makes me.

Smack!

Smack!

Smack!

I hold still, internally praying that the spanking is already over, as Gavrill cups my right butt cheek, molding it to his palm before smacking it. He repeats the motion with my left, his movements slow and methodical. Thoughtful. As if he's realizing something. I feel the training belt recede, uncovering me completely, and I moan.

He plumps one cheek, and I suck in a breath. I'm practically dripping on the floor. He's got to notice—it's only a matter of time.

His fingers stray lower, and my lower half twitches.

"You're still enjoying this." He sounds a little surprised.

"No!" I crane my neck. He's examining the sticky wetness on his fingers, a satisfied little smile on his face. His armor shimmers—changing colors?

"Commander," one of the warriors pipes up.

"A moment," Gavrill growls and jerks my shimmery robes over my bare skin, covering me up against prying eyes. The training belt slides over my ass and pussy again, cool against the heat of my bottom. Oh, so now he's concerned about privacy?

He swings me upright, propping me between his knees facing him. I can barely meet his eyes. His suit shifts to a more neutral grey, but there are small flashes of gold that nearly match his skin. I know from my training that the gold is arousal.

"We will continue this later." He strokes my hip, and I shiver, trying not to imagine all the punishments he might think up in the meantime. "You will take your place as my Tribute and *keep quiet*."

I bite my lip and nod. He makes a chiding noise, and I add quickly, "Yes, Master."

I'm in a good position to learn about the ship up here on the bridge, so if I can just keep my mouth shut, then maybe I can take the first steps in escaping from here eventually.

Nodding in satisfaction, Gavrill shifts me off his lap. This time, I obediently kneel on the large cushion—which is surprisingly comfortable. By the time I've lowered myself down, I realize he must have told the truth about my knee, because it didn't even twinge when I put my weight on it.

As Gavrill conducts his business, I review my circumstances. I'm the captive of a large, dominant alien, but he's only going to spank me if I've been bad, and otherwise I think he'll treat me pretty well even if he thinks of me as a pet. Things could definitely be worse, right? Studying the other warriors out of the corner of my eye, I'm not sure I'd be better off with one of them. Certainly not with the big one at the station to the right of Gavrill's chair. When he's not addressing the Commander, he's scowling at me. I recognize him from the presentation ceremony. He was standing behind Gavrill along with another, older Tsenturion.

"Bodgan," Gavrill says, and the glowering warrior snaps

his attention from me to the Commander. "You found sign of the Vgothas?"

"Yes, sir. Along the edge of the Boral Nebulae. Likely, they are trying to use its energy as camouflage for their ships. It is effective, the trail is very hard to follow, and it looks as though it's leading towards Outer Rim space, where they are sure to have allies. We will likely not have an opportunity to engage them from such a position of power again." Bogdan lowers his gaze to me again. If looks could kill... I duck my head and scoot closer to Gavrill's chair, using the commander's thickly muscled leg to block some of his warrior's malice. Gavrill reaches down and strokes my hair absently. I should be pissed at him petting me like a cat, but I feel safe and protected instead.

"There will be plenty of opportunities to engage the enemy, especially if we bait them."

Bogdan's suit abruptly lightens to a cloudy silver.

"Send coordinates to Arkdhem. Tell him to send out the scouts. They should cloak their ships and cruise along the meteor belt. They're authorized to use firepower to clear a path."

"The Vgothas will sense the weapons' emissions."

"Yes," Gavrill says, sounding suddenly fierce. I almost lift my eyes up to look at him, feeling just the tiniest bit afraid at this other side to him. "Then we will engage them."

"You propose we use subterfuge?" I can't tell if Bogdan is happy or disgusted.

"The enemy is stealthy. They will not expect it of us." Gavrill settles back in his seat with a satisfied grimness that makes me glad his attention is on the Vgothas and not me. "Then we will destroy them."

～

GAVRILL

MY TRIBUTE'S eyes are downcast when we enter my chambers. She's been quiet since her little outburst on the bridge. While I appreciated her silence there, I find I am growing more uncomfortable with it. She was certainly not quiet when she woke up, so why is she now silent?

I stride to the edge of our resting place, snap my fingers and point to a spot in front of me.

With a wary gaze, she approaches and stands before me, eyeing me warily. She's intelligent enough to be nervous, and yet she still obeys.

"Good girl," I murmur. Her lips press together, and I can tell she's aggravated by the praise for some reason, but I enjoy it almost as much as her reluctant obedience. I like her strong spirit, as long as she obeys. For her, my will is law. Always. Still, disobedience will give me reason to punish her, which I also enjoy thoroughly. I do not wish for it to occur again in front of my men though.

When I'd had her over my lap, I'd nearly forgotten they were all there, gazing upon her... coveting her. Feeling their eyes on us was why I'd cut her punishment short. She is *my* Tribute, I don't have to share any part of her, not even the sight of her, if I don't wish it.

Her very presence has also been a distraction from matters which need my attention. It was easier when she was on the cushion and I hadn't actually had my hands on her.

"You disobeyed me on the bridge, my Tribute. But I am fair. I will give you a chance to explain before finishing your punishment."

Her shoulders lift and fall, slumping a little. She looks

like she is trying to appear meek, but she looks more sulky than anything else.

"Speak," I order, goading her. "You are a sentient being. You have language. Use it."

Her mouth knots into a defiant pout. Red stains her cheeks. She might not know her hands have curled into fists, but I notice it—along with her heightened body temperature. Sensations seep into me, conducted from her Trainer to my suit. She's angry... and aroused.

"With all due respect," she says, straightening up and daring to look me directly in the eye. I shouldn't like it, but I do. "You don't treat me like one."

"What?" My suit flashes with surprise.

"A sentient being. You don't treat me like one. You treat me like a pet." She indicates her necklet and lead. "A collar? A leash? I'm not your fucking dog."

"What is a dog?" I ask, frowning at the unfamiliar word as I attempt to approximate her pronunciation. 'Pet' I understand, we had those on Tsentur, but 'dog' does not translate.

"It's... it's a pet." She stammers out the words, caught off-guard. "An animal. A smart one which can be trained but is not equal to a human."

Just as she is not equal to me, but I choose not to point that out. It would be rude and possibly even cruel to highlight the superiority of Tsenturions to humans.

Still, I shrug. I am the master, she is the Tribute. Of course, I treat her differently than I would one of my men. Tsenturion brides were often courted in a similar manner until they are mastered, after which they were allowed more liberties... but she is not a bride.

"You are my Tribute. You belong to me. If I choose to declare my ownership to my men by marking every inch of your skin, it is my right."

Her chest flushes pink, and she looks away, casting her eyes downward. The joining of our nanotech seems to be more complete than anticipated, as I can actually feel her growing ire, though she tries to hide it.

"You might as well. It won't be as embarrassing as walking around practically naked with all your men staring at me." Her shoulders hunch in.

Jealous heat flares through me. I recall every warrior who laid his eyes on her exposed form, and I'm ready to march to the com and order all of them blinded. It pleases me that she obviously prefers to be covered in front of them, that she does not wish for them to look at her.

"Very well. To be clear, in the future you will respect your Master. You will not argue with me in front of my men. In fact, you will not speak to me when I am on duty unless given permission."

"I thought you wanted me to use my language?" There's a slight edge to her voice, a little hint of sarcastic sass, and I have to hide a smile. Why I find her attitude endearing, I cannot say. There are very few of my men who would dare to address me so, but she does it without fear, though her bottom must be burning from the spankings. It was still very pink when she was over my lap on the bridge.

"Not in public. But you are right—I have contradicted myself. But I trust I have made myself clear now. If you think you are unable to follow my orders, then I will procure a gag for you."

Fear flickers across her face and then is gone, but I can still feel it. She is very brave, my Tribute. An admirable quality.

"Wonderful," she mutters. "Thanks for making it clear."

I allow myself to smile. She glances at me and shivers. I smile broader.

"Now that the matter is settled, I owe you a punishment," I say calmly. Inside, I'm quivering with glee as I sit and pat my knee.

She hesitates, then begins to reluctantly move, very slowly. I reach out to take her hand, pulling her forward faster, and she allows me to draw her small body over my legs.

I take my time arranging her, undoing the binding from her hair and spreading the shimmering mass over her shoulders. The blue fabric of her dress slides off her pearly skin, exposing the darker pink between her legs.

Her gown really is not sufficient to hide her from my warrior's scrutiny. I will order the replicator to design more concealing garments for her to wear outside our chambers. It will make her appear more like a bride than a courting Tsenturion female but... she *has* been claimed by me. Even though she is not Tsenturion, in a manner she is now my bride. A fitting argument if anyone dares to speak up.

Inside our quarters, it will be an entirely different matter. Perhaps I will order her to go without clothes. Yes, and command her to disrobe within the first minute of entering or face punishment.

Punishing my Tribute is far too enjoyable. Even now she is squirming in anticipation. The color of her bottom has faded somewhat to a soft pink, but I can tell it is still sensitive to my touch as I caress the soft mound.

When I clear my throat, she ceases moving, going quite still in fact, almost as if she's hoping I will somehow not notice her.

"Your skin still has color from your previous sessions," I announce proudly, thinking she will want to know. The manuals indicated that human females have an interest in knowing what their bottoms look like after punishment.

"Because there was some ambiguity to my statement, I will make this brief. Next time you disobey publicly, I will be much harsher."

Little grunts and huffs of air escape as I smack my broad hand over her small, tight cheeks. I pay special attention to the crease between her leg and rounded buttocks, an area I had attended to before but not focused on. Every time my palm lands on that sensitive area, her breath catches and she lets out a little cry. I pause, wondering if I should push this session further. The manuals outlined the benefits of spanking a Tribute until she releases emotion. After all she's been through, she might need a good, hard cry.

Yet I find that, like before, I am eager to move on to the next part of a spanking. My cock, *seela*, and *prime seela* all press against my suit, threatening to burst out, eager to be inside of her once again. And I'm not the only one who notices.

My Tribute wriggles, pressing herself against my cock. I know she is attempting to incite my lust and end her spanking sooner. Amused, and highly aroused myself, I decide to indulge her. Apparently, I am feeling *very* lenient now that we are alone. And her bottom is already a nice, hot pink, thanks to having been attended to earlier. The cream between her legs is a clear indicator of her arousal.

Lifting her up from my lap, I move her to the side so that she is bent over the edge of the bed. My armor sends a message to the bed, and she lets out a little noise of startled surprise as the bed begins to rise until she is at the perfect height to receive my cock. The new placement means she is barely touching the floor with the tips of her toes, leaving the full weight of her body resting on the bed.

Once she's impaled on my cock, she won't be able to

move, she will be pinned between the bed and myself. I smile, greatly pleased by her predicament.

"Master... please... wait," she begs. "Let me turn over..."

"No," I say, gripping her hips and shoving my cock into her wet heat.

6

Dawn

I CRY out as Gavrill thrusts inside of me, hard and fast. I knew I was going to be sore, both inside and out, but that hadn't been why I'd wanted to turn over. Just as I thought—feared—the long tentacle above his cock immediately probes around the entrance to my ass as he holds himself inside of me. I try to lurch forward and away from the intrusive touch, but in this position there is nowhere for me to go. All I can do is try and wriggle to the side as he holds himself deep inside of me, groaning. His *seela* stroking my pussy lips while the long one circles my anus.

It feels better than I want it to.

Invasive. Perverse. Pleasurable.

I try to clench my cheeks, but my position doesn't allow for it, and I make a high-pitched whining noise as I squirm uncomfortably.

Yeah, I read about this stuff, but I've never actually *done* it. Some fantasies are supposed to remain just that —fantasies.

Yes, I'd been trying to distract him from spanking me again—I would much rather have sex than take any more punishment—but I thought he'd put me on my back again. It hadn't occurred to me what I was risking until he had me bent over the bed and the way everything would line up had flashed into my mind.

When he pulls back, I relax slightly until he's pushing forward again, burying himself inside of me. Every time he does, I can feel his long *seela* probing, exploring... and I don't dare say anything because I don't want to give him any ideas he hasn't already had. Considering the reading material, I don't have a whole lot of hope for keeping my ass virginal, but I'll cling to whatever hope I can.

But, as usual, my fantasies aren't helping me one bit.

The more his tentacle teases my tiny hole, the better it feels, and the more my mind starts racing with all the scenes from my favorite books. The dominant alien master demanding his human slave's submission, probing *all* of her despite her protests, and finally taking her ass... maybe even making her enjoy it, but maybe not.

His hard body slaps against my tender cheeks as he rides me, reigniting the sting in a way that makes my pussy clench around him. Despite how sore I am, both inside from our previous encounter and outside from the spankings, I respond readily to him. The ridges massage the inside of my walls, that odd-shaped head fluttering inside of me and stimulating me in all the right places.

I don't know if it's the training or if I've gone full-on Stockholm syndrome, or if it's just the fulfillment of my fantasies, or some unholy combination of all three, but it's like my entire universe has narrowed down to this one room, to this one moment. I spasm around him, my back arching slightly, my pussy lips plumping under the massage of his *seela*. The embarrassment and trepidation I feel about having my virgin ass probed seeps away as my pleasure rises, the sensations coming from that area contributing to my growing ecstasy.

My sense of helplessness only increases my arousal, and I moan as he takes his time, obviously enjoying riding me. Each thrust brings me a little closer to orgasm, but he's so deliberate, each stroke so measured, that it's starting to drive me a little out of my mind. I'm clawing at the sheets as I strain towards an orgasm I can't quite reach yet.

"Please..." The plea escapes my lips, my pussy clenching around his thick shaft, trying to drag him in deeper, hold him there longer. "Please..."

Gavrill

The sweet sound of my Tribute's begging incites me.

I had been taking my time, testing my control after the wildness of my first time with her, and had been reassured that it had been an aberration. That it allowed me to wallow in the pleasure of her body was an added inducement. But when she begins to beg... I can feel my urges growing again, responding to her submissive plea.

Groaning low, under my breath, I begin to move a little harder and faster, my *seela* writhing and stroking. The small, crinkled hole which so disturbed her when it was touched winks at me from between her pink cheeks as they jiggle against my thrusts. I have many plans for exploring that opening, one that Tsenturions do not possess, but which figures prominently in all the texts of her people.

My *prime seela* probes at its tightness with every thrust, and I can only imagine how pleasurable such a narrow channel would be, especially as my Tribute whimpers and submits beneath me, very much as she is now. Her wetness increases with every thrust, her moans becoming louder as I plow into her from behind, my hands gripping her hips, pinning her to the bed and holding her in place while I take my pleasure.

She is obviously enjoying it as well, and it is as though my need is feeding off hers... my control is slipping from my fingers, and I don't care anymore. My entire focus is on the sweet clasp of her body, her delicious cries of pleasure as she begins to spasm and clench around me, and my own urgent desire.

I rut her harder, faster, groaning with pleasure as she sobs out her own climax. The way her legs kick, I can tell she is becoming overloaded with sensation, and it only spurs me to take her harder. I grip her hips, pinning her down and holding her in place while I fill her, over and over again. The walls of her body tighten, trying to hold me in place, but she is too slick and my thrusts too strong.

Her cries have become incoherent, filling my ears and feeding the dark craving that her presence has created. I growl, low, pumping relentlessly until my own orgasm finally surges. My seed spurts as I bury myself inside of her, letting the spasms of her body milk me of my offering. My *seela* have latched onto her again, pulling at her body and keeping us firmly joined as I empty myself into her. Panting, I shudder, groaning, and she whimpers delightfully beneath me, her breath coming out on a ragged sob.

My own body feels oddly slack, my satisfaction so overwhelming that I would be alarmed if I didn't feel so good. So right.

Bemused, I run my hand down her back and over the soft cheeks of her bottom, which are still slightly warm to the touch. The noises she makes are so quiet, I can barely hear them, just enough to let me know she's still conscious and responsive.

When I lean back slightly so that my fingers can explore the area my *prime seela* was probing, she becomes much more responsive.

~

Dawn

"WAIT!" My voice comes out in a high squeak, making me sound like a cartoon mouse as one of Gavrill's big fingers pokes at my rear entrance. My legs kick, but my muscles are so watery and weak after my orgasm that I might as well have just lain there. Not that it would have made much of a difference even if I wasn't feeling so pathetically limp.

Ignoring me, his finger dips down between our bodies to where he's still embedded inside of me, gathers the cream there and returns to push at my crinkled hole. I'd finally gotten used to the sensation of his tentacle thing circling and teasing me there, and then the way it felt like it had actually been sucking on the tender bundle of nerves that I hadn't known existed, but it hadn't actually gone inside of me.

"No..." My cry of protest is barely a whimper as the tiny hole stretches and his finger slides inside. Embarrassment flushes through me as he probes the virgin entrance to my body, his finger burrowing inside and making me uncomfortably aware that it doesn't feel entirely unpleasant. The slight burn of stretching isn't enough to truly hurt, and being so full feels almost good.

I whimper as he pumps his finger, exploring, and my body clenches down instinctively, trying to push him out. All that means is that I can feel every millimeter of his digit as it moves inside of me.

"You are very tight here," he says, sounding pleased. "I look forward to finishing your subjugation by taking you in this orifice."

The very formal wording he uses for the act only makes it sound even more depraved. I'm also not super happy about him calling it my 'subjugation', but I can't bring myself to argue either, because that's exactly what it feels like. Like he's literally fucking me into submission with his strange, alien cock.

A cock which had been softening inside of me but is now beginning to harden and thicken again. The uber-sensitive walls of my pleasure-soaked pussy can feel the difference easily, and I whimper. I can't possibly take any more pleasure. Humans aren't meant to. I don't care what upgrades Frllil gave to my body to ready me to be a Tsenturion Tribute, if Gavrill fucks me again, I think I might die.

Unfortunately, Tributes don't get a say.

I sob as he begins to thrust again, my sore pussy fluttering in protest and my ass clenching around the finger he is now pushing in and out of my bottom.

GAVRILL

BY THE TIME Bogdan calls to ask if I am coming to the bridge for my shift or not, his voice full of disapproval, my Tribute is nearly insensate. I have pleasured her into complete submission. Her nipples are reddened from the attentions of my mouth and fingers, her pussy lips are just as red and swollen and marked with many purple circles from the suction of my *seela*, and she didn't even protest when I used the training belt to fill her bottom, stretching that tight hole for my eventual use. Tsenturions do not have the "plugs" which her manuals mention, but I have used the belt to create what I think is a good approximation.

I have lost count of the number of orgasms I've had; much less how many I've given her. Learning her body, exploring what she does and does not enjoy, how to make her climax hardest, has utterly consumed me. I have also lost count of the hours. Unheard of for me. For the first time in my life, I am late to my shift.

Yet, I still find myself oddly reluctant to leave her, though she is no longer in a position to entertain me. While I feel energized, it is obvious that she requires rest. Probably food as well.

Frowning, I make a fast decision and hail Arkdhem. While I would like to bring my Tribute with me to the bridge, that will not be very restful for her and will be distracting for me. But I do not wish to leave her alone, especially as she may awaken hungry or thirsty after all the rigorous activity. Indeed, I will be ordering someone to bring me some sustenance as soon as I am on the bridge.

Out of all of my men, other than Medik, I trust Arkdhem with her the most. He is the commander of our scout ships and young for the post, but it was well-earned. From the beginning, he was vocal of his support for the Tribute program, but he does not have a covetous personality and looks up to me as an older brother. None of my men would disrespect me or harm my Tribute, but... Arkdhem will be the most respectful and least envious.

"Yes, Commander?" Arkdhem answers my hail immediately.

"Arkdhem, I have a new assignment for you, if you are willing to accept it."

"Yes, Commander," he says without hesitation. "Whatever it is you wish."

"You might want to hear it first," I reply, somewhat amused. "I am on duty on the bridge, but I do not wish to leave my Tribute entirely unattended. She is currently sleeping but will likely require sustenance when she awakens. I would ask you to be her escort on the ship while I am otherwise occupied."

"Commander, it would be an honor." The sincerity in his voice confirms my choice. "I will return to the main ship immediately."

"She is in my quarters. I will give you access before I leave."

It will not take him long to dock his ship and make his way here, and it is unlikely my Tribute will awaken anytime soon. As much as I enjoy the look of her the way she is now, I exert my will on the nanotech, and it spreads downwards from the front of her belt and upwards over her pussy from where it's embedded in her secondary entrance. I leave it inside of her there, to facilitate my eventual breaching. All of the manuals indicated that being filled there would help human females remain in the submissive mindset, reminding them of their helpless vulnerability to their Master.

Once the nanotech is in place, I pick out the most covering of her garments, an opaque pink gown with slits up the side, and dress her. She barely murmurs as I move her about on the bed, other than a small whimper when I caress her breast before covering it. Arkdhem has still not arrived, but I cannot delay any longer.

Shoving down my unanticipated reluctance, I force myself to leave the room. It feels wrong to separate myself from her, which only increases my determination to do so. This swiftly growing attachment makes no sense and is not at all convenient.

Just how much so becomes more apparent when I reach the bridge and face Bogdan's glower. My second is fuming, his armor dark and streaked with simmering red, and he does not even bother to contain his emotion.

"Is this going to be the new way of things now that you have a Tribute?" he asks, his voice full of demand.

Normally I would not allow him to question me in such a manner in front of the crew, but they all deserve an answer.

Calmly, I meet his gaze, my own armor not flickering one iota from its neutral grey. I actually feel quite serene now that I am on the bridge, more focused.

"It will not happen again," I say. "However, I will recommend that in the future, those receiving Tributes also receive some time off. It is unlikely any of us will be able to resist indulging deeply after such a long period of abstinence. Perhaps it is unreasonable to expect that things will continue completely as normal when a Tribute first arrives."

My statement makes quite a few of the crew brighten. Whether they are excited by the idea of their own Tributes or by the idea of additional time with the females once they arrive, I am unsure. Bogdan just looks angrier than ever.

"So you are saying that that human is now your first priority?" He is practically seething, and his accusation makes some of the excitement in the room dampen.

I scowl back at him, my own armor darkening slightly.

"My first priority is, and always will be, our people. I came the moment you called earlier, did I not? As I always do and always will. But allowances must also be made for the change in our situation."

His jaw clenches, and he is obviously not entirely appeased by my answer, but I have no other to give him. Having a Tribute is more consuming than I had realized, and I think my men will find it so as well at first. The fascination for something new will fade, even the urge to copulate should grow less as my desires are satiated, and Bogdan will eventually see that.

"You will understand when you have your own Tribute and are able to sate your needs," I tell him.

"I do not *want* a human Tribute," he spits out, his voice full of disgust and derision, before storming off the bridge.

Silence reigns in his absence, and I resist the urge to rub my head. I don't know why Bogdan is behaving like a child, but I will not chase after him either. Obviously, he needs rest.

"I'll take his if he doesn't want her," Vander, my pilot on duty, pipes in. Laughter breaks the tension in the room, and even I chuckle.

"We'll see. Now update me. Where are we on the search for the Vgotha?" I ask.

Still looking, since following the trail through the ion pathways of the outer edges of the cloud is difficult, and so far they have not taken the bait our scout ships have offered. As the bridge reports in, Arkdhem sends me a message that he has arrived at my chambers and my Tribute still slumbers. A small part of me I hadn't even known was tense now relaxes, and I am able to focus entirely on the matters at hand, knowing she is watched over.

Dawn

I COME AWAKE WITH A GROWL. Not that I'm growling, my stomach is. I'm *starving.* Not too surprising considering the last time I ate was before I was presented as a Tribute, and... well, I have no idea how long Gavrill had erotically tortured me, but it had been a long time. My pussy feels thoroughly abused, my thighs feel like I'd run a freaking marathon, and though I've been asleep, I still feel really drained.

I am also very... full... in a place that I'm not accustomed to being full.

Reaching down, I groan when my fingers meet the hated training belt, which is covering me underneath the filmy dress I am now wearing. I have a fuzzy memory of Gavrill eagerly watching my expression as he pushed the belt's nanotech up inside my ass, making me squirm even though I had been practically dizzy with exhaustion by that point. The control he had over the belt was more than a little terrifying, since the belt was *on* me.

The dirty pervert had then fucked me while my ass was full, and I'd come so hard, I'd seen stars before practically passing out.

"Tribute? Are you awake?" The deep voice came out of the darkness and makes me shriek and scramble... what exactly I'm scrambling for, I have no idea, but my hands and legs go every which way.

"Who's there?" I ask, my heart pounding. That was *not* Gavrill's voice, and I don't think it's one I had heard before. Although, it's not like I've been memorizing voices. I think I would remember the angry one on the bridge though, Bogdan.

"Cabin, lights." At the order, the lights in the cabin come on, and I blink rapidly as my eyes adjust. Sitting on one of the couches in the main area of the cabin is a Tsenturion warrior, fully armored except for his head. His armor is a light grey, almost a sky blue. It's a very unthreatening color, and I relax again.

"Greetings, Commander's Tribute, I am Arkdhem, and I am here in case you require anything while the High Commander is on the bridge."

I nearly giggled at his eager formality, except...

"Please, call me Dawn, not Commander's Tribute or Tribute." I plead, already anticipating that he'll turn me down, but instead he nods his head and looks like he's concentrating.

"Very well, Dawn," he says, sounding out my name the same way Gavrill did when I made the request of him. A request that he has since ignored. "Is there anything I can do for you right now?"

As if on cue, my stomach growls.

"Food?" I ask hopefully. "And water? Maybe something to brush my teeth?"

For a Tsenturion, Arkdhem turns out to be pretty easy-going. He kind of reminds me of an eager puppy. He shows me how to use both the shower and cleaning facilities in the bathroom, although I only actually use the latter for now. While I definitely need a shower, I need food first. Brushing the sleep out of my mouth felt good though. I feel a little odd just rinsing my mouth out with a flavorless liquid that basically just seems like it's water, but I can feel it tingling, and my mouth does feel cleaner afterwards.

Food is in the cafeteria. Arkdhem offered to order it

brought to us, but I wanted out of the cabin. If I'm ever going to escape, I need to explore, right? When I tell him I'd rather see more of the ship, he's completely amenable and escorts me right out of the door. Walking on wobbly legs, I tell myself that this is a good idea. My muscles could do with some movement that doesn't involve my legs being spread or hanging uselessly. Fortunately, the training belt is soft against my pussy, or else I would be a lot more uncomfortable.

Truthfully, I feel way better than I should. My limbs are long and loose, like I've done a satisfying yoga session. I can't help but wonder if it's the tinkering Frllil did to my body to prepare me for being a Tribute.

Gavrill's collar is still around my neck, but Arkdhem didn't attach a leash, to my relief. Apparently, that's a right reserved only for my *master*. I'm definitely not complaining.

Out in the corridors of the ship, I look around at everything, and, since Arkdhem is so accommodating, I ask as many questions as I can think of. Not that any of his answers are very helpful to me.

Where are we in relation to my galaxy? *No idea.*

Does he know how I got here? *Through an unstable wormhole.*

How does someone travel through a wormhole, much less an unstable one? *Through a portal or a pod designed by the Jabols. But as far as he knows, I'm the only being who has ever travelled through one.*

It quickly becomes apparent that he has no problem answering my increasingly unsubtle questions that would help me escape because there *is* no escape. The Tsenturions don't even know the general vicinity of Earth, because they had nothing to do with picking me up. To get back to my home, I need the Jabol. To get back to *them*, I'd need a ship and a navigator.

Hopelessness is swamping me by the time we make it to the cafeteria.

"Don't worry," Arkdhem says gently, patting my shoulder with his huge hand. "You'll be happy here with us. The High Commander is the best of the best, and he will treat you well."

"Right." Bitterness wells. "I just have to accept that I'll never see my home again."

For a long, solemn moment, Arkdhem studies me. "I know you don't think I understand, but I do. We all do."

Shame rushes through me as I realize that he does. They all lost their entire planet and everyone on it. At least I know Earth is still there. My beloved house still stands. My yoga class students are going on about their lives as if everything is totally normal. And I don't have any immediate family, no one who would be significantly hurt by my abduction. My life has completely changed, I've lost everything... but at least I know it's still out there.

"Sorry," I whisper.

He just smiles and pats my shoulder again before leading me to a machine in the wall. There's an opening there with a tray in it. I assume this is how they get food. Frllil used to just bring me trays, so I don't know where he was getting it from, but at least I had some time to learn what I like. Arkdhem also insists on adding a few of his favorites that I haven't tried before—it wasn't like the Jabol ever provided me with a buffet or anything.

It's nice having someone care what I want, even if it's just for a meal. I don't want to admit it, but some little part of me aches, wishing it was Gavrill beside me, helping me try new food and not Arkdhem.

7

Gavrill

WHEN CORIN ARRIVES on the bridge to take over command for the next shift, Arkdhem and my Tribute are still dining. They have been there for quite some time and I frown in concern as I stride down the hallway. Do humans take an abnormally long time to eat, or has something else detained them?

When I reach the dining hall, the scene that greets my eyes is unexpected and not entirely welcome.

My Tribute sits at the center of a group of my warriors, all of them watching as she bites into what looks like a piece of korrun fruit. Immediately, her eyes widen with delight at the rich flavor, her entire face lighting up.

"It tastes exactly like chocolate!" She shoves the rest of the fruit into her mouth, looking almost blissful and humming with a noise that is far too close to the sounds she made in my bed.

Jealousy rips through me, so hot and fast that my armor actually flickers with the bright orange color, as if it's been shot through with meteors. Seeing the color, I push down my unruly emotions before the color streaks can catch anyone's eye. There is no reason for jealousy, just because they can hear her. No one is touching her, they are just watching her.

Listening to her.

And they seem as enthralled by her as I am.

It is only understandable, I tell myself. They are curious. And she is beautiful. Interesting. Exotic. The first of the Tributes. The hope for the future.

Despite my logic, I can still feel my possessiveness, my jealousy, seething underneath the surface of my forced calm. At least none of it shows on my armor where my warriors can see it. Not that any of them seem to have Bogdan's attitude, but I am the High Commander, and I would not display any weakness by choice.

In control of myself again, I start forward, and the movement catches Arkdhem's eyes. He immediately stands and salutes, thumping his hand against his chest, which causes a chain reaction as the rest of my warriors notice and do the same. My Tribute looks startled at the sudden formality— which is not strictly necessary when in locations like the cafeteria or on the bridge when work is being done. Arkdhem tends to salute when he sees me, regardless of what he's doing, unless it would be dangerous to do so.

"High Commander," he says. "I did not realize how much time had passed. We were introducing Dawn to more of our cuisine than the Jabol had provided."

"So I see," I respond, nodding my head. "She seems to be enjoying the korrun fruit."

My eyes drop to hers, and she smiles hesitantly at me. Hopefully. I do not understand what it is she hopes for, but she appears pleased to see me, and that pleases me, as well as soothing some of my jealousy.

"It tastes just like my favorite dessert back home," she says, almost shyly, as though she is wondering whether or not it is appropriate to speak. I am even more pleased that she is obviously already adjusting to the expectations I have set down for her.

"Then you shall have as much of it as you like," I say, feeling rather magnanimous. "Right now, I'd like to go back to the cabin. If you are still hungered, then we can bring some with us."

There is no sign of disappointment by the males around us, but I can feel it like a palpable thing. But they have had my Tribute's attention for long enough.

My Tribute shakes her head. "I am finished, thank you. Master."

The honorific is tacked on to the end as if she almost forgot, but I will be lenient, as she is still learning, and it does not seem deliberate. My warriors begin to disperse as I move to her side and clip the leash to her collar. As soon as I've done, so I can feel myself relaxing even further, as though having her physically attached to me in some manner has completed something that was missing within me.

I am uncomfortably aware that some of Bogdan's accusations may have been closer to the truth than I want to admit.

～

Dawn

STUPID LEASH. The sound of it clicking into place is heavier than a door slamming shut. The brief illusion of being myself again is gone.

Worse, there's a part of me that felt joy at seeing Gavrill walking up and that now feels a sense of satisfaction at being leashed by him. I had been happy to see him, although slightly wary since I definitely wasn't being quiet and the blank expression on his face hadn't seemed particularly promising. But he didn't seem angry.

For some reason, I get the sense that he's feeling possessive, maybe even jealous, but I can't imagine where I'm getting that from because I can't read that in his expression or body language at all.

"Thank you for taking care of my Tribute," he says to Arkdhem. Again, I'm torn into two Dawns—the one that wants to bristle at being dehumanized back to 'Tribute' and the one that is stupid enough to feel special about being called *his* Tribute.

He would have called any woman that, I remind myself. *If something happened to me, they'd probably just replace me with another woman, and then he'd call* her *his Tribute.*

I'm stupid enough that the thought actually hurts. If Stockholm Syndrome was water, I'd be swimming in the ocean right now.

"It was my pleasure, High Commander," Arkdhem says, absolutely sincere. I smile at him. I like Arkdhem; he seems like a nice guy—a nice Tsenturion.

After relieving Arkdhem of his babysitting duties, because that's pretty much what it feels like right now, Gavrill leads me back to his cabin. He's silent the whole way, and so am I. Talking with the other Tsenturions hadn't been easy exactly, because they'd all been strangers, but somehow it had been easier than talking to this particular Tsenturion. I hadn't cared what they thought of me except in a very general way.

As much as I didn't want to admit it, I definitely cared what Gavrill thought of me.

I was also torn between a sense of relief and peace at being in his presence again and being annoyed as all hell at being on a leash again. I'm also getting tired, and as he leads me into the cabin, I yawn.

His dark, sharp eyes immediately take in the action. "You require more rest?"

"Probably," I say, trying to hold back what feels like another yawn coming on. "I think being hungry kind of woke me up before I was finished sleeping. Master."

The look in his eyes sharpens. I feel my heart rate pick up a little as he steps forward, looming over me slightly. His fingers cup my chin, tilting my head back so he can look me in the eyes.

"It is your first day, and you are tired, so I will be lenient," he murmurs, his voice gentle but firm. "But you will learn to call me Master, or you will be spanked until you remember."

"Yes, Master," I say immediately, the honorific coming very easily now when he's looking at me like that and holding me like this. I am suddenly very aware of my body, the cheeks of my bottom tingling in a kind of anticipation despite still being sore from earlier, my nipples hardening, my pussy lips plumping, and my ass clenching around the nanotech plug the training belt created.

I want to fight the reaction, but how can I fight myself?

"Good girl," he says, and warmth flushes through me. Dammit, I shouldn't like it so much when he says that. I shouldn't care what he thinks, because my complaisance is supposed to just be an act.

But I do care. And I do like it.

Then he's pulling on the leash, drawing me in closer to him using the leash and collar around my neck, as his mouth lowers to mine for a kiss. How I can still be horny after being fucked multiple times, I have no idea, but arousal immediately flares within me, and I can feel myself becoming slick and swollen in the belt.

He groans against my lips, picking me up and carrying me over to the bed, one arm around my waist, the other holding the back of my neck as I wrap my legs around him for balance. His armor is already flowing back and disappearing into his spine, leaving bare skin behind. He practically rips the flimsy dress I'm wearing off my body, the training belt immediately receding from my pussy, but not from my ass.

I moan as it moves inside my rear channel. Not growing, exactly, and not fucking me, but just rippling inside of me and creating an entirely new sensation that is pure pleasure.

GAVRILL

I TRULY HAD MEANT to let her rest without having her again, but when she called me 'Master' so sweetly, especially after my jealousy had been roused, my cock and *seela* had immediately come to life. I wanted—needed—to possess her again. To truly master her.

My Tribute whimpers beneath me as I manipulate the belt's invasion of her rear entrance, approximating the movements of my cockhead inside of her tight ass. Grasping her wrists, I take them both in one hand and hold them down above her head as I cup one of her ample breasts with the other. The soft flesh is pleasing in my grip, and I lower my mouth to her nipple as my cock dips between the lips of her pussy.

"Oh...oh please..." she moans, arching slightly as I begin to push inside of her. "Too full... please, Gavrill... Master... I'm too full..."

I should punish her for calling me by my name, but I find I like to hear it on her lips. Immediately, I make the decision that as long as she addresses me properly in public, I will not punish her for what she calls me privately, in the throes of passion.

Ignoring her plea, knowing she can take it, I feel the wet clasp of her heat and the ripples of the belt through the thin lining between her channels as I push deeper. Laving her nipple with my tongue, I gently nip at the tender bud, making her clench around me as I suck it deeper into my mouth. She writhes, her arms pressing upwards against my hand as though she is trying to break free, but to no avail.

Next time I take her, I will use bindings to secure her to the bed, so I may have my hands free to do what I wish, but right now I am too impatient to be inside of her again. I hold her down with my own weight as I begin to thrust, groaning with pleasure around my mouthful of breast flesh as the muscles of her pussy ripple around me.

My *seela* stroke her pussy lips and clit, my body having already learned the way she likes it the best. Being inside of her again gives me a relief that is almost indescribable; the closest I can come to it is saying that it feels like coming home. She strains beneath me, arching, as I pump in and out of her, manipulating the training belt so that it begins to grow and recede inside of her. While it cannot thrust, it is the closest I can come to approximating fucking her ass with it.

The sensations of it moving alongside my own shaft are incredible. The feel of her beneath me, around me, the scent of her filling my nose... it is everything I want, everything I need, and I become lost in her.

~

Dawn

THIS TIME I'm sure I'm really going to die from an overload of sexual pleasure. I am completely dominated by him, totally overwhelmed by what he's doing to me.

I can't even protest as I sob in growing ecstasy.

I'm so full, so sensitized. Every single one of my nerve endings has turned into a receptacle for pleasure. The movement in my ass matches his thrusts into my pussy, creating perverse and satisfying sensations that drives my rapture higher. My clit is begging for mercy even as it swells under the attentions of his *seela*. Thankfully, whatever soreness I had felt when I first woke up had dissipated while I'd been eating, and my body is ready to receive him again.

Even if it hadn't been, I'm not sure he'd be able to stop.

His thrusts are relentless, his hands and lips possessive, as if he's drinking me in, as if he can't get enough of me. I know how it feels, because I feel the same. My legs spread wider, my hips tilting up to receive his thrusts, my body greedy to feel him as deep inside of me as I can, to be even fuller although I already feel as though I'm about to burst.

When the belt begins to vibrate inside of me, I scream as

sheer erotic ecstasy rips through me, untamed and unyielding even as it overloads my entire nervous system. The waves of rapture sweep over me, curling my toes, my legs, and arching my back against Gavrill's rough thrusts, each one sending me higher and higher on planes of pleasure. The vibrations shake the very core of my existence, and my entire universe narrows to just the two of us.

There's a moment where I can feel his pleasure, his need, his loneliness and his possessive joy at having me...

My climax hits another intense wave, and I feel his body latch onto mine, his tentacles sucking at my pussy lips as he swells inside of me, throbbing as his seed spills into me. I'm blinded by the white-hot ecstasy, the sensation of being *one* with him in every way, and even as I writhe in orgasmic euphoria, the dark of unconsciousness begins to drag me under, saving me from the intensity of the physical and emotional frenzy I'm experiencing.

GAVRILL

I AM WRAPPED around my Tribute, her exhausted body tucked against mine, when my com beeps. I have been awake for a while but loathe to move when I am so comfortable with her warm, soft body cuddled so close. Tsenturions seems to require less sleep than humans—or perhaps I am just more used to large amounts of vigorous physical activity.

The message is from Medik, who wishes to speak with me about my Tribute and the Tribute program in general. I am not opposed. Back on Tsentur, warriors transitioning to their civilian phase of life would often have a mentor to help them through the process. Although I am not transitioning, and my Tribute is not a Tsenturion bride, I do have a few questions for a male who has been mated before. I would also like him to examine her and reassure myself that her exhaustion is normal and she remains healthy.

As I am composing my own message back, another one arrives.

Bogdan, with the same desire as Medik. Although I doubt his thoughts on the program align with Medik's.

I respond to both of them—we will dine all together before my next shift. It will be interesting to see Medik and Bogdan's opposing arguments, and I will be able to stay well out of it while sifting through their points and thinking through their merits without having to take either side. When we have the time to plan our military excursions, I have found such tactics to be a useful tool in making my decisions.

Fortunately, there are several hours before I need to meet with them.

Laying here with my Tribute is not the most productive use of my time, but my motivation to do anything else is very low. I cannot think of anything else that *requires* my attention. There is no shame or wrong in focusing on her during these moments when I am not on duty. Perhaps doing so will aid in focusing on my mission when I am on the bridge.

Once I am used to having a Tribute, she will no longer be so distracting.

8

D awn

"FOR OUR NEXT MEAL, we dine with company. I trust you will behave."

As he instructs me, Gavrill runs his large hands over my naked body. I can't keep from shivering with pleasure at his touch. The trainer hums between my legs, and I moan. I can't believe I'm still horny.

I should be sore. Chafing even.

But instead he woke me up with soft caresses and the belt vibrating against my clit and inside me, and I'm squirming on my back. I also woke up with my hands bound to the headboard of the bed, leaving me completely vulnerable to whatever he wants to do. Apparently, what he wants to do is torment me by touching every part of my body but not actually bringing me to satisfaction. The fact that his armor is on, concealing his bare skin, makes me wonder if he's going to fuck me or just drive me mad with need.

"Yes, Master," I answer dutifully. I struggle to think rationally as Gavrill's hands continue to roam. I force myself to focus. "Who will join us?"

"My second, Bogdan, for one."

Great. The glowering warrior from the bridge. Sounds like fun.

Gavrill must have picked up on my dismay, for he adds smoothly, "Do not worry, Dawn. Obey me, and I won't let any warrior speak against you."

"Thank you, Master. I will be good," I whisper, a very Tribute-like answer. There's a part of me that is insisting I'm just playing the part I need to in order to survive—preferably survive without more spankings—but deep down I know that I also don't want to jeopardize his standing with his men, and I want him to be proud of me, as Stockholm-Syndrome-y as that sounds.

"If you are, then you will be rewarded," he says smoothly, his hands sliding over my stomach. My muscles quiver beneath his palm, making me whimper. It doesn't tickle exactly, but it's close. "Bogdan may try to antagonize you. It is his nature. Follow protocol, and even he won't be able to speak against you."

"Follow protocol." I sigh. For all my determination to play the good little Tribute, even I know I haven't been great at that. Tsenturion protocol, as explained by Frllil, is ridiculously strict. My understanding is that it's not meant to be followed *all* the time, but apparently in my case... "In other words, be quiet and obedient like a good little trophy wife."

His big hands pause. "What is a trophy wife?"

"Similar to a Tribute," I say quickly, not wanting to explain in any detail. They are close enough after all, but as

Gavrill and the others seem to revere the idea of Tributes—even if I'm being treated more like a pet than a human being —I don't want him to think I'm disparaging Tributes. I doubt that would go over well.

Accepting my explanation, his hands begin to move again, stroking the sides of my breasts as he explains.

"During our meal, you will be required to be obedient, yes. Silent, no. Our second guest wishes to engage you in conversation. Medik is the most well-versed among us when it comes to mating and bonding. He had a family and a mate before the Great Attack. On his advice, I instructed the Jabol to search the universe for suitable brides."

So I have the doctor to thank for my abduction.

Despite the arousal humming through my body, my anger stirs.

Gavrill places a finger at my lips as if to wipe away my frown. "You will treat him with respect. Medik is my oldest and closest friend, as well as a mentor."

"Is Medik his real name?" I ask. "My translator makes it sound like 'doctor', and it seems like that's the position he fills for you..."

"He is our physician, and his name *is* his title. We all called him that while he was on duty, and his true name was lost with our world. He does not wish to be called by it." His eyes unfocus, as if he's thinking hard about something. "I do not even remember what it was."

I barely keep from shaking my head. The closest thing to a friend Gavrill has in the known universe, and Gavrill doesn't even know his real name. If that doesn't warn a girl off from getting emotionally attached to him, I don't know what would. Unfortunately, I'm not sure it will be that easy.

I don't *want* to like him, but I do.

Not just because he seems intent on pleasuring me into the stratosphere either. Yes, he's spanked me, put me on a leash, and treated me like a pet... but he's also obviously a good leader, he can be exceedingly gentle, he looks at me with something like reverence, and he's incredibly straightforward. I'm not sure Tsenturions even know how to lie. From everything I've seen, they're all completely sincere in everything they say and do.

There is definitely something appealing about all of that.

No guesswork, no games.

Which means it's very clear right now that Gavrill is enjoying tormenting me for his own amusement.

"Mealtime approaches. Soon it will be time to make ready." His hands fit over my hips and the trainer recedes, baring my pussy. My ass, on the other hand, is still full, and I can feel the thin strip of it leading down between my cheeks from the belt part. Instantly my body seizes, my pussy creaming even more than it had for the belt in anticipation of him taking me again.

"Are you primed for me?" Gavrill murmurs. One hand strokes my labia, while the other covers my right breast. Since he's been touching me everywhere *but* those places for what felt like hours, the sensations feel doubly intense and I arch against his fingers. They slip inside my pussy, testing my wetness and probing just inside my lips.

"Yes..."

"Yes, what?"

"Yes... Master." My breath comes in little pants. Sensual need ripples through me, pulsing at my nipples and between my legs.

"I don't know." If I didn't know any better, I'd say he was teasing me right now. But he's too stoic for that... isn't he?

"Perhaps I should leave you primed and waiting until tonight."

I whimper as he pinches my nipple, the hot sting of pleasure zinging straight down to my pussy and making me clench around his fingers as they slide deeper inside of me. The idea of him leaving me on edge like this makes me feel manic. I know I've gone through worse, while Frllil was priming me for him, but right now that doesn't matter... I want my orgasm, and I want it *now*.

"If you let me come now, I won't be distracted during the meal," I point out. As aroused as I am, it's amazing that I can form a logical argument.

"Or you'll be focused entirely on me, waiting for the command that allows you to cum."

I flush at the idea of being brought to orgasm in front of an audience, unsure of whether I'm more horrified or just more aroused. I don't really want to find out. "You don't want me to... perform for them, do you?"

His reaction shocks me. At first, I think I must be imagining that I can actually feel what he's feeling, but the darkening of his suit and the way his jaw clenches makes me wonder if I'm right... if I can actually feel the violent possessiveness gripping him. I gasp as my skin prickles almost painfully, as if reacting to the strange surge of outside emotion.

"You will never perform for them." His dark eyes spear me, his hand tightening on my breast, fingers thrusting deeply into me. I gasp, arching, my wrists tugging against the restraints at the pleasurable and painful sensations tingling along my nerves, and it's only getting stronger as he speaks. "Do not speak of it again. Do not even think it."

"Master," I gasp as the buzzing energy along my skin grows. I feel like I've been Tasered or struck by lightning. If every hair on my head isn't standing up, I'd be very surprised. It *hurts*. "I meant nothing wrong. Please—"

The electric current dies away. Gavrill pauses, steadying me as I choke on air. The possessiveness gripping me, making my skin too tight, relaxes, and I slump, gasping for breath. The hand on my breast has relaxed, and his fingers slide out of me, no longer trying to punish me with rough thrusts.

"Forgive me," he says, and I jerk in surprise. An apology was the last thing I'd expect from my stern master. Judging by the dismayed look on his face, his behavior has shocked him, too. "I did not mean to upset you. It has been a long time since I possessed anything so rare and treasured. I do not wish to share."

Jealous. I'd asked if he wanted me to perform sexually for his friends, and his response was a jealousy so intense, it nearly choked me. Although he didn't seem to realize what had been happening to me. Had I felt his emotions? Or had what I thought were his emotions actually just been him manipulating the training belt? Could it do that to me?

He runs his hands over me, stroking what now feels like raw skin.

I whimper again, and he hushes me, his voice and hands soothing.

"You are *my* little Tribute. You belong to *me* and me alone." His armor recedes as he shifts above me, spreading my legs with his palms. The electric current left me both sensitive and wanting more. Being bound before him only makes me wish I could touch him, and yet it arouses me that I literally can't. His cock brushes over my clit, moving toward my entrance, and I moan. "Shhh. I am your master. I will take care of you and give you pleasure, and you will want for nothing."

I cry out as he thrusts inside of me, my hips rising off the bed, silently begging for more.

GAVRILL

I AM out of control again, but I do not care.

The idea of my Tribute showing this side of herself to others... of them hearing her soft moans, seeing the way she throws her head back in ecstasy, has inflamed me with passion, possession, and anger. For the first time, I understand the Tsenturion impulse to mark our mates, so that all may see who she belongs to. I almost wish it were possible to do so with a human, even though everyone already knows she is mine.

It is an illogical desire.

But that does not matter to me in this moment.

Growling, I fuck her harder, feeling her hot wetness clasp me tightly as she writhes beneath me. Having her hands bound is just as enjoyable as I'd imagined it would be. While I am not averse to being touched by her, having her so helpless is exhilarating.

I can feel the head of my cock flaring inside of her, stroking her walls, and my *seela* writhe. The lips of her pussy have little marks all over them from how often I've climaxed inside of her, my body attempting to fully bond with hers. Sliding my arms under her legs, I spread her wide so that I may watch my cock sliding in and out of the plump lips of her pussy. All the little marks I have left on her there fill me with a sense of supreme satisfaction, as well as a desire to leave more on the rest of her.

Leaning forward, I practically bend her in half, pounding into her as I bite down on her shoulder. Not hard enough to draw blood, but hard enough to make her gasp. I suck, pulling at her flesh, the same way my *seela* pull at the lips of her pussy when I climax. I can taste her skin on my tongue as I suck. The manuals said that doing so would leave a mark.

It is not the mark of a Tsenturion, but it will be *my* mark on her.

"Please... oh please... Master..." Her body tries to move against mine, despite the restraints on her wrists, and I can feel her muscles beginning to flutter around my cock as her climax approaches.

I release the mouthful of her shoulder, seeing the dark red blotch that I've left on her skin with a sense of keen relish.

"Come for me," I say, demanding more than giving her permission. "Come on my cock, Dawn."

Her name slips out, unintentionally. It sounds odd and feels odd on my tongue but also seems very right. In the manuals, during the penultimate moment, the master would often use his female's name. Especially when ordering her to come for him.

The high cry she utters as her body clamps down around me is everything I want to hear. She is coming apart beneath me as I move harder, faster, my body urging me to fill her, claim her, *own* her.

Mine... she is mine... all mine.

My *seela* latch on to her pussy, my cock swelling against her clenching walls as the head goes rigid. I let loose my own deep groan of intense ecstasy as I begin to throb, my seed spilling into her, filling her. She pulses around me, pulling at my cock, like her body is hungry for whatever I can give her. I hunch over her, panting as each spasm of her body causes me to jerk against her, my *prime seela* pulling at her clit and catching us in a circle of passion which feeds off each other's reactions.

By the time I am spent, my Tribute is drowsy again with pleasure, whimpering slightly as I gently dislodge myself from her body. Her pussy lips are freshly plumped, the marks from my *seela* standing out against the paleness of her thighs, but not as much as the deep red mark my mouth has left on her shoulder. I look at it, both pleased and yet... unsatisfied. Something about it is not enough, though I know more is not possible.

As I am contemplating how to satisfy myself—perhaps by making it larger?—my com beeps and I realize we are late for our meal. Bogdan is hailing me, obviously annoyed at the delay.

Immediately, I instruct the training belt to cover her again, obscuring the delightful sight of her pussy. I wish it had enough tech to cover her body fully, but such a need had not been anticipated.

At least more opaque dresses had been delivered to the room earlier, while she was still slumbering.

"Come, my Tribute," I say, getting up and going to fetch one of them. The red one, I decide, to match the mark on her shoulder even though it will be hidden beneath the fabric of the garment. "We must hurry, we are late for our meal."

Medik will not mind, but Bogdan is liable to be more surly for it.

I am also unsettled. Tardiness is not something I tolerate in myself or in anyone else. What disturbs me the most is my annoyance at being interrupted from being able to cuddle my Tribute. It is not the reaction I would have expected myself to have.

But this is just a meal, not a duty, I remind myself. I would be more upset at becoming so distracted and less annoyed about the interruption if I were tardy to the bridge again.

Then again, before meeting my Tribute, I would have thought that about being tardy to anything.

An unsettled feeling trickles through me as I watch my Tribute pull on the red dress. I am changing, and I am not sure what to think of it.

∿

Dawn

GAVRILL IS silent as he swiftly leads me to the room where we'll be eating. It's not the cafeteria, it's a smaller room near the cafeteria. A meeting room? An officer's mess? I'm not sure.

Both of the other Tsenturions are there waiting when we enter, both standing rather than sitting. Actually, it kind of looks like they were arguing, both of them stepping away from each other as we come in.

After what Gavrill told me about Medik, I'm not sure how to greet him. While I want to be angry that he is responsible for the Tsenturions requesting the Jabol find them mates, it's not like it was something that was personally done against me. Plus, Gavrill describing him as his 'oldest and closest' friend instinctively makes me want to make a good impression on him. So when Gavrill leads me to be introduced to him first, I flush and bend my knees in a small curtsey as Gavrill proudly claims me as his Tribute... and then immediately feel stupid as all three of the males look at me with confusion at my genuflection. But the old alien's eyes are kind.

"Tribute," he greets me in a deep, slightly reedy voice. "I have waited a long time to greet you. On behalf of myself and the remnant of the Tsenturion race: welcome." Placing a hand on his chest, he bows his head to me. It's not quite the same as the salute the warriors give to Gavrill, but it still feels ceremonial. Tongue-tied, I jerk my head up and down and half-curtsey again before I realize what I'm doing.

I look helplessly up at Gavrill, who didn't prepare me for anything like this. Neither did Frllil for that matter. Nope, Frllil was all "keep quiet, be submissive, please the Commander", and Gavrill was all "sex, sex, sex." No one told me what good manners for communicating with a Tsenturion who actually wanted to *talk* to me would be. Gavrill just looks back at me, expressionless. I have no idea what he's thinking.

Behind him, Bogdan snorts in derision. Yeah, no guesses as to what *he's* thinking. The dark-suited warrior salutes to Gavrill and completely ignores me, marching past me to his seat at the large table. At least he didn't say anything rude aloud. He's still a jerk though. I bite my tongue to keep from sticking it out at him.

As I look back at Medik, the Tsenturion gives me a slight smile that crinkles the corners of his eyes. He's like the Tsenturion version of a grandfather, and the small moment between us makes me feel better.

"Please, sit, Medik." Gavrill rests his large hands on my shoulders, steering me towards the table; the firm weight of his touch settles me. "You do us honor to join us at our table."

"A celebration is in order, is it not?" The doctor straightens as much as his stooped shoulders will allow. His movements are a tad stiff and slow, compared to the warriors' stride. He must be much older.

The table is shaped like a triangle. Bogdan stands on one side, the doctor takes another. That leaves one side for both me and Gavrill. My face heats as I realize I might be delegated to a cushion on the floor. So much for proving I'm a sentient being. I grind my teeth, determined not to say anything. While Gavrill got pretty possessive about having me do anything sexual in front of his friends, I don't know whether or not that will extend to being spanked as well.

He'd already demonstrated that he's perfectly willing to punish me while there's an audience.

I stumble a little as Gavrill maneuvers me into position. There's no cushion, but there's only one seat. The High Commander sits and pats his knee. Cheeks pulsing hot with embarrassment, I twitch to the side and perch gingerly on his lap. At least I don't have to sit on the floor.

Spots on the table glow, and platters of food appear. A whole smorgasbord of completely weird looking dishes, only a few of which look familiar from what the warriors in the cafeteria had shown me. I want to reach for the delicious korrun fruit, but Gavrill pulls a different dish towards us—several multi-colored mounds with the consistency of ice cream, if ice cream came glowing in jewel tones. The doctor peers at me from around what looks like a stack of green sea crab legs with red thorns.

"I consulted the Jabol for food of your people," Medik says. "The nanos changed your system to accept nutrition from our foods, but food is more than nutrition, wouldn't you agree? "

I nod and gulp. If I'd really thought about it, I should've

prepared myself for a feast of strange dishes. I'd already learned in the cafeteria that Frllil hadn't exactly shown me all the things the Tsenturions eat.

The plate in front of Bogdan holds what looks like a hunk of charred meat. A long claw-like razor extends from the warrior's suit, and he uses it to hack into his meal. Purple goo oozes out from the blackened carcass. That is definitely not something I've seen before. I close my eyes for a moment and tell my panicking stomach to calm down. I don't have to eat that.

9

G avrill

.

I CAN FEEL my Tribute's tension as she examines the food in front of us. The memory of seeing her in the dining hall with my warriors rises in my mind, and I immediately want to be the one to introduce her to new things as well. I pick up one of the severill balls, sure that I had not seen one of them when she was trying new foods earlier.

As I move to hold it for her to eat, she begins to reach for it with her hands and I making a chiding noise. I will provide her with what she needs. Catching my eye, she quickly lowers her hands to her lap and obediently opens her lips, pleasing me. Even the act of feeding her arouses me, despite my recent release. Everything she does arouses me.

The expression on her face as she tastes the sweet and sour flavor makes it appear as though she is unsure whether or not she likes it. Certainly, she'd enjoyed the korrun fruit much more, but I want to show her things she didn't taste for the others.

"Perhaps in time we can teach you how to use the replicator," Medik says to her, obviously also watching her eat. I do not mind, as he has a vested interest in her health.

Bogdan mutters something about 'wasting time catering to the weak,' but Medik ignores him. I shoot Bogdan a dark look, which he avoids, although he re-focuses his attention on his own meal, obviously aware that he has sparked my displeasure. It is also unlike him to be so derogatory towards those weaker than us. Tsenturion warriors are built to be protectors, and there is nothing dishonorable in not being a warrior. Perhaps my tardiness for the meal has stoked his ire even more than I thought.

"It will ease her transition if she can surround herself with familiar things. And we will make use of the settings again and again, with each new Tribute." The doctor takes one of the thorny vines and starts to peel it. "That is, if you deem the program a success and decide to continue it."

"Yes," I say immediately, tightening my grip on my own Tribute. I may have just acquired her the previous cycle, but our compatibility has already been demonstrated. Whether or not we will be capable of procreating has not yet been proven, but I trust the Jabol's assessment, and I will not deny my warriors the comforts and relief of Tributes of their own just to wait for it to actually happen.

"Wait!" My own Tribute sits up straight in my lap, interrupting. I frown—not because I am displeased, but because I feel her distress and I don't understand it. "You don't mean you want to bring *more* women here?" She sounds appalled, and I do not know how to answer. Surely, our aim was obvious.

"The survival of our race depends on it," Medik says quietly.

"No." She turns on my lap, her distress growing with every word. I should punish her for being so outspoken—though I had told her she did not need to be quiet, she is verging on disrespect—but the strong swell of her emotion is affecting me, and I do not know how to react. "You can't do this. The women you'll take--they'll have lives, maybe even *families*..."

"Commander, if I may speak," Bogdan puts in, but my Tribute talks right over him, not even glancing at him. I do not look at him either, I am studying her face. Her blue eyes are filling with tears, her cheeks flushed with the strength of her upset.

"You can't just rip women from their lives and expect them to settle down with a Tsenturion. I don't care how many orgasms you give her, she will never forgive you."

"Did you have a family, Dawn?" the doctor asks in his quiet voice. The question jerks both of our attention to him. I already know the answer, and I know he does as well, but he is trying to make a point. I decide to let him take the lead, although I am not sure where he is going with this yet, but our aims are the same.

"No. I mean, I did, but they died when I was younger." She twists back to me, her blue eyes large and imploring. Strangely, I feel her plea tugging at me, even though I know what my answer must be. "*I* didn't have anyone, but the next woman might. You might take her from her children—"

"What if we take women who do not have ties to Earth?" Medik interrupts. "The program is designed to lure unattached females." It was done so on purpose. Tsenturions do not want females who already have mates or children.

"How is that possible?" She throws up her hands. "If they're from Earth, they'll have ties."

"Did you have ties?" Medik presses. He's not upset or trying to be cruel. His face is patient, even a little sad. I feel the same melancholy. Even Bogdan has become more subdued, unwilling to interrupt. While he might not want more Tributes from Earth either, the subject is bringing up the stark loneliness we endure. He has stopped eating, his gaze turned towards the windows and the emptiness out there.

No Tsenturion has ties to a planet or a family anymore. Those of us who are left are each other's family, but it is not the same. We would never deprive someone not an enemy of the same by choice.

~

Dawn

"It was different for me," I tell Medik. "I was more alone than most people."

It's true. The revelation had hurt when Frllil pointed it out to me, but it doesn't anymore. If anything, I feel relieved that there's no one on Earth who would miss me. I didn't have regular friends or ties to anyone. Funny how it took being sucked into another galaxy where I'm the only human for me to realize how alone I'd been.

But it's better this way, because while I'm determined to get home eventually, I'm also pragmatic enough to realize that might not actually be possible. I'd rather no one be desperately searching for me, without answers. People go missing all the time, and it leaves devastation in their wake;

at least my disappearance won't do that to anyone. I wouldn't call myself resigned to my fate, but I recognize this might be it for me.

At the very least, I have to keep this from happening to anyone else.

"I was alone," I repeat, a little desperately. "But with the next woman, that might not be the case. You can't keep doing this."

"We have no choice, Dawn," the doctor says, his voice tired and heavy. Gavrill's hand suddenly rests on the back of my neck, over the collar, in an almost comforting gesture. I can feel tears welling as I realize they're in earnest. "We have been alone too long. The warriors almost don't remember what it is like to be around a female. Now that you are here, they remember. They have begun to desire a mate, and, for the first time in countless cycles, they have hope. We cannot stop the program now."

A weighty silence fills the room, and I can almost feel the sadness hanging heavy in the air. Even Bogdan is affected, although his gaze cut to the doctor when he said they could not stop the program now. All of their armor shimmers silvery grey, and I swear, I can feel Gavrill's emotions again. That or the nanotech is somehow tuning me in to his feelings.

He's sad, but it goes beyond that. A deep grief that feels old—memories of his lost loved ones? And something fresher, more familiar, a pain that mingles with his own regret. The regret is his, but the pain feels like mine. An echo of my own feelings. I turn to stare at the hard angles of his face without seeing him. Am I feeling what he's feeling? And if I am—is he empathizing with me?

"Commander," Bogdan cuts in as Gavrill and I look at each other. "If I may. I object to the program."

Well. Never thought I'd agree with Tall, Dark, and Moody. Silently, I turn to look at him as Gavrill changes his focus to his second-in-command. The sad grey is gone from his armor already, and it has darkened to a more neutral gray. How I can tell the difference, I don't know, but I feel sure of it.

"I am aware," Gavrill answers him, his voice serious. "But having heard Medik's conclusion, what is your argument?"

"These Tributes are not necessary to our mission." Bogdan waves a hand in my direction. It wouldn't look so menacing if the claw he used to cut his food wasn't still sticking out of his suit arm. Red streaks momentarily through his armor. "They are a distraction. They will not aid us in our objective."

"And what is our objective?" Medik asks, turning to face Bogdan and raising his eyebrows. I'm reminded of a teacher, facing off with an unruly student.

Bogdan's large hands clench into fists, his dark eyes fierce. "To destroy our enemy."

"And then what?" Medik asks. "What do we do once the enemy is gone? Continue on our mission to protect the Jabol? What about our species? The needs of the warriors for life outside of revenge? For deca-cycles we have lived as warriors, protecting the weak and bringing order to the galaxy. But when is it their turn to have a life? A family?"

Bogdan's suit is so black, it seems to suck light into its obsidian depths. "Commander, we do not require—"

"I disagree," Gavrill says, his fingers stroking the back of my neck. "The warriors are fascinated by my Tribute. Many of them already want their own now that we know it is possible. We've gone too long as warriors focused on one objective. Many of the warriors are tired. Our memories are long, but revenge cannot sustain us forever. We need something to fight *for*, and I believe the Tributes will provide that."

"And when they don't want to fight at all?" Bogdan asks, growling his response as his eyes flash. "We retired our warriors when it was time for them to mate for a reason. One cannot be both a warrior and a mate."

"That has been true in the past," Medik acknowledges. "But our circumstances have changed. We no longer have the luxury of separating our lives the way we did before."

"But—"

"I agree with Medik," Gavrill says, interrupting whatever argument Bogdan was about to make.

Bogdan's boots thump the floor as he rises. Red slashes skitter like lightning across his armor. "If it's already decided, then I see no point to my presence here."

I sit quietly on Gavrill's lap as Bogdan storms out of the room, obviously irate at Gavrill's decision. It sucks because I want the same thing as him, although for a very different reason. On the other hand, I can see what Medik and Gavrill are saying. What was that old *Star Trek* saying? Something about the good of the many coming before the good of the one or something.

They are willing to sacrifice the lives of a few human women for the good of their entire people. It's really more than a few, but Frllil had told me there were only several hundred Tsenturions left now. Compared to the number of women on Earth, that's a drop in the bucket. And without them, the Tsenturions will become extinct.

There is no right answer, and it makes my heart hurt.

"Give him time. He'll come around." The doctor helps himself to a piece of the blackened meat on Bogdan's abandoned plate. The purple goo has hardened and turned...

orange. Eww. "He feels things more deeply than most. So he likes to pretend he cannot feel anything at all."

"Perhaps," Gavrill murmurs. He picks up another disc thingy to feed me, but I push it away. Still unsettled about the feelings I'm feeling—my own amplified and mirrored back to me—I shake my head. Nausea rises up in the back of my throat. Even though I know it's hopeless, even though I understand their reasons why, I have to ask again.

At least I know what happened to all of my relatives when they left me. I can't imagine how awful it would be to have someone I love disappear and not know what happened to them... to *never* know. And for that person to be clear across the universe, wondering what their loved ones back home are thinking, what they're doing...

The Jabol got it right with me, but who says they'll get it right every time? Even one mistake would be too many.

"Promise me you won't continue the program." I blink back tears, placing my hands on his chest and looking into his eyes, pleading with my own. "Promise."

Gavrill's eyes turn black as Bogdan's suit, a deep well I could drown in. Endless, empty space. The emotions I've been feeling swell, like our solitude, our loneliness, is feeding off each other the same way our passion does.

Suddenly, I'm gasping, choking on tears, a deep desolation draining me and leaving me empty... a thousand years of heartache, of isolation, of hopelessness, and I'm drowning in it. The darkness of his eyes expands and swallows me whole, and I'm falling, falling.

Two thoughts rush through me, filling my empty body:
I'm all alone.
And... the barest whisper....
I don't want to be alone anymore.

GAVRILL

As MY TRIBUTE passes out in my arms for the second time in two cycles, I am nearly undone. Surely, it is not normal or healthy for her to be unconscious so often. There must be something wrong with her. Although I trust the Jabol, I worry that perhaps they did something to her detriment through ignorance. She is the first human either of our species has seen, after all.

"What's wrong with her?" I ask, trying not to sound as frantic as I feel. Medik is already standing, a frown on his face, as he moves around my side of the table. I push back so that he can examine her with the scanner he always carries. Panic is rising in my chest, making it tighten painfully.

"Patience, Gavrill," he mutters as he holds the scanner up against her and begins to run it from her shoulders down to her hips, checking her vital signs. Calling me by my name rather than my title is a sign that he recognizes my distress, although he is not rude enough to comment on it.

My armor is a burgundy red with shimmering violet overtones, displaying my upset and anxiety for him to see. Medik makes an odd humming noise under his breath as he looks at the scanner's readout.

"What?" I ask.

"Nothing."

"It is not nothing, tell me what's wrong with her," I demand.

Medik glances up at me, his eyes kind. Patient. "I am not trying to hide bad news from you, there is literally nothing wrong with her that I can see. Her body is in perfect working order, other than being unconscious."

As I watch, he moves the scanner up beside her head, and that's when his eyebrows lift.

"There is something wrong with her, isn't there?" Fear grips me, the kind I haven't felt in deca-cycles. "Can it be fixed?" Had going through the wormhole harmed her? Or something the Jabol did? Or, worse, something I had done?

"Nothing permanent," Medik says firmly. He gives me a look, lifting his eyebrow. "This is actually very interesting. These are similar to the kinds of readings I would expect from a Tsenturion female in the process of bonding with her male. I think some of the changes to her brain waves may have overwhelmed her."

I am surprised to feel a pang of disappointment at his description of it being 'similar' to rather than the same. Also, a touch of worry that it would cause her to faint. That didn't happen to Tsenturion females, did it? I realize I do not actually know. I was never interested enough in attending the mating festival to learn the specifics, although I had the general knowledge from watching my parents and other bonded pairs before I had begun my military service.

"That... would a Tsenturion female react to the bonding process the same way?" I ask curiously.

Medik dashes my hopes immediately.

"No," he says, shaking his head and tapping at something on the scanner. "They were Tsenturion after all, their brains would go through a maturing during courtship as the bond grew, but biologically we were all designed for it. Not being Tsenturion, it is not surprising that Dawn would have some different reactions. She seems unharmed, although I'd like to take her to the med bay for closer observation. We can learn a lot about what to expect for the future Tributes from her."

"Of course." Immediately I heft her in my arms, feeling slightly calmer as she sighs and nestles against me even in her unconscious state. I hadn't even realized I'd begun to harbor a faint hope for a full Tsenturion bonding, but it seems unlikely now.

Still, perhaps there will be a facsimile of one, as she is going through a 'similar' process. Whatever she manages, and the influence of the nanotech which has already allowed me to sense much of her physical reactions and interpreted her emotions for me, will have to be enough.

We are nearly to the med bay when my comm hails me. I open the line, already feeling impatient with whoever feels the need to speak to me *now*.

"High Commander?" The uncertain voice of Corin, currently captaining the ship while Bogdan and I are off duty, fills my ear. I frown, because normally Corin is just as confident as myself or Bogdan, otherwise he would not qualify to sit in the Captain's chair.

"Yes, Corin?" I try to keep my impatience out of my voice.

"Ah, High Commander, I ah... well, third shift has started and..." His voice trails off, uncertain and hesitant, because it is difficult to tell the commander of what is left of the entire Tsenturion race that he is late for his shift.

I close my eyes, torn between my duty and the female in my arms. That I feel so is shocking to me... but I am protective of her. Not only is she mine to care for, but she is so helpless and weak. How could I be anything but protective? I cannot allow that to interfere with my duty, and I know it. The impulse to stay with her makes no sense to me, yet I feel it keenly.

"High Commander? I can call Bogdan to the bridge instead, if—"

"No." I cut Corin off immediately, my voice sharp. The last thing I need is for Bogdan to know that I was late for my duty because of my Tribute. He requires no more ammunition for his arguments against the Tribute program. I will have to be better about demonstrating our ability to balance our lives as warriors with our Tributes. "I will be there momentarily. My apologies for my tardiness."

"Yes, High Commander."

I can practically feel Corin's salute through the com.

Medik raises his eyebrows at me as we turn into the med bay. "Is there a problem?"

"No," I say stubbornly. I will not allow it to be a problem. "But I must go; it is my shift on the bridge and the ship requires its High Commander. Do what you must for her. I will send Arkdhem to escort her when you are finished. We will have to continue our conversation about the program at some other time."

"Very well. Please lay her over here," Medik says, gesturing to one of the empty beds.

Gently, I lay my Tribute down. Her pale face tugs at my heart, and the desire to stay by her side until she opens her beautiful blue eyes again is overwhelming. My feet feel heavy as I turn and head for the door, but I force myself to keep moving anyway, already sending a communication to Arkdhem. It grates that I cannot care for my Tribute myself, but at least I can provide her with a suitable escort—one who will immediately report to me when she awakens.

D awn

BEEP. Beep. Beep. A machine chirps in time to my heartbeat. I open my eyes to a grey-beige blur.

"Be at ease, Tribute."

"Dawn," I mumble. "Please. I am so freaking tired of being called Tribute, like that's all that matters about me." Especially when I'm flat on my back, vulnerable, and aching, I want to hear my name. My real name, spoken by someone who pretends to care.

"Dawn, then," the deep voice repeats, gentle and filled with what sounds like sincere care. My vision clears as I blink back the moisture suddenly threatening my eyes. The Tsenturion doctor hovers over me, his lined face soft with concern. "Stay calm. You are well."

"What happened?"

His lips quirk into a smile. "Actually, I was hoping you

could tell me that. As an outside observer, it seemed as though you were talking to the Commander before you rather suddenly passed out. The scanner indicated new brainwaves that I have not recorded from you before, closely matching those of a bonded Tsenturion female, but I need more information before I can say anything definitive."

New brainwaves? That sounds vaguely terrifying. Was my brain actually changing?

Strangely, despite the fact that he's a Tsenturion and I don't really know him, I feel just as comfortable with Medik as I did with any of my doctors back home. I instinctively trust him, too, and I just want him to tell me what was wrong and how to fix it... but what he says makes sense.

I blink as I push myself up to a sitting position. Immediately his hand hovers near me, in case I should need assistance, but I manage to sit up on my own.

"I... I just remember looking into Gavrill's eyes, and they were so dark, and then it felt like I was falling into them. I felt so alone, too, though I was sitting on his lap, I felt overwhelming loneliness and sadness and grief... but it didn't feel like those emotions were really mine, if that makes any sense."

To my shock, a smile blooms across Medik's face, wide and joyful and making him look about ten years younger than the seventy-something human years he currently resembles.

"You felt his emotions!" The excitement in his voice takes me aback slightly. "A side effect of bonding. The bond can act as a mirror between partners. If two partners share the strong emotion, the feeling is amplified between them. This most often manifests itself as passion, but... in this case obviously it was otherwise. You must have accessed the Commander's emotions while you already were experiencing your own influx of feelings. Your body was unable to handle it and shut down. A simple loss of consciousness."

I stare at him, with no idea what to say when he's obviously so excited and I am so confused.

Practically chortling, he turns away, and when he turns back he has a glass of water in his hand. "Here, drink. You will need to keep hydrated, well-fed, and rested. Obviously, the bonding process is harder for a Tsenturion-human pairing than for two Tsenturions."

Obediently, I take the glass and drink as I try to remember the moments before I passed out. What was I feeling? Loneliness. Extreme, soul-crushing loneliness. The sort I never let myself dwell on. On Earth it was easy to pretend I was an introvert or super independent, that I was too busy for more than a quick chat with a student while refilling my water bottle at the yoga studio. I'd told myself I was happy that way.

Out here, in deep, alien space, without a human or anyone I know, I can't hide from the feelings anymore. And when they were amplified by Gavrill and his own deep, untreated angst...I literally had all the feels.

"So basically I fainted." Thanks, nanotech. Not enough that I have to deal with my own emotions, now I might have to deal with someone else's? And exactly how deeply permanent is this bond going to be? "Is this going to be a common occurrence?"

The doctor waves a disc-shaped instrument over my body, hovering a moment over my heart until it gives a satisfied beep. He shrugs. "As your brainwaves seem to have adjusted, I do not think it will happen again, although we must make allowances for your biological differences."

"You mean the fact that I'm a human and not made for bonding."

"Not made for it, perhaps, but obviously it is possible," he says, smiling widely again, obviously overjoyed at the prospect. "If you felt his emotions, then the bonding is already progressing further than I would have guessed."

I fidget. I'm not sure I want to get used to the bond, but honestly, I can already feel something tugging at me, demanding to know where my master is. Even if I don't want to necessarily think of him as my master or my mate. "Where's Gavrill?"

I want to know what he thinks of all these sudden revelations.

"He wanted to be here," Medik says, his voice turning sympathetic. "His presence was required on the bridge, as it is his turn for a shift. Arkdhem is already waiting for you in the next room, and he will escort you to wherever you wish while the High Commander is captaining the ship." With a wave of his hand, Medik summons a floating chair so he can perch close to me. "You are certainly well enough to go, but before you leave, I wished to have some time to speak with you."

I eye him warily, and he makes an amused sound, close to a chuckle. "Nothing invasive, I assure you. I merely wish to see how you're settling in."

"Really?" Despite how nice he's been right now, despite his relationship with Gavrill, I can't help but glare at him. This... male who suggested the Tribute program in the first place. Who is just thrilled that I'm successfully bonding to an alien master I never wanted. Who insists that other women should also be abducted and put into my position. I don't want to be nice. I want to rant. "You want to know how I've been treated? Imagine being transported from your home in the middle of the night. Imagine waking up in a strange place millions of light years away and being told you can never go back. Imagine a big, strong, weird but hot alien doing all sorts of things to you that you'd only read about—only it's twenty times more intense in real life—and he's going to do it over and over again no matter how many times you orgasm or beg him to stop—and worse! He makes you like it..."

I stop to catch my breath. I've been shouting, but the doctor doesn't seem to mind. I've also gotten myself worked up in other ways. My body is primed from just thinking about Gavrill's 'bonding' methods. "And then you're expected to be with him forever, with no say so in your future, and have his babies and wear filmy dresses while he parades you around on a leash and... hell, I don't know. This whole thing is a fantasy gone way, way too far. That you want to bring more women here is just... look, I get it, but this whole situation is fucked up. It might be a good solution on paper, but that doesn't make it any less wrong."

There's silence as the doctor waits to make sure I've finished. Then he nods, sighing. Some of the joy has leaked out of his face, which makes me feel a little better.

"I understand, and I do not disagree with you, but being on the other side of the equation, I do not feel we have a choice. And things are not too bad, are they? You appear to be adjusting admirably. The courting rituals of your people are very close to the rituals of ours, so perhaps that accounts for some of it."

I shake my head, rolling my eyes. "Those books are not our courting rituals."

"But they come from your manuals, and the methods outlined in them seem to be working, though, even better than I thought they would. Gavrill requested them, and I suspect he's been following them to the letter, although I encouraged him to use more... intuitive methods. You must realize, he's been a soldier for deca-cycles. He thrives on rules and regulations, especially during times of crisis. And we have been in a crisis for a long, long time."

"Since your planet was destroyed," I blurt and mentally kick myself at the doctor's wince. His face goes blank in a way that makes me suspect he's hiding great pain.

"Yes," he agrees softly. "The greatest catastrophe any species has borne. You cannot be too hard on him."

"Says you. You're not going to be... biologically bonded to a guy who thinks that spanking is required foreplay!" I blush but forge on. "All these years floating around space, and he never found the time to learn about relationships. He doesn't even know your name!" I throw up my hands. Medik looks on patiently and doesn't correct me. "And when it's time to learn about bonding, he reads BDSM novels as his guide—"

"The Jabol informed me those manuals were widely read. They are popular, no?"

I flush. "Well, yes, but—"

"The Commander wished to integrate your courtship rituals into our own. He was pleased they were so well-structured."

"Look, those books aren't talking about relationships manuals. They're fictional, meant to be read for pleasure, not as guides."

"But surely you want your bonding to include pleasure." Medik looks confused.

Argh, why is this so hard to explain? Maybe Tsenturions don't have a concept of fiction?

"Well, yes, but not like that...I mean, I don't want that sort of pleasure all the time." Great, now I'm blushing and talking about my sex life with a guy who looks like a grand-father, but I started it, so it's hard to complain.

Medik makes a sound I translate as disbelief.

"Well, maybe I do. In the bedroom. But I want him to treat me like a person, not a pet."

Now Medik looks even more confused, his head tilting to the side as he waits for me to continue.

"I mean, you want me to be the savior of your race. The one who starts this whole breeding program. Half the time, Gavrill treats me like a... naughty little girl, and the other half like a thing, a trophy on a shelf or a prized pet he can show off and sit on his lap and feed..."

"You dislike this treatment? Your responses say otherwise." Medik gestures to the machine just as it gives a smug beep. He still appears confused. "Our females have always been pampered and protected. They too enjoyed the courtship rituals."

Crap, I'm making a muddle of this.

"I just want him to treat me like a person. I'm not totally opposed to the... structure. The punishment/reward games. But deep down, I need to know he respects me. Wants me—and not just for my body. For my... for who I am. For me."

"Ah," Medik tilts his head. "You are speaking of bonding."

"Bonding... is that like..." I can't quite bring myself to say "love." I take a deep breath and start over. "You were bonded, right?"

Again, the blank face, shielded against showing pain. "Yes."

I swallow my apology. He shouldn't have abducted me if he didn't want a troublesome Tribute on his hands. "How does it work?"

"Bonding happens in stages."

For the first time, he looks away from me. The expression on his face is a little distant, like he's seeing something that's not there.

"How long were you bonded?" I ask curiously.

"Almost twenty deca-cycles."

I calculate quickly in my head.

"Two hundred years," I whisper in shock.

Medik smiles. A sad smile, his eyes still staring at something that I can't see. "We met at a mating festival, but it took several meetings before I was able to begin the courtship. Once we pledged to each other, the bonding was swift. It was the most glorious experience I will have in this lifetime."

I swallow. "Did she...?"

"She was on planet, along with our offspring."

"I'm sorry."

"It was quick, at least." He passes a hand over his face and murmurs so quietly, I wonder if I'm supposed to hear him. "I only regret I that was not with them."

I sag back on the floating table and cover my own face with my hands. Giving myself and Medik some semblance of privacy. As much as I want to be angry with him, it's really hard. If he were a hardened soldier, or as much of an ass as Gavrill can be sometimes, it would be easier. But he's very open and very patient and kind. He's just trying to do what is best for his people, just as I am for mine. And he's doing it while grieving his family and probably dealing with the biggest case of survivor's guilt in the galaxy.

My emotions are running through me too fast to catch or understand.

I try to break things down logically as I catch my breath. There's been a lot of new information in a very short period of time.

Fact 1: I am an alien captive and will probably be one for the rest of my life.

Fact 2: I belong to the High Commander, and he is doing everything he can to bind me to him. But apparently, the bond goes both ways.

"If Gavrill and I fully bond... there won't be any chance of me going back to Earth, will there?" My voice isn't as bleak as I thought it would be. What's happened has happened, and I can't think of anything I can do to change it. If anything, I'm becoming resigned to that fact.

The look Medik gives me is sympathetic. "A broken bond is more than painful. There would always be something missing, a void that could never be filled. That's if it were physically possible for you to even return. The wormhole the Jabols used is unstable. Just one journey is perilous. I doubt the path can be reversed, but even if you could return that way, you probably would not survive a second trip."

I gape slightly at him. Yeah, I remember how much it hurt to be brought through, but I hadn't imagined it was quite that dangerous—just painful.

"But you will keep bringing women through it?" I ask, and—again—I can hear the resignation in my voice, along with a hefty amount of censure.

"We don't have a choice. We need females to bear offspring, or our race will not survive. You have made good points though. I will speak to the Jabols and make sure the screening process selects women who don't have any strong ties to Earth. Who display fortitude as well as an interest in the Tsenturion way of life and indicate a willingness to live the life they read of."

"You're basing all of this off a few stories on an e-reader."

I face palm, because seriously, what else is there to do? "It's not a foolproof process."

"The Jabols studied your race from afar. They determined the most effective way of communication is through story. They also experimented with sound waves and frequencies, but felt the messages weren't clearly received."

"Wait, what? Sound waves? What kind of sound waves?"

"A form of entertainment that your species uses. I believe they called the experiment 'electropop'."

"Oh my god." I wrack my brain for everything I know about the 80s music style that involves synthesizers. "You mean the members of Daft Punk are really aliens?"

"They received the first messages, yes. The program was changed when the Jabols found the transmissions were better received when translated by female humans. Two messengers became very popular. One was called 'Madonna', and the other was referred to as 'Lady Gaga'."

"No way. Madonna and Lady Gaga's music was inspired by alien transmissions?" I think about it for all of a second before nodding. "That explains a lot."

We look at each other, and I finish off the water in my glass, trying to think of something else to say. I can't think of anything though. Medik still has something left that he wants to address though.

"I take it your worry about the Tribute program is for future Tributes and their ability to assimilate their duties. But what about you, Dawn? Do you think you could be happy as a Tribute?"

I blink at the kindly old alien. He's basically said out loud what I've been afraid to admit. I'm not totally hating my experience as a captive alien bride. There's been lots of kinky punishments and erotic pain, yes, but Gavrill hasn't really hurt me. The sex is fantastic. The male is... well, if I'd met him on Earth, I might have found him stodgy and bossy, but there's also a lot to like about him. And part of me even likes the stodgy, bossy parts.

Not that I'm actually falling for him. No way. But the reassurance that my alien master will care for me, keep me safe, and treat me well is important. It's simple self-preservation.

Even if it feels like more.

"Tell me this. Do you think he'll ever..." I choke on the word, "c-care for me? Not as a Tribute or for what I represent, but for me, as an equal? The way he would for a Tsenturion woman he bonded with?"

"I think, from what I've learned today, that you two have a chance of completing a full bond, in the Tsenturion manner. Emotionally as well as biologically. And once the bond is complete, yes, he will care for you, although I cannot say that his treatment of you will drastically change." The doctor watches me carefully. "Is this what you wish? That he care for you?"

"Yes." As I say the word, I realize that yes, that's exactly what I want. Not just to make the best of this situation, but also because I actually am coming to care for him. Sure, there's some part of me that cynically thinks my brain chemistry has been all messed up by everything since I barely know him... but at the same time, I feel a stronger attachment to him than I ever have to anyone on Earth.

Maybe that's what the bond is, a way to join two beings together in a much faster manner than we do it on Earth. That's certainly how it sounded to me when Frllil explained it during my training. Like soulmates. I'd been skeptical at the time, but now I can't deny that I feel a physical and emotional yearning for the High Commander. I can't think of another way to explain the depth and strength of that yearning after so short a period of time.

I want the bond. I want him to care for me. Because I want him to feel the same things I am. And maybe once the bond is formed, I'll have more influence on him. Medik already seems open to being more selective about choosing Tribute candidates. Since I'm already stuck here, I just have to do what I can.

I lick my lips. "What can I do to, um, facilitate the bond forming?"

"Exactly what you have been," Medik says, smiling almost like a proud father. "The bond usually manifests physically at first. From the amount of time you've spent in his cabin, I would say you're well on your way there. Our courtship rituals truly are not so different; the more possessive and protective he feels over you, the deeper all of his emotions become. I have read your manuals. Submitting to him in the manner of your people is close enough to Tsenturion courtship rituals, but do not make it too easy on him. Not that I can see that happening."

So there's some hope. We could have a full bond. He might come to care for me, even love me in the Tsenturion way... but it sounds like the courtship has to be more than just hot sex, even if that's where it begins. Somehow, I have to teach a big, dominant alien who is over a thousand years old and has never had a real relationship, to emote. No biggie.

I take a deep breath, clenching my fists together in determination, and I nod. "Okay. I can do this."

Medik looks at me, his eyes filled with so much hope, it's almost painful, because it's not just hope for me—it's hope for the future of his entire people. "If anyone can teach him how to bond, Dawn, it's you."

11

G avrill

ARRIVING ON THE BRIDGE, I relieve Corin of duty, extremely thankful that Bogdan is not on duty and hopefully knows nothing of my lateness. If I am truly lucky, he will never learn of it. My second is the only one capable of reprimanding me, and he would be correct to do so.

Fortunately, Corin does not know why I am late and—unlike Bogdan—does not demand an explanation. In many ways, Bogdan is more like a sibling to me than an underling; other than my Tribute, there are none other in our fleet who would challenge me the way he does. I doubt he would appreciate the comparison, although my Tribute might.

Dawn.

Her name echoes through my mind even as I read through Corin's shift log.

Medik used her name. So did Arkdhem. I used it when I

was pleasuring her... perhaps I should do so more often. She did ask it of me in the beginning, I remember. While her name does not give me the same visceral satisfaction as calling her *my Tribute*, there is something intimate about it.

My Dawn.

I will think on it.

But for now... I force myself to focus on the readout Corin left behind. It doesn't make any sense.

Frowning, I look up at Corin, who has been standing off to the side waiting for me to read his log, rather than quitting the bridge. Obviously, he anticipated I would want to speak of the strange events he reported. I could feel the crew glancing at us from the corners of their eyes, probably waiting for my reaction. They've been on duty for a while, although not as long as Corin—it would not do to have the entire bridge crew changing shift all at the same time—so they are well aware of the anomalies as well.

"They aren't attacking at all?" I ask, completely baffled by this change in Vgotha tactics.

They have never had compunction in the past about attacking when they know they have a chance of winning. The only reason the ship we'd been pursuing had fled without a fight had been because it was outgunned and engaging with us would have been a suicide mission. What I was seeing here was completely different. One of the scouts reported that he practically ran into one of their advance guard—which meant that he was hopelessly outclassed and should be dead. Instead, he'd been allowed to slip away. The tone of his report sounded as confused as I felt.

"No, High Commander," Corin says, shaking his head. "All the reports are the same. The scouts have become more and more reckless, almost as if they're daring the Vgothas to come after them and yet... nothing other than sightings."

"What are they up to?" I murmur, scrolling through the readout, my disturbance growing.

New tactics that make no sense are far more concerning than even a fully armed armada. Changes that cannot be anticipated, for reasons unknown, can do far more damage than a frontal attack, even by a larger force.

"I thought about hailing you, but I did not know what to say." Corin sounds exasperated. "*High Commander, I need to report that the enemy has been sighted but they have not engaged... we have no casualties...*"

"Well, it would have gotten my attention." My lips quirk. "But none of this is exactly urgent, is it?"

"No, and I did not want to interrupt your time with your Tribute." Now there is a thread of envy in his voice, which I do not begrudge him. Still, as much as I appreciate the sentiment, I know I cannot allow it to continue.

My duty must come first.

"Next time, if something unusual is happening, report in." I closed the readout and meet his gaze. "I may not come to the bridge, but I do want to know." I realize that I would not have appreciated the interruption, but having seen the readout and reports for myself, I am uneasy about what the Vgothas are doing. Besides, before Dawn arrived, Corin would not have hesitated to hail me. I should not allow her presence to change that.

"Yes, High Commander." He nods smartly, his fist coming up to pound against his chest in salute.

"Dismissed. Enjoy your break."

As Corin leaves, I turn my attention to the current situation. The scouts *are* being reckless, but I cannot blame them. Still, we need to know what the Vgothas are up to. I am about to hail Arkdhem when I realize I have re-assigned him to watch over my Tribute rather than command the scout ships. I send my communication to Rorick, second in command of the scout ships, instead.

"Bring up the vid screen, with the information Rorick is about to send," I command. Immediately, the screen on the far-left lights up and a moment later is filled with the patterns the scout ships have been flying and where each Vgotha ship was spotted along the lines... and where they dropped out of sight again.

Examining the display, I feel my jaw clench.

Some of the places the Vgothas have been disappearing from make no sense. There is nothing there that should hide their ships or the trails.

"High Commander?" The hesitant voice of Borodem, one of my communications officers, interrupts my thoughts. His focus is also on the display, his worry writ clear across his face—and he is not the only one. "The Vgotha... they have some kind of new camouflage technology, don't they? That's the only explanation for this." He waves his hand at the display, his question bolstering my own conclusion after examining the data.

"Unfortunately, I think you may be correct," I say grimly.

What I still don't understand is why they're using it to play with our scouts rather than blowing them away.

Still, I contact Rorick again. The scouts need to be extra careful. While the Vgotha are playing with them for now, there must be some endgame coming up that we can't see. They are doing it for a reason, which means we must be extra vigilant and not play into whatever plot they've concocted.

I am surprised that the emotions welling up inside of me as I try to determine the Vgotha's motivations are as much anxiety and protectiveness as they are determination. I have always considered myself protective of my warriors—we are all each other has after all... or, at least, we were. I realize now that I have lost the edge of that worry.

There has been so much death over the years, so much loss, and as we continue our quest for revenge we mourn each life ended as it happens, but it is *acceptable*. Each warrior knows the risks, each gives his life willingly so that we may obtain our ultimate goal—justice and revenge for our people and safety for the rest of the universe from the Vgotha scourge.

Now though...

I have someone to protect who isn't a warrior. A life on board who did not choose to be here. Who did not sign up for revenge or justice. A helpless female life, who has already roused my protective instincts more than once.

I have been so focused on attacking for so long, realizing that I now have something to defend... no wonder my anxieties are sharper. But knowing the reason does not help to allay them.

Silently, I send a non-verbal message to Arkdhem, requesting an update.

I receive a response in a matter of moments.

Dawn is conscious but still in with Medik; they are conversing.

I am relieved to hear that she is awake, but not entirely soothed. My immediate impulse is to return to the med bay, no matter that I am on duty, to look her over for myself. For a moment I am tempted to direct Arkdhem to bring her to the bridge when she is finished in the med bay, but doing so would not be constructive. It would definitely be distracting.

As the leader, I am the one who must set an example for my warriors, especially since I have decided the Tribute program is to continue. They will witness how I handle my own Tribute and follow my example. We cannot have a bridge full of Tributes, so I will not bring her here again.

While we cannot separate the two parts of our lives—warriors into civilians with mates and families—we can at least separate our Tributes from our time on duty. Even if the desire to have her by my side makes me feel as though I am perpetually missing something.

THE FEELING of relief when Bogdan comes to take command of the bridge is overwhelming and unsettling. Normally I am reluctant to take leave of the bridge, now I am practically impatient to hand over command and find my Tribute again. Just the thought of knowing I will soon be able to touch her again has my *seela* beginning to writhe beneath my armor.

The difficulty I have in controlling my emotions is also unsettling, although I manage to keep my armor to a light, neutral gray, letting none of my impatience show as I update Bogdan on the situation.

There were several sightings of Vgotha ships while I was on the bridge, none of them engaged with our ships. Not even the pilot who decided to pretend he was having some kind of shields malfunction, making him the perfect target. Bogdan is as confused as I am, although no less vehement in his passion to eradicate the Vgotha threat.

"Perhaps we should engage in force," he says, studying the map the scouts' explorations have created, as well as the pattern of appearances by Vgotha ships. "They appear to be testing their capabilities rather than engaging, but the size of these ships would not be able to withstand an assault by *this* ship. The scouts' firepower isn't enough, and so far they haven't approached any of the fighters."

"Or perhaps that's exactly what they want," I murmur, frowning at the map. Even as I feel the tug to go and find my Tribute and bury myself inside of her, to feel her presence beside me, I force myself to focus on this threat. It is a threat to her as well. Bogdan has made a good point, which is why he's a good second, but I do not agree with his instincts to rush in. "See if we can get any fighters close to their ships... we will continue to pursue them at a slower pace for now, unless one of their destroyers appears. So far we've only seen the smaller ships, but there must be one that they're reporting back to. Send the scouts further out to see if they can locate any larger ships. I want to see what they do next."

Bogdan grimaces but nods his head in agreement, seeing the wisdom of letting events play out. While we can take on a destroyer—and win—it will not necessarily be easy or without loss of life. Caution may not come naturally to him, but he is smart enough to recognize when it is needed. We will go forward with our eyes peeled.

Done with my duty, I barely recognize myself in the eager warrior who practically races from the bridge. Normally I would linger, although not too long so as not to undermine Bogdan's authority now that he's on duty. Instead, I am walking as quickly as I can without feeling rushed, my tech already reaching out to hail Arkdhem.

As usual, he responds immediately.

We are back in your cabin, High Commander. She asked for any texts on our history and customs and has been reading them for a while now.

I am more than pleased with Arkdhem's response. Both because of her interest in learning more about us, beyond the information Frllil would have imparted during her initial training, and because she is in my cabin. While I would not confine her there unless necessary or if she needs to be punished, the possessive need riding me is soothed a little by knowing she is alone and in my rooms.

Not that my stride slows at all, for I am still eager to join her, but my chest feels a little less tight and my shoulders relax. Although Ardkhem had informed when they'd left the med bay, I had not felt as though I could ask for frequent updates while I was on duty. The rest of the crew would surely have noticed. I must set the example for how Tsenturion warriors with Tributes should act, for I will not require my men to behave differently than I myself do. Once we have more Tributes, the crew on duty cannot be constantly checking in on their Tribute, therefore I cannot do so.

Perhaps it would be wise to designate a room in the ship where Tributes whose warrior is on duty may stay so that the warrior will know where she is and will not be distracted by wondering, the way I have been. The idea has merit.

When I arrive at my cabin, my Tribute is sitting curled up in the corner of the couch, while Arkdhem sits on the other side, both of them reading. The translator the Jabol gave her should allow her to read any of the texts I possess, and she seems engrossed.

As always, Arkdhem jumps up to salute me when I enter. "High Commander."

"Arkdhem," I respond, acknowledging him. "Thank you for escorting my Tribute. You are relieved."

"Thank you, High Commander," he says before turning. "Farewell, Dawn."

"Bye," she says, smiling at him, placing the book she is holding down and rising to her feet. As she turns her blue eyes towards me, I can already feel my body responding to being in her presence. My *seela* begin to move, my cock engorging. I barely take notice of Arkdhem leaving the room.

"Dawn," I say in greeting and am rewarded with her entire face lighting up. She does like being called that. Very well. It does not satisfy me as much as claiming her with her title, but I do enjoy seeing her pleasure.

"Master," she says, smiling up at me. My armor flashes gold before I order it to recede, and the nanotech flows over me to my back, leaving me naked and erect in front of her. Her eyes widen as they drop to my groin, and I can practically taste her arousal as it surges.

"Come here," I command, holding out my hand. She moves to me, but to my surprise she does not take my hand. Instead, she drops to her knees in front of me, her hand reaching out to wrap around the base of my cock, caressing the sensitive bulges located there which hold my seed. I groan at the sensation of her delicate fingers caressing me, and my *seela* immediately reach for her hand, stroking it. When I speak, my voice is strained. "What are you doing, Dawn?"

"Something that we do on Earth, but which I haven't heard or seen mention of here," she says. There is something almost mischievous in her expression, and I am unsure of what to do.

Then she leans forward and licks the flared head of my cock, and the sensation is exquisite. I groan, my hands coming forward so that I can sink my fingers into the pale strands of her hair, holding on for all I'm worth as she begins to explore my cock with her *tongue*. It's an act I had never even considered, and when she opens her lips and takes the tip of my cock into her mouth, my knees buckle.

Hot. Wet. But deliberate. Her tongue moves like a *prime*

seela, stroking and exploring, and eliciting the most exquisite pleasure. It was perverse, there is no breeding benefit, and yet... I don't want her to stop. While the manuals had made mention of this activity, it had not particularly appealed to me at the time. Human cocks are different, and I had no interest in a Tsenturion woman's mouth, so I did not think I would have one in hers.

I was wrong.

I groan, thrusting my hips forward, my hands tightening in her hair. It is just like in her texts. The very unusualness of the activity adds a piquancy to it that I find greatly appealing, on top of the physical pleasure running through me. She hums with pleasure, and I shudder, thrusting more deeply and causing her to pull back slightly.

"Enough," I growl, because I do not know how much more I can take without losing my control and I do not wish to harm her. My fingers grip her hair, pulling her mouth off my cock, with much reluctance on my part.

I pull her up against me, taking her parted lips in a fierce kiss as I begin to yank her dress from her body. The fabric falls easily away, and I carry her to the bed, her legs around my waist, and she whimpers as the underside of my cock rubs against her wet heat, my *seela* stimulating her plump lips.

We practically fall onto the bed, her touch and kisses frantic, as if she is as desperate for my touch as I am for hers. I feel as though I have waited another thousand years for her, my need is so great. I do not bother with bindings or tormenting her, having her mouth around me had been enough torment for us both. Instead, I pull back my hips and thrust home, making her cry out as she clamps down around me in happy ecstasy.

Just being joined with her fills me with satisfaction, a

sense of rightness, of gratification, that I have never found anywhere else.

Once I am inside of her, some of my need is soothed... just enough to allow me to keep my initial thrusts slow and steady, rather than pounding into her without care. She writhes underneath me, a sob rising in her whimpering cries as I move, stroking her insides with my cock and her outsides with my *seela*. I grunt, fisting my hands beside her head, pumping in and out of her and doing my best to hold onto my control.

"Yes... please... Gavrill... Master... *harder, please!*"

My name on her lips, her desperate plea, and all my careful efforts at holding myself back are undone. I oblige, taking her as hard as I want to, enjoying the high cries of her pleasure filling my ears. My *seela* latch on to her as she clenches around me, and we both tumble into erotic oblivion.

∼

Dawn

CUDDLED up against Gavrill's side, I stroke my fingers over his broad chest, enjoying the moment of intimacy. He has me tucked up against him, my head resting on one arm while he strokes my lower back, his other hand caressing my bottom and the leg that he has draped over his hip.

I know that I only have a limited amount of time before the quiet moment turns to ardor again. Is it just his libido, or is it the physical influence of the bonding that Medik referenced? I can only hope it's the latter. As much as I enjoy having tons of orgasms, I want the physical connection to lead to an emotional one. I want the bonding... I want Medik's hope to be realized, because I think that's the most likely path to happiness for me. It might even be the only path, because of the way my own emotions are becoming engaged; if they aren't returned, it's going to hurt. A lot.

"Master, why is there no mention of the Vgothas in any of your books?" I ask.

I knew what Frllil had told me, and so I understood the references the other Tsenturions made toward their enemy, but I'm still curious. I don't know what they look like, how formidable an enemy they are, or how likely the Tsenturions are to be able to get their revenge. I did know that we were currently chasing Vgotha ships, but that was about it.

His muscles tense beneath my fingers but relax again as I continue stroking.

"We did not know anything of them when those books were written," he answers, his voice quiet. Sad. "Before they destroyed our planet, we had never even heard of them. They targeted us because they discovered the Jabol had reached out to us for protection."

That, I knew from Frllil. According to him, the Vgotha had been trying to either enslave or eradicate the Jabols for a long time. The peaceful race was very intelligent, scientifically superior, but they were not warriors. So they'd gone searching for protectors and found the Tsenturions; but the Vgotha were so merciless, so cruel, that they thought nothing of massacring an entire planet to keep the Jabols vulnerable.

"Have you ever seen one?" I ask.

"Why do you want to know?" Gavrill leans back so he can frown at me. There's some suspicion in his expression, although I can't imagine what he thinks he should be suspicious of. I swear I feel a touch of jealousy as well. I almost roll my eyes at the irrational idea that he would feel posses-sive or jealous because I'm asking about his enemy, but with him looking directly at me, I don't dare.

"I'm just curious," I explain. "This is a whole new idea for me. I've never had an enemy before, and now we're chasing after a whole fleet of them."

"You are not, my warriors and I are," he says, almost fiercely. I might have taken offense at being left out if I couldn't sense his sudden surge of protectiveness. I squeak as I find myself being turned over onto my forearms and knees, his hands coming down on top of mine to pin me in position with my ass high in the air. I can feel his *seela* stroking against my bottom as his cock hardens. "You will be protected and cared for, and the Vgotha will never be close enough for you to worry about them."

I would explain that I wasn't worried, but I don't think it would matter. The moment of intimacy is over; I've riled both his need to protect and his possessiveness.

He thrusts deep, his *prime seela* immediately rimming my anus, and I groan as he ripples inside of me. With his body over and around me, I can't help but feel surrounded and completely protected, as if he's created a haven for me with his muscles.

"My Tribute," he says, and as much as I prefer it when he calls me by my actual name, I can't help but hear the pride, possessiveness, and—dare I hope it's not my imagina-tion—affection in his statement. But his next words make my heart soar. "My Dawn."

12

———

D awn

As TIMES PASSES, I go from being resigned to my fate to feeling almost hopeful about it. Medik's hypothesis that physical intimacy will lead to a deepening of the bond and more emotional intimacy seems to be coming true. There are times I worry that I'm imagining things or reading too much into things, because my own emotions are growing, and I don't want to be the only one feeling this deep attachment... but I swear there are times I can feel Gavrill's emotions.

I don't even get annoyed with being called "my Tribute" anymore, because he seems so pleased, so possessive when he does so, but not in a way that makes me feel like an object. I swear I can feel the affection he has for me when he does so, the way calling me that is like an endearment for him. My favorite is when he calls me "my Dawn," but both feel good.

When he is on duty, I have begun to get to know some of the other Tsenturion warriors. Despite how intimidating they are, they're nice guys—pretty desperate for feminine attention, which makes me feel kind of bad about being against the Tribute program. They deserve mates and happiness as much as anyone else... but does it have to come at the cost of a woman's Earth life?

Unfortunately, I can't think of an alternative.

"Why don't you work with Medik on it?" Gavrill asks when I express my continued unhappiness with his plans, his fingers stroking my hair. Our pillow talk often comes between bouts of kinky hot sex and his delight in experimenting with my training belt to see exactly how much it can affect me, so I have to get the conversation in when I can. Every time he returns from the bridge, it's like he's desperate to reforge our physical connection, and my own need matches his.

Being apart from him makes me feel antsy and almost itchy with need to be reunited with him. No matter how short the time period of separation, it spurs a compulsion to be as physically close to him as I possibly can. Honestly, it's a minor miracle I'm not sore and chafing from all the sex, but I can't seem to get enough of it, and neither can he.

"Work with Medik?" I ask, confused. "On the Tribute program?"

"After you spoke with him, he told me he wants to revise some of the parameters to assuage some of the concerns you had. If you work with him, you can address your misgivings with the specifics of the program directly."

Immediately, I am torn by conflicting emotions. Be directly responsible for the women who are chosen? On the other hand... isn't it better that those women at least have someone like them advocating for them if the Tsenturions are going to bring them here regardless? The idea of having a purpose, beyond being fucked to unconsciousness on a regular basis, also appeals, especially since Gavrill spends long hours on the bridge.

I've filled my time with doing yoga, keeping my body strong and supple, even when it's hard to concentrate on the poses when I have the training belt as a constant reminder of my master and his ultimate control of my body. It certainly makes some of the poses *way* more interesting.

I also read more about Tsenturions from their own texts, getting to know the others on the ship, and asking Arkdhem questions about Vgothas, but that's not the same as having something to *do*. Something meaningful. And the moment Gavrill suggests it, I realize that I want that.

In fact, if I think about the consequences of my involvement in such a project with so many repercussions for both Tsenturions and humans, this might be the most meaningful thing I could *ever* do. That Gavrill suggests it, that he would trust me with such a task, means more to me than I can say.

It feels like proof that he really sees me for me. As a person with valuable input, a person who can do something useful, who can make a difference, and more than that, a person whose feelings matter.

"Yes," I say, answering him with so much enthusiasm, it surprises both of us. "Yes, I want to do that."

Pressing my hand against his chest, I lift myself up slightly so that I can give him a kiss. Despite my physical desire for him, I am rarely the aggressor when it comes to sex—I don't need to be. For the first time, I am the one on top. Well, sort of on top. Leaning over him, at least.

One hand comes up, sliding into my hair to cradle the back of my head as our kiss deepens. His other hand, which had been on my hip, moves until he is cupping my ass cheek, squeezing and kneading the soft flesh while his fingers work closer to the small hole he is so fascinated with. Something that I learned through a Tsenturion biology book—they don't have the same digestive system humans do, and so they don't have an anus.

Which explains at least part of why Gavrill is utterly fascinated with mine. His finger presses against the crinkled star, pushing inward and making me squirm. I've gotten used to the sensation and to the belt stretching that hole, and I know it's only a matter of time before he uses his cock there. I don't know whether I'm more aroused or frightened by the idea at this point.

I whimper as his finger pushes deeper, the lack of lubrication making the insertion burn a little more than usual, and my pussy pulses in response to the erotic sting. His finger feels even larger than usual, and I'm practically humping his thigh as he moves it gently, delving a little deeper with each pass. With the way he's holding my head for the kiss, I can't verbally protest even if I wanted to.

GAVRILL

MY SWEET TRIBUTE'S alternate entrance grips my finger tightly as I probe deeper, although it opens easily thanks to the training with the belt that I've been doing. She moans against my lips, her arousal wetting my thigh as she moves against me.

Excitement rises as I realize the significance of her kiss, of her rising passion. Not that she has been passive to my advances, but this is the first time she has clearly initiated our joining. I have finally mastered her fully, by giving her a task. The irony is that she will be helping me by completing it, but that does not seem to matter to her.

Her submission is offered up to me, her body ready for the final claiming, and I respond immediately. My grip on her roughens, the way she likes it, and she whimpers in the back of her throat as mutual desire sweeps through us. After a long, deep kiss, I slide my finger from her bottom and switch our respective positions, pushing her arms up above her head so I can bind her to the bed.

"Oh... no, Master, please, I want to touch you," she begs, but I shake my head. When she touches me, I lose control too quickly, and I want to make sure I can go slowly, for her own pleasure, as well as to savor this moment.

"No," I say firmly, running my hands down her bound arms to her breasts and cupping the soft mounds. I run my thumbs over her nipples, making the hard buds swell even more. She makes a whining noise, and I pinch the tender nubbins in response, feeling her shudder beneath me as the erotic pain mixes with her pleasure. Her breath is now coming in soft pants as I manipulate her body, rousing her need along with my own.

She writhes slightly, arching and trying to rub herself against me. I chuckle.

"Naughty Dawn," I say, for I have found that using her name at such times elicits more of a response than calling her Tribute or even 'naughty girl' like the examples in the manuals. "Do not try to manipulate me."

Moving away from her and ignoring her sound of

protest as I abandon her breasts, I easily flip her over so that her bottom is high in the air, ready for spanking.

"I wasn't—!" She starts to protest, but my hand is already coming down on her vulnerable bottom.

Smack!

The manuals all made it clear that her bottom should be a nice, hot pink, if not red, before I claim it. The spanking I give her will not be punishing, because I know she was not truly trying to manage me, but by now she also knows I need no excuse to redden her bottom if I wish. Indeed, I have found that turning that particular area nice and pink has a most salutary effect on the level of ecstasy she can reach.

Smack! Smack! Smack!

Realizing that I'm not actually disciplining her, my Tribute drops her head and lifts her bottom higher, inviting more swats, her soft moans encouraging me to swing a tad harder and sting her soft flesh a tad more. Her hips wag up and down, her bottom cheeks clenching slightly, and the tiny hole between them looks more inviting than ever.

Her feminine lips are swollen and marked from my *seela*, the sight filling me with satisfaction. I have come to enjoy leaving marks all over her, especially her neck and breasts, in lieu of the mating mark she is incapable of wearing, but the small circles on her sex are my favorites. My *seela* stamp her in the Tsenturion manner, at least.

Smack!

I deliberately aim for paler patches of skin on her bottom and the crease between that sweet curve and her thighs. Her cries are a little higher every time my hand goes lower, slapping that sensitive area. The cream coating her inner lips is glossy, announcing her growing arousal.

Exerting my influence on the nanotech, I send the belt

upwards in thin trickles to her breasts. I cannot see them, but I know they have created a line from the belt to her nipples, where they tighten around the little buds, creating an all-encompassing, painful erotic pinch that even my fingers couldn't duplicate. Another thin tendril slides down to her clit, covering the swollen nub with the nanotech and doing the same thing, giving me total mastery over her pain and pleasure as I prepare to claim her completely.

MY NIPPLES and clit throb in the confines of the nanotech, which squeeze so tightly that I hover on the edge between pain and pleasure. The growing heat in my ass has me squirming and bucking against Gavrill's hard hand. Each swat by itself is not particularly punishing, but the overall effect of stimulation has me gasping for breath as I'm bowed submissively before him.

I can feel my pussy creaming as the erotic stimulation of all my most sensitive parts fuels the need growing inside of me. I cry out as the tech begins to pulse, squeezing and releasing rhythmically and confusing my senses as to whether I'm feeling pain or pleasure. All the while, Gavrill's hand continues to come down in firm, measured swats designed to drive me wild.

"Please..." I beg, my toes curling as my ecstasy rises, but nothing he is doing is quite enough to bring me to orgasm. I swear he's made a science out of figuring out exactly how far he can go before I tip over that sweet edge, and he enjoys keeping me teetering on it for as long as possible. "Please, Master, I want you inside of me."

I can feel his usual sense of satisfaction at the honorific, his nearly savage satisfaction at reducing me to pleading for pleasure at his hand. I don't care; I get my own satisfaction from pleasing him, and my arousal is only enhanced by his domination.

"Good girl," he says, his hand smoothing over the hot curve of my ass, rather than swatting it again. "My sweet Dawn. I am truly your Master now."

"Yes," I agree eagerly, my wrists tugging slightly at the bonds around them as I lift my hips up, knowing how much the sight of my reddened bottom will entice him. The nanotech pulls at my nipples and clit, like tiny mouths sucking on them almost too hard, and I moan, wagging my bottom.

A moment later, his cock presses against my opening—just not the one I was expecting. I gasp, trying to surge forward and away from him as the tapered tip of his cock pushes into my ass. Even though I had half-expected this moment, I can't help but try to flee from it.

His fingers curl around my hips, holding me in place easily as he pushes forward.

"Please, not there, Master," I beg. "Not yet, Gavrill, please!"

"Yes, my Dawn, now," he says, and his cock thrusts in, making me cry out as I'm opened.

It doesn't hurt as much as it might have, because I have become accustomed to the invasion of the nanotech, but the flared head of his cock feels very different. It stretches me, moving inside of me, and pushes deeper as I squirm and moan in ambiguous pleasure. Feeling him filling me, claiming me, in this intimate manner is affecting both of us.

I can feel every ridge, every bulge of his alien cock as the strange shape pushes past the tight ring guarding my channel. My muscles flutter around him, clenching, trying to grip him. He slides backwards, and I cry out again at the strange dragging sensation, only to choke on my cry as he thrusts in even deeper than before.

GAVRILL

MY TRIBUTE'S bottom is more exquisite than I could have ever imagined. The crinkled star of her opening has stretched to create a smooth ring around my cock, gripping me so tightly, I know I would not be able to move if it weren't for the additional lubrication I had received from my armor before entering her. Now I understand why the texts had been so adamant on that point.

She is not wet here, but she is hot, and the spasming walls of her body feel incredible. My cock widens as it nears the base, and I can hear the sob rising in her voice as I press deeper, rocking my hips back and forth, thrusting a little deeper each time. While there is some pain in her voice, there is pleasure as well, and by now I know when something is truly hurting her.

This is pain she is taking for me, enduring because she wants to please me, to submit to me. Pain that will eventually turn to pleasure, I believe.

To assist, I instruct the nanotech on her clit to vibrate, and I feel her clench around me in response as she squeals in surprise. Her grip loosens, and I thrust deeper, stretching her to her widest point yet as my groin nestles against her hot bottom. Both of us pant for breath, moaning as her muscles play over the full length of my shaft and my *seela* stroke her spread cheeks. The sight of myself buried in her unusual hole, hearing the strain in her voice as she adjusts to my invasion, is gloriously erotic.

After holding myself still for several long moments, doing my best to memorize exactly how her reddened cheeks look split by my golden cock and stroking *seela*, I begin to thrust.

Her moans are ambiguous, but I can hear her pleasure as well, I can practically feel it as she quivers under my hands. There are no more pleas for me to stop, only willing submission as she slowly loosens, able to take my cock more easily with every thrust.

Now I understood what the manuals had meant. There was an intimacy to this act that I could feel, though it was unknown to Tsenturions. Tsenturions were focused on procreation with our pleasure, but this... this is nothing but pleasure. Her mouth had been similar, but she couldn't take me between her lips as deeply or as fully as she could in her ass. It didn't cause her the same kind of discomfort, which she was now enduring solely for my pleasure.

There is something pure about being offered this gift of her body, of knowing there is no guarantee for her own pleasure and no possibility of breeding. It is an act done completely for me, for my enjoyment and domination over her body... I can feel her submitting to me, giving over to me, and it's an ecstasy that outweighs even the physical rapture.

～

Dawn

THE EROTIC BURN of Gavrill's cock filling my ass while my pussy spasms emptily makes me feel as though I'm splintering apart. I'm wracked with need even as I want to beg him to stop. I can't tell if it hurts or if the sensations are just so overwhelming that my body can barely handle them.

I can feel his cock moving inside of me, his *seela* gently stroking my cheeks each time he slides home. The ridges and bumps on his cock rasp against my delicate insides, my nails dig into the mattress as I cling to it for dear life, feeling like I'm adrift in an ocean of sensation in the middle of a storm. The pain from my pinched nipples is nothing, barely a drop, but when the nanotech around my clit begins to vibrate, I can feel my toes curl as a whole new dollop of pleasure is added to the chaos consuming me.

If it wasn't for Gavrill's firm grip on my hips, I'm sure I would have collapsed beneath his heavy thrusts by now.

Agony.

Ecstasy.

Two sides to the same coin, and I'm caught in the middle.

Not just claimed, *consumed*.

My orgasm slams into me, and I keen with the intensity of it, my ring clamping down tightly around his cock and burning at the sensations as he shoves himself deep inside of me one last time. I can feel the hard suck of his *seela* as they latch onto my skin, the throb of his cock as he begins to come, and his possessive triumph as he fills my ass with liquid heat.

13

Gavrill

THE SOFT CURVES of my sweet Tribute are nestled against me, her breathing slow and steady in her slumber. I have worn her out utterly. Her little nipples are soft now but still reddened, as is her clit, and even her bottom hole appears pink and well-used. I am not much better off. I feel drowsily content, as if I could lay here in this bed beside her and never move ever again.

Which is why the furious message from Bogdan, informing me that I am late for my shift, feels like a slap to my face, bringing me back to reality.

Late.

Again.

Cursing under my breath, I pull myself away from Dawn, resentful at having our time together interrupted and yet knowing I am being illogical to feel so. These emotions, this urge to stay by her side is becoming stronger the more time I spend with her.

I had thought by now I would have myself more under control, but to be late again...

Worse, to wish that I didn't have to go to the bridge at all...

I don't need Bogdan to tell me that the situation is getting out of hand. Not that it will stop him from doing so. He is waiting for me outside of the bridge, his armor a dark black that flashes with occasional streaks of red in his fury. Normally I would stand my ground against his temper, but knowing I am in the wrong has me inwardly flinching in a way I haven't done since I was a raw recruit.

That he is waiting for me—and not on the bridge—tells me all I need to know about his intentions.

Worse, I deserve the dressing down.

I still try to bypass it.

"I know," I say, growling out the words the moment I'm within earshot, letting him see my own upset at myself as my armor flashes with emotion. "It won't happen again."

Red streaks across his chest.

"It has already happened multiple times," he says, stepping in front of me to block the door. I hadn't realized he knew, and I mentally curse whoever told him. There is heat flashing in his eyes, contained rage, and the fact that he is actually controlling his temper drives home exactly how angry he is. This is no vent and steam, this is righteous, justified anger. "I know about the last time too, I saw the log. I did not say anything, but now I think that was a mistake. Someone needs to hold you accountable since you are apparently no longer doing so for yourself."

My jaw clenches in anger. Not at him, but at myself.

He faces me, fists clenched, his fury contained but

palpable. "The Vgotha are taunting us, engaging in tactics we have never seen from them before, and we still don't know the reason why, and instead of focusing on them, instead of leading our people, you are distracted by that human. You say we must protect our future, but there will be no future if we are all killed in the present. How can you be our leader if you aren't even thinking of us half the time?"

I have no answer for him.

He is right.

I *have* allowed myself to become distracted. I *haven't* been focused on the threat the way I should be. I *haven't* been thinking about the present. Not only have I failed in my duty, but I am putting us all in danger—including my Tribute. I am behaving in a manner that is not only unfit for a Commander, but for a warrior.

Bogdan holds himself stiffly, looking me directly in the eyes. "I do not want your position, High Commander. I do not."

Don't make me step into it.

The words hang unspoken in the air between us. I know Bogdan does not want to be High Commander. He often wants his way, he often wishes I would choose his line of thinking, but he does not want my rank. Nor do I want him to have the position. I know I am the best suited for it... at least I was.

Before I received my Tribute.

Before I became distracted.

Before my attention was torn.

My first duty must be to my Tsenturion warriors, in the present, but my eyes have been entirely to the future as if the Vgotha threat is already eradicated. I have been indulging myself with pleasure while Bogdan and Corin and the others worry over the Vgotha's new antics. I have forgotten what it means to be in command, what it means to be holding all of our lives in my hands.

"It will not happen again," I say softly. My armor shimmers to a bluish-grey, a deliberate show of contriteness for him. "You are right. I have been distracted. I will fix it. There is time for the future when the present Vgotha threat is eradicated."

His expression lightens with relief, as does his armor. Not much, but enough to know that he at least believes my sincerity. I cannot help but feel grim as he steps aside to let me pass. I have neglected my duties too much in favor of my Tribute.

My words to Bogdan echo in my mind as I enter the bridge.

It will not happen again.

~

Dawn

WAKING up alone in bed sucks. On the other hand, I'm just a tiny bit relieved because I'm so freaking sore all over. Thankfully, Gavrill didn't have the belt do more than cover all my lady bits before he left me. I don't know if I could have handled having something inside my ass right now.

I sigh, knowing that he must have had to go to his bridge shift.

As soon as I make the noise, I hear Arkdhem's voice.

"Dawn? Are you awake?"

"Yes, hello, Arkdhem." I try to sound more enthusiastic than I feel. I like Arkdhem, but it would be nice not to have a constant babysitter. I don't know why I feel so irritated right now. Especially since I'd probably feel kind of lonely without him.

Apparently, my emotions are sort of out of whack.

"I will leave the room so you can dress," he says cheerfully.

When I hear the door whoosh shut, I think about what I want to do. I don't know when Gavrill left, but it's unlikely he'll be back quickly. His on-duty shifts are long, which does currently have the benefit of giving my body time to recover. I take a moment to perform a few sun salutations, concentrating on my breathing as my body flows from pose to pose. There's a hollow in my gut, almost like the emptiness I felt when I lost my mom and grandma. I take my vinyasa, seeking the peace in fluid movements. On an alien ship a million light years away from everything I've known, I need the balance between my body and my breath more than ever.

By the time I'm done, the ache in my chest has shrunk to a pea-sized throb. I bow and whisper, *Namaste* to the wall. Away from my master, the pain never truly goes away. Only sex will soothe it completely. I'd chalk it up to the Pavlov-type training, except that I felt the same hollowness on Earth.

Pulling on a deep violet dress, I decide I want to go visit with Medik and talk with him about the Tribute program. Arkdhem has no objections, and after he takes me to eat, we go straight to the Med Bay. It turns out that Arkdhem also has a lot of good thoughts about the program. I definitely wouldn't call him soft—I wouldn't call any Tsenturion warrior anything close to that—but in a lot of ways he's more empathetic and open than his compatriots. Definitely more so than Bogdan or Gavrill. While he's excited about the Tributes and wants a female for himself, it's obvious he would prefer one who *wants* to be here.

"Why not have them click on something that's an actual agreement?" Arkdhem suggests as Medik and I wrangle over the questionnaire that I think women should have to answer so that we don't end up with anyone who has a significant other or children or other strong ties to Earth. What constitutes strong ties is somewhat up for debate, with Medik having a much looser definition than me.

I sigh. "No one's going to take that seriously. They'll think it's a gimmick. We'll get all sorts of women clicking it just to see what the link takes them to."

"We could do both." Arkdhem tilts his head as he looks over the screen of notes Medik has been taking. "It would narrow the pool..."

Medik gives him a stern look. "Do you want a Tribute or not? The pool can't be too narrow."

"I think you'll be surprised how many swipe right," I mutter under my breath. I'm self-aware enough to know that I would have. Although I don't know that I would have been any happier about showing up on an actual Tsenturion ship and expected to be a warrior's mate. But I would have clicked.

"Swipe right?" Both males are now looking at me with confusion.

"Don't worry about it."

Neither of them lets it go that easily, and I found myself explaining about how humans *actually* hook up, which led to a fair amount of confusion on their part.

"I'm starting to think we're doing Earth females a favor," Arkdhem says, shaking his head after I finish explaining 'ghosting.'

Despite the fact that Earth women would definitely

rather choose their own mates, even if sometimes our choices are terrible, I'm having trouble coming up with a good rebuttal. Ask a woman what she wants out of a relationship, and a strong, loyal, kind male who is completely devoted to her and gives her multiple orgasms on a regular basis is going to sound pretty damn good. Granted, some of them might have issues with the collar, leash, and spankings... but maybe not.

Medik strokes his chin thoughtfully, his eyes focusing on me. "Do you think women will 'swipe right?'"

I sigh. "Yes. I think there will be plenty. Even if they don't believe that it's real."

My stomach gurgles, and I realize I'm hungry again. I frown. How long have we been here? If I'm ready to eat again, then surely Gavrill must be off duty by now...

"Arkdhem? Is Gavrill still on the bridge?" I ask. For some reason, now that I'm thinking about *my* Tsenturion mate, I feel strangely bereft. I can't quite pinpoint the emotion, and I definitely don't know why I'm feeling it, but it feels like more than the longing I'm used to experiencing when we've been apart for a while. That's still there, but instead of feeling a return of it, I feel strangely empty. Like something is missing.

Both Medik and Arkdhem frown as they check the device they use as a clock—which I still haven't figured out how to read.

"No, he should be done by now," Arkdhem says. "Would you like to go back to your cabin?"

"Yes, please," I say. Anxiety is rising in my chest as I wonder why Gavrill hasn't already summoned me there.

~

GAVRILL

BLACK SPACE STRETCHES BEFORE ME, an endless road I have travelled since taking my first orders. I was so young when I joined the Tsenturion forces, pledging to serve and protect. If I had known the chance to settle into a civilian life would be wiped out in a horrible instant of Annihilation, would I have made a different choice? Would I have embraced a simple life, mated young, produced children, and died in a flash of fire during the Great Loss?

I never would've known the loss of my world. I never would've known the empty years, protecting the Jabol race as I could not protect my own.

I never would have met Dawn. Never held her in my arms, demanded her obedience, commanded her pleasure.

I wouldn't be wishing I was with her now.

But my duty must come first, no matter how it makes me ache inside. I have pushed down my emotions, my desires, because I need to prove that I can, even if it's only to myself. Arkdhem has reported in to me that he has escorted my Tribute back to our cabin. I have stayed away as an exercise in self-control. It is both harder and easier than I expected.

I have neglected my duties, including spending time with my warriors, and there was much I needed to catch up on. They were happy to see me again in my free time and had many questions for me—both about the Tribute program as well as the Vgotha. Morale is not low, but there is palpable concern over the new tactics and what it might mean. Concern that I did not even know about until today, because I have been spending all my free time with my Tribute and not my warriors.

I had meant to find a balance, but now I can see I have done a poor job of it.

That helps motivate me to stay away.

My body yearns for her. My chest pangs with a painful emptiness each moment I am away from her. Yet, I know it's necessary now, for the good of us all. Bogdan is correct. If the Vgotha kill us all because of my distraction, I will have failed not only my people, but her as well.

She did not come all this way just to die at the hands of my enemies. If that is what happens, the guilt and shame will burden me into the afterlife.

Eventually, I do return to the cabin—I must rest after all. Arkdhem has reported that she seems sad but has fallen asleep. I feel relieved. Surely, she must be less distracting when she is slumbering.

But when I slide into the bed beside her, pulling her against me, my body rouses with a passionate fury, as if suppressing all my emotions has allowed them to build. She comes awake with a whimper as I roll atop her, my hard cock seeking her opening, my hands already rough on her breasts.

"Gavrill—" she starts to say, and I catch her lips in a kiss, silencing her.

Our joining is hard, rough, and she is just as desperate for my touch as I am for hers. Once isn't enough. I take her again... and again... until she is limp beneath me and my seed bulges are emptied. Curling around her, I hold her tightly as the darkness draws me down.

But when I wake, I force myself to leave immediately rather than waking her again or cuddling her close in her sleep.

I am early for my bridge shift, and Bogdan actually

smiles with relief. He's not the only one, compounding my guilt. My warriors have missed my presence and leadership.

I vow to do better by them.

Perhaps it had been a mistake to accept my Tribute so early, before the Vgotha threat is eradicated... but now that she is here, I will protect her with my last breath.

Nodding to Bogdan, I look up at the screens, seeing the new patterns of the Vgotha Raider ships as they play hide and seek with our scouts and fighters, putting Dawn from my mind.

14

Dawn

I WAKE UP ALONE.

Again.

This is bullshit.

I want to feel angry, because that would be a hell of a lot better than the sad loneliness creeping through me, but somehow I can't muster the energy.

"Dawn?" Arkdhem is here, sitting in the darkness. My watchdog. "You are awake?"

"Yes," I say heavily as I roll onto my back, staring up at the ceiling that I can't actually see. I don't know exactly how well Tsenturions see in the dark, but I know it's better than humans do. My inner thighs and pussy are sore from Gavrill's visit last night, although at least the ache there is pleasant, not like the empty ache currently residing in my chest. "I am awake."

"You are well?" he asks tentatively, obviously hearing something in my voice that worries him.

Physically? Yes. Emotionally? Not so much.

Rather than answering him, I ask my own question. "Arkdhem, is something going on that I should know about? Something that's keeping Gavrill busy?"

I would have much preferred to ask Gavrill last night, but he hadn't exactly been interested in talking, just fucking me into oblivion. I feel like I had something precious almost in my grasp, only to have it snatched away.

Reaching up, I scratch at a spot on my shoulder while I wait for Arkdhem's answer.

"The Vgotha have changed their tactics," he says immediately. "No one knows for sure what they're doing or why. It is worrisome."

Immediately, I feel terrible. I hadn't even noticed that Arkdhem was worried or anyone else. "What are they doing?"

"Toying with us," he says grimly. "The High Commander believes they may be testing their camouflage capabilities. They do not always show up on our scanners."

Well, that is scary. No wonder Arkdhem is worried. It makes me feel a little better about Gavrill's abandonment except... vague memories from the one time I'd been on the bridge, my very first day on board, prod at me.

"How long has this been going on?" I ask.

"Since you arrived."

Okay, so that doesn't explain Gavrill's absence. Unless...

"Are they attacking now or something?"

"No," he says, almost absent-mindedly, like he's thinking about the Vgotha and what they're up to. "So far there have been no casualties at all. It's actually making us all very anxious, because we can't understand why they aren't engaging."

I feel both relieved that no lives have been lost and even more forlorn, as well as a little pissed, that Gavrill's suddenly changing how he's treating *me*. Does it have anything to do with the Vgothas? Or is it something I've done?

Does he suddenly not respect me since we had anal sex?

Or does he think his 'job' in claiming me is done, so now he's going to stop spending time with me?

The thought makes my entire body chill.

I vow to talk to him about it the next time I see him again, but he doesn't come until after I fall asleep. Again. And again, I awaken to his hands and mouth on me, his cock thrusting inside of me. Again, he uses me until we both pass out.

Again, I wake up alone.

Staying awake the next night doesn't help either. When I angrily try to demand he speak with me, all I do is I earn myself a spanking before his cock is sliding into me again.

Even as I scream in ecstasy, I can feel my heart breaking.

GAVRILL

"COMMANDER, DO YOU HAVE ORDERS?"

I stare at the swirling black matter. Vast and beautiful, and potentially deadly. Emotion bursts in me, as the sight of it seems to echo the gaping hole in my chest, and my fingers curl around the com desk. The pain I feel in my hearts has worsened every time that I tear myself away from my

Tribute and focus on my duty. It is the burden I must bear. Loneliness... and something more.

"Commander?"

"Skirt the edges," I say. "We need more information."

Sholtorin nods, peering at the screen the same way I am, as if we might actually be able to see inside the cloud of nothingness.

"Do you think they could be hiding inside?" he asks. "Where would they have gotten the technology?"

"Stole it, probably," Bogdan says, standing at my side. He should have taken over command already, but once the Vgotha ships disappeared right outside the mass of black matter, I hadn't needed anyone to tell me that I needed to stay on the bridge.

We were dealing with the unknown.

"Maybe that's what they keep testing," Sholtorin mutters.

It is possible. If they have new, stolen technology, then that could explain some of the Vgotha's current antics. That doesn't mean anything good for us.

"Send probes," I order tersely. "A few from different points. Bogdan, you have the deck. Hail me if we find anything."

Bogdan nods, already stepping into place and giving orders.

As has become my usual habit, I make rounds of the ship, speaking with my warriors and hearing their concerns and thoughts before making my way to my cabin. Tonight, I move a little faster. There is a strange feeling in my chest, brought on by seeing the black matter and the disappearance of the Vgotha ships.

As I approach my cabin, the strange feeling grows. Something is wrong.

The door slides open, and Arkdhem straightens from his position on the couch. The room is dimly lit, but not darkened the way it is when she is sleeping. He gives me a short salute before retreating from the room, leaving us alone. I frown at the small lump on the bed.

"Dawn?" I ask softly, in case she has fallen asleep. "Dawn?"

The lump moves as I approach, and Dawn sits up. Her hands flutter over her face, wiping at her eyes. Her skin is flushed, and she does not meet my gaze. It almost looks as though she has been crying, but I do not see any actual tears.

"Master? Do you need me?" There is a touch of irony in her voice, almost as though she is mocking me. "You are back early." Now I hear a hint of accusation, and she still won't meet my eyes. She is displeased that I have spent so much time away, but tonight she does not try to chide me. The spanking she received for being waspish corrected that behavior.

My body responds at the sight of her, my cock stirring, but the great weight on my chest does not move. Perhaps my suit is malfunctioning. Well, I shall make things up to her now. I will pleasure her, and she will not feel the lack of my attention.

I move to the bed, my armor already retracting into my spine.

She is so pretty and pleasing, even with her eyes downcast and hiding her emotions.

"I wanted to see you," I say, crawling onto the bed toward her. Everything in my body is yearning to touch her.

Her face starts to lift, then crumples again. She clenches her jaw. "Did you? You've been very busy lately."

"I have," I agree, reaching out to take her by the wrist

and pulling her to me. As she seems sad rather than angry tonight, I am gentle as I wrap her in my arms and begin kissing down her neck. There is a red angry spot on her shoulder. "What is this?"

"Just an itchy spot," she mutters, somewhat stiff in my arms.

"Have Medik see to it," I order her, tipping her head back to take her lips in a kiss. She turns her head away, making me frown down at her.

"Do you not wish to spend time with me anymore?"

"It is not about my wishes. I have a duty to my warriors and my people," I tell her, beginning to grow frustrated. I am here with her now, and she wishes to remonstrate with me instead of enjoying ourselves? "Just as your duty is to me. You are my Tribute."

"Yes." Why is there such sadness in her tone? My frustration grows and then ebbs. If she is sad, I will cheer her up. She will writhe and cry out for me, and then she will be happy again. After so much attention and pleasure, the adjustment to my new schedule must be harder on her than I realized.

I stroke her back, breathing in her scent. I feel her arch against me slightly, squirming under my touch. My hand strays to her front to caress her soft curves under the gown. Her breath quickens as her nipples bud against my palms. My rod swells under her sweet bottom as my *seela* begin to writhe.

I touch my lips to her neck. "I am already primed for you, my Dawn."

She shudders against me as my hands slide under her gown and begin to rove, hungry. I want to feel her, all of her.

"I will make you feel better now." I squeeze her breasts, pinching her nipples to arouse her further, and feel her sudden intake of breath. I rock my hips against her, seeing the future I so desire laid out in front of me, as soon as our enemy is eradicated. "When we defeat the Vgotha, then I will be able to attend to you properly and you will bear my children."

She suddenly breaks away, throwing her body backwards, leaving my hands and lap empty.

"I'm sorry," she says, her face knotting in the way that heralded tears. "I can't do that. I don't... I don't want children with you. Not like this. I'm sorry." She rolls away from me, rejecting me, rejecting her future with me.

I should punish her. Tributes should not reject their masters. I could use an enforcer or her training belt to punish her. I could spank her. There are so many things I could do to her for pushing me away.

Instead, I stare at her shaking shoulders as she curls around one of the bed cushions, her back to me, for the sadness is back, a black despair that I can feel all through my chest. The pain of loss.

And Dawn is the source.

If she were not so upset, I would marvel at the wonders of the nanotech, how attuned it has become to her and how well it transmits her emotions to me, mimicking the bond. I do not know what to do now that she has rejected me.

I still do not want to leave her though. Not until I have to again.

"Lights down," I say, and darkness descends on the cabin.

We lay there, side by side but not touching, lonely even as we are together.

～

GAVRILL

THE SADNESS LINGERS, following me for a tsencycle. My officers fall silent as I take my post on the bridge. Bending over their workstations, they pretend not to study me, perusing my suit for a hint of my emotions. Their entire chance at a mate rests on the success of this Tribute program. I cannot let my emotions dictate the outcome between me and my... Dawn.

I clench my fists on the panels alongside my command chair.

I will train my Tribute. I will breed and bring her to heel. I will do my duty to uphold the breeding program and ensure the survival of our race.

My determination does not quite fill the void inside me. Nothing can replace the warmth of my Tribute's regard. But I cannot allow her moping to derail my duty. She will learn her place, in time. Her needs belong firmly behind those of my mission and my men.

"Commander, we located a warship!"

The screen fills with the space craft we've spent a millennia trying to discover. Their warships are not as big as our destroyers, but they are closely guarded. We still don't know why.

"A warship," I say, half -rising from my seat as if that will give me a closer look. The enemy tech is dull and unassuming, almost blending in with the surrounding space. Small and remarkably fast, the Vgothan ships have a habit of hiding in dust clouds or meteor belts, refusing to stand their ground and face us—even before they had the cloaking technology we're facing now. Despite tsencycles of fighting, we have few visuals of their warships.

Now we've come upon one just sitting here, on the other side of the mass of black matter. There is no sign of the hunter ships and raider ships we were following, although it's possible they've retreated to the bowels of the warship rather than remaining outside of it.

"Scan shows no evidence of hyperdrive or engines." The warrior continues with his report. "And the sensors aren't registering any heat signatures that might mean armed weapons."

"They're scuttled. They've run out of fuel or life-resources. Or both." Bogdan almost sounds gleeful. His suit is the lightest I've ever seen. "Permission to destroy it?"

I stare at the enemy ship, still and silent as if waiting. My senses prickle as if the nanites are trying to tell me something is wrong.

"Keep scanning," I order. "I want to know why they're sitting in open space."

"Yes, High Commander." The science officer bends over his panel, pressing buttons and frowning at the strange readings.

I wait for Bogdan to protest, but the big warrior is also frowning at the exposed enemy ship, much more concerned now that he's had a moment to think about why a warship would just be sitting here. Waiting for us, right where the smaller ships had led us.

My instincts are right, I know it. Something's wrong.

"High alert," I announce. "All warriors to their post."

~

Dawn

. . .

I TRACE the outline of the stars on the glass. So small, so infinite. It is hard to look at them and feel that, in this great swirling galaxy, one matters.

Gavrill doesn't care about me. He cares about his precious tribute, but that could've been any woman. I am a trophy, a toy to take down off the shelf and admire. An object to show off. He doesn't care about Dawn. For all I know, he's incapable of caring. Of love.

This is my life now, a toy to a male who will give me great pleasure, but who will never love me in the way I wish he would. The way I love him.

Gathering up my skirts, I stride from the massive viewing deck, unable to bear the sight of the stars anymore. Arkdhem follows at a discreet distance, obviously realizing my wish to be alone. Which is almost funny, because the truth is I don't want to be alone at all.

But I don't want to talk either. Definitely not to any Tsenturions.

I retreat to the cabin, my silent escort shadowing me. I decide to read, because then at least Arkdhem won't try to entertain me or talk to me.

I don't know how much time passes when an alarm blares. A light over the door flashes from green to purple. My head jerks up from the book I've been sitting and reading. Well, pretending to read. I've had some trouble focusing on it, but at least trying to read helped pass the time. When the light came on green a few minicycles ago, Arkdhem didn't seem concerned, but now he's tense.

"What's happening?" I ask him when it doesn't look like he's going to say anything on his own.

With a slight shake, he faces me, trying—and failing—to give me a genuine smile. "What do you mean, Tribute?"

I sigh. Sometimes he can take the protecting me thing

way too far. "Something's wrong. That light has been lit for fifteen minutes—uh—minicycles, and it just changed color."

"It is an alert for all warriors to report to their stations."

"Why?" I prompt, sitting up and setting my book down. "What is happening? Are we being attacked?" I'm trying to stay calm, but I can feel anxiety rising up in the back of my throat. Which is probably exactly what he was trying to protect me from by not telling me in the first place, but not knowing would just make me even more fearful in the long run.

"You should ask the High Commander." Arkdhem fidgets with his armor.

I grind my teeth. "I would ask him, but he's not here. He's hardly ever here anymore. He keeps leaving me with you."

"The High Commander has many duties—"

I shoot to my feet, pacing to the end of the room in a savage burst of energy.

"He would be here if he could," Arkdhem calls after me.

"No, he wouldn't," I half-laugh in despair.

"Tribute..." Arkdhem's voice trails off.

"You know it's true. He's avoiding me."

"He is very busy—"

"Then maybe he's too busy for a Tribute," I snap.

"It will be different once you have bonded—"

"It's not going to happen. I've tried. I can't bond with... a robot." Gavrill has feelings somewhere, deep down. He just refuses to show them.

"The High Commander is not a machine," Arkdhem frowns.

"He certainly acts like one sometimes. The pilot light is on, but there's no one home."

Arkdhem's suit shimmers as he tries to figure out what I'm saying. I'm not sure myself. The doctor seems so sure Gavrill is capable of bonding, but the more I fall for the Commander, the more he pulls away. Maybe the nanites have taken over and he's only a shell of a Tsenturion. A lean, mean, fighting machine, steady and reliable and as emotionally available as a refrigerator. I would've noticed his lack of emotion sooner if he didn't also have the stamina and orgasm-inducing ability of a Sybian.

"The Commander regrets his duties have called him away for so long. He wished for me to tell you." Arkdhem sounds desperate for me to believe him. Poor guy. It's unfair for me to take my anger out on him. He's such a nice guy.

Too bad I'm not his Tribute. I eye Arkdhem's muscular form, perfect and balanced under the bronze suit. I've never seen any other warrior's suit get as light as his; he must always be in a good mood. And with his strong jaw and long lashes, he's pretty, too.

But even if I could get Gavrill to give me up, I know I can never love another. My master might be incapable of loving me, but my stupid heart is lost to him, my body enslaved along with it.

"The Vgotha are executing an attack," Arkdhem keeps explaining. "Until we know what they are up to, the High Commander must remain on the bridge."

"What if we went to him?" I ask, hating myself for even considering seeking the High Commander out. Do I want to go running to him, curl up at his feet on my little cushion and hug his leg as he works? Am I that pathetic?

My pussy tingles and drips a little at the memory of being on the bridge. Apparently, I am.

"Oh no, Tribute, we must stay here. These quarters are at the heart of the ship. Perfectly safe." Arkdhem laughs nervously. "If the enemy breaches them, we are already lost."

"Fine," I say and drop down on the couch in a swirl of floaty silk. I pick at the filmy folds with a perfectly manicured fingernail, feeling useless. Just a pretty little trophy, lounging around in a powder pink dress while the menfolk are off fighting.

"Perhaps we can play a game," Arkdhem offers, and I sigh. He is trying. I don't know what's worse: being left alone like a house bound pet or having a babysitter.

"I can use the replicator now. Would you like something to drink?"

"Yes, thank you, Tribute."

I rise and head to the silvery machine in the corner. I should order some Earth drinks for him. A juice or a soda. A root beer float or a margarita with a tiny paper umbrella. Maybe he'll be impressed.

I could test the limits of the replicator. This dress I'm wearing is soft, but I'd love a pair of yoga pants. If Gavrill likes dresses, he can wear one. I'll even replicate one for him. I don't have his size, but I can use Arkdhem; if I can get my warrior babysitter to drink enough margaritas, I bet he'll agree to it. We can have a party—a luau with grass skirts and flower leis. We can turn the giant tub into a hot tub and make Gavrill jealous.

It's official, I think glumly as I reach the replicator. I'm so bored, I'm designing clothes and mentally throwing elaborate parties. Maybe I'll produce a new reality TV show: *Desperate Housewives of Tsentur.*

I'm so preoccupied, I don't notice the warning lights over the door flashing red a second before the doors explode.

The blast lifts me off my feet. I hit the side of a blush-colored couch and sprawl on the ground.

"Tribute," Arkdhem cries, throwing himself between me and the door. I pick myself up, coughing as smoke billows through the room. My ears are ringing, my vision filled with sparks.

"What—" I cough.

The smoke clears, swirling around a shadowy form just beyond the door. Not human, not Tsenturion, but something strange and massive. In the acrid aftermath of the blast, I shrink back against the couch as the intruder moves through the door, stepping closer on a giant clawed foot.

15

G avrill

"COMMANDER, OUR WEAPONS ARE READY," Officer Kalexston reports.

"Hold fire." I tap my earpiece. "Hail Medik. Come to the bridge. High alert." Medik confirms that he received my message, and I end the transmission. I turn back to the science officer. "Sholtorin, have your crew scan all surrounding space for life forms. As soon as you have readings, make a report. I want to know *why*, after a lifetime of hiding, a Vgotha *warship* is sitting in barren space as if waiting for us."

"Commander!" Bogdan's voice is somewhat strangled as he points at the screen in front of us.

The warship is beginning to move.

Away from us.

Lumbering through space like an injured animal.

"Something's wrong with their thrusters," Sholtorin mutters under his breath. "At least... I think there is. The scans are spotty, and there is interference from the black matter cloud."

"What about the hunters and raiders?" I demand, turning towards him. The tension on the bridge is palpable. We all want to attack and bag one of the few warships that the Vgotha have... but we're all aware it could be a trap. "Are they on the warship? Or are they hiding around us?"

"We don't know." Sholtorin's voice is grim.

Beside me, Bogdan mutters a curse.

Medik arrives on the bridge as we all stare at the warship. His steps falter as he takes in the scene.

"A warship," he says, sounding just as awed as I feel.

Turning to him, I nod a greeting. "Medik. You have the most knowledge about the workings of the mind. I would like your opinion on the situation."

Dawn

I SHRINK behind the couch as the giant rectangle fills the doorway. Smoke streams around what must be a shield covering all but the clawed feet. Whatever it is, it's taller than Arkdhem.

"Tribute—run!" Arkdhem orders, but where am I supposed to run to? The attacker is blocking the only avenue of retreat. Arkdhem rises, his weapon humming. The laser hits the shield, and the thin red line redirects, cutting into the wall. Smoke and the smell of charred machinery rises.

"Surrender, Tsenturion," a deep voice reverberates through the room. The voice is almost... wooly. It gets in my head, expanding until it fills every corner. I put a hand to my face to relieve the pressure.

"Come closer, and I'll shoot," Arkdhem rasps. A front panel of his helm hangs askew.

"And risk hitting the Tribute?" The amused tone is the voice of reason. "Lay down your weapon." That voice, slipping between my ears. All I want to do is lay down my weapon. I don't even have a weapon.

"You won't take me alive," Arkdhem grits out.

The creature lowers its shield slightly. "Warrior." Its voice is almost a purr. "I do not need you alive."

The intruder pads closer, shield sagging to reveal a behemoth shoulder, muscled and covered with intricate patterns. Its face is a mass of tubes—some sort of helmet that covers everything but a narrow goatee. Above the mask, black antlers rise proudly. The spiny rack is so tall, the thing dips its head to enter the door. Poking out from the coil of tubes are pointed ears, tufted with fur.

I search frantically for a hint of familiarity, a mark or hint that would let me figure out what it is, but the thing looks more like a beast from *Where the Wild Things Are* than any species from Earth.

"You cannot fight me. Embrace oblivion." The voice rolls out, echoing as if at the bottom of a deep well. *Oblivion, oblivion.* My eyelids weight, and I sway a little at my seat on the floor.

Arkdhem's gun wavers. He's succumbing to the voice, too. It reverberates through my head, the wooliness making my thoughts feel as though they are stuffed with cotton.

The creature lowers its shield completely, revealing something out of a nightmare. Tattoos scroll across a broad chest divided into deeply grooved muscle. A dark mane with a greenish tint tumbles down its back between its antlers, reaching a tattered loincloth suspended over enormous thighs. Furred limbs end with clawed hands and feet. More fur tufts from the ridges of its elbows, shoulders, knees. The rest of its body is part-fur, part-green-grey skin, thick and leathery, covered with black markings. As it steps into the light, its tattoos writhe in a hypnotic dance.

Balanced on clawed feet, the monster advances. *Oblivion.* The echo of its last whisper conquers the very air.

Slowly, as if moving through water, Arkdhem's gun tilts down.

The smoke scrapes down my throat, making me choke. A dagger of pain in my lungs is exactly what I need to shake off the intruder's spell.

"Arkdhem," I hiss. "Wake up!"

My Tsenturion protector shakes his head, mouth slack and eyes dazed, even more affected by whatever is happening to us than I am. The creature's face twitches towards me. The gigantic body stops in its tracks. Not a hair moves as it studies me. I recognize the preternatural stillness of a predator waiting to pounce. I cower alongside the couch, my fingers grasping at my silky robes, the only protection I have between my skin and the creature's glowing white eyes.

I marshal my breath, welcome the pain and let it clear my head. Tightening every muscle I have, I open my mouth and let loose the only weapon I have—a scream.

~

GAVRILL

. . .

THE VGOTHA WARSHIP SITS EXPOSED, tempting us. I've never seen one out in the open like this before. Unguarded. Vulnerable. "What are they planning?"

"Maybe they wish to surrender?" Bogdan offers. A thin chuckle ripples through the bridge, breaking some of the tension.

The Vgothas and Tsenturions have been locked in mortal combat for a millennia, ever since the Jabols hired us to protect them from the bully race. We embraced our mission with even more vigor when planet Tsentur was destroyed.

"Why would they be waiting there for us to fire on them?" Medik's voice is a murmur

Bogdan's eyes are fixed on the dun-colored ship on screen. "If we fire, we give away our position," he murmurs, but not as if he's rejecting the notion, just weighing the option.

"What could they do with that intel?" I ask.

My second officer shakes his head, still staring at the enemy ship. "If there are no other ships in the area... nothing."

"The readings report a single life form. One. A large one." Kalexston keeps checking his readings, searching for an explanation.

Medik and I exchange glances. He has long entertained a theory that the Vgothas ships are actually alive, a planet-based symbiot evolved to be useful in space travel. That allows the Vgothas to spread their forces wide, because partnering with the symbiot means it only takes one or two Vgotha to pilot a ship.

"Why would they abandon a warship?" I muse aloud. If the tech was truly a living symbiot, abandoning it would be like cutting off a limb and losing an entire battalion of warriors all at once.

Beside me, Bogdan makes a sound of annoyance. "Does it matter why? They would not have done so unless they had no choice. Our weapons are superior. We must fire on the ship and destroy it."

Beside me, the doctor makes a noise of agreement.

We cannot just leave a warship here. They might come back for it. They might be trying to find a way to repair it. Or it might be a trap, but we won't know until we spring it.

"Lock weapons on the Vgotha ship," I order. "You may send a warning shot. Fire at will."

"Firing," Bogdan says gleefully as the image flares with a sudden bright explosion.

The whole screen lights up for a moment, blinding us. Someone cries out as the floor under my feet vibrate, tossing as our ship is hit by the biggest blast I've ever felt. The entire bridge shakes, tossing warriors to the ground.

Alarms blare. Bogdan's crowing turns into a curse. I reach out and steady the doctor, helping him find his feet.

"Report," I shout.

"Sensors down." Kalexston sounds shaken. "Commander, the ship detonated some sort of energy pulse.

"They have a new weapon," Medik murmurs.

"Whatever they hit us with, it's affecting our sensors. My team needs to recalibrate them," Kalexston says.

"Do it now," I order.

"Commander, we must lock weapons again and destroy them," Bogdan snarls. "This is our chance."

I meet Medik's gaze. We've destroyed Vgotha ships before, but never one that's scuttled. Something doesn't feel right.

"Lock weapons on their coordinates again," I order.

"Die, alien scum," Bogdan says, his armor practically glowing, seething with righteous victory.

The bridge hums with the powering up of our weapons, almost drowning out the science officer, who whirls from his com desk. "Commander! Our shields have been breached!!"

~

Dawn

THE ROOM SHAKES like something hit the ship.

I kick backwards, scuttling across the floor. My dress rips. The creature reaches for me.

A roar blasts my ears along with the sinister hum of a weapon. Arkdhem is upright, firing.

The creature angles the shield, and the laser reflects back on Arkdhem, slicing into him until he falls.

"No," I scream. I race to Arkdhem's side, whimpering in sympathy at the gash in his suit, peeling away from his burned body.

"Tribute," he rasps. "You must run. You must survive this." His eyes flutter closed. "Tell the High Commander I fought well." His suit dims as if shutting down.

"Arkdhem," I whisper, planting a hand on his chest to feel the slight movement of his breathing. He still alive, I think, but unconscious.

Dammit, where are the other Tsenturion warriors?

Blood rushes from my face as I remember what I was told—*These quarters are at the heart of the ship. Perfectly safe. If the enemy breaches them, we are already lost.*

Oh my God… is everyone else dead? Is Gavrill dead?

The horned creature stalks forward. I've seen sketches of

the Horned God, leader of the Wild Hunt according to fae-lore, a giant satyr-type god with a stag's head. This alien looks exactly like that pagan deity come to life. Terrifying and intimidating and...

And it's coming for me.

I hoist the gun and rise, scrabbling for the trigger even as a scream rises behind my clenched teeth. But I'm too late.

The creature rips the weapon out of my hands and wrenches it apart. I throw up my hands to shield myself from the spray of gun pieces, staggering backwards.

If I can run and reach the adjoining room, maybe I can lock myself in and radio for help.

A few steps, and a claw yanks me back, whirling me around. Another claw closes around my throat, and the creature hoists me in the air. I grasp at the rigid arm holding me aloft, my feet kicking wildly, looking for purchase as I choke. Spots swirl before my eyes, and I put all my strength behind one desperate kick to the alien's gut. It drops me, I think more out of surprise than the force. A second later, I'm cuffed and thrown against the couch. My head is numb from the blow, and I can already feel a bruise forming over the side of my face.

"I see. You must be the High Commander's Tribute," the creature murmurs thoughtfully. A purring hum rumbles from its chest, the soft sound at odds with its powerful body.

It reaches for me. I kick again, much more weakly this time, but it's much faster as it grabs me and scoops me up. Not by my throat, in fact it cradles me almost gently, and I don't understand the change in its demeanor. I meet its blazing white eyes in terror.

"Peace, little creature," it growls, and the voice fills my senses again, trying to make me sleep. There's a shushing sound, an exhale, a rush of soporific fog enveloping me. It's a gas, not a spell, and if I can just tear off its mask, the creature won't be immune. I try to hold my breath, but my limbs are already feeling heavier and heavier, like I'm trying to push through Jell-O as I lift them.

As my fingers reach the knotted coils, my head lolls on my neck and darkness rises to swallow me whole.

GAVRILL

THE SHIP on screen flares with light, and the bridge shakes with another pulse. Consoles light up, and the alarms whine louder in protest.

"They can reverse the weapon's path and send an energy pulse back! Disengage!" I order. Suddenly, the scuttled ship before us doesn't seem so harmless.

"Get me readings. I want to know what just hit us."

"The pulse blew our sensors offline for a moment, but they are returning," my operations officer, Miths, reports.

"Weapons are disengaged," Bogdan adds gruffly. "Permission to take a pod to engage the enemy personally." My second looks ready to grab a gun and storm the enemy ship all by himself.

"Denied. We need to know what we're dealing with first."

"No change in the enemy ship," Kalexston says, his eyes on his beeping panel.

"Keep running scans." I turn to my operations officer. "Miths, did we sustain damage?"

"Negative, Commander. All sensors are functioning

again." He frowns. "Except for some slight damage to an exterior portal near the lower right quadrant."

"Exterior portal?" Medik asks. "Was there a breach?"

Miths frowns. "I'm trying to gather more data. My crew informs me there's a number of sensors offline in that area. They're headed onsite to repair them now."

An alarm clangs in the back of my mind. "Was the portal damaged with the pulse?"

"Unsure, Commander. My crew should arrive to secure the area soon." He pauses to listen to his crew's report before continuing. "There's a row of damaged sensors extending from the exterior portal down the halls leading towards the core. The aft quadrant."

"The aft quadrant," Medik repeats. "That's near the officer's quarters."

I'm on my feet a second before Miths cries out, "Commander, we've found wounded Tsenturions."

"High alert," I shout. "The enemy breached the hull! Kalexston, report." An enemy on the ship is unthinkable.

"My crew is working to secure the area. We've found six Tsenturions down in the halls. They appear to have been overpowered by their own weapons."

Drakk. The enemy is here, on my ship. And instead of calmly accepting this and sending my crew to kill the intruders, I am seized with fear. The situation below decks requires caution. I have a Tribute, a defenseless female I've sworn to protect. I cannot risk her being caught in the crossfire.

For the first time in a thousand tsencycles, I have something to lose.

We wait in tense silence. Medik looks like he might say something but bites it back at the last minute. Every muscle in my body is rigid. The moment I decide to grab my weapon and run down there to save Dawn myself, Miths stiffens as he receives a piece of news.

I know what he's going to say even before he turns around. "Commander, we've found evidence of a Vgotha intruder. He entered one of the portals, found his way to infiltrate your quarters, wounded Officer Arkdhem, and left via the same exterior portal."

"The Tribute?" Medik asks before I can find my voice. His face holds all the fear I refuse to show.

"Gone," Miths looks at me, his armor flickering sickly, and I feel my hearts sink in my chest. I already know what he's going to say, and it's all I can do to keep from howling at the pain already ripping into me. "The Vgotha took her."

16

D awn

THERE'S something cool plastered on my face. It feels good on my bruised skin, tingling lightly. Healing me? I definitely don't hurt as much as I expected to. Gingerly I pluck the cloth from face, sitting up and tossing it to the side so I can see where I am.

The space is dimly lit and close, the air a mix of humidity and mist, a warm, flower-scented gloom. The walls look like a blend of moss and some sort of fungus, almost... breathing.

I lay on a soft mass that shifts slightly under me. It feels like a cross between a bean bag and a water bed. The supple form has a soft, slippery skin that's bright yellow.

A giant shadow moves out of the corner of my eye, and I stiffen. My tattooed captor paces forward on large, clawed feet. The mass of tubes that were a sort of gas mask are gone from its head, leaving a more humanoid face with a pointed, goatee-tipped chin and wide cheekbones framing large, limpid eyes. Back on the Tsenturion ship they were glowing white, but now they're a comfortable brown. Beneath the tattoos is a gray-green skin that reminds me of stone.

I've been abducted by aliens—again.

He opens his mouth, and sharp teeth flash at me. "Are you awake?"

There's a buzz in my ear as my translator works overtime to interpret what the creature is saying. The voice seems to go directly into my head.

I nod, then realize it might not understand the gesture. "I'm awake."

"Are you hurt?"

I reach up to touch my face where it hit me. The soreness is gone, though a slight numbness lingers. "No. I'm good."

The creature settles on its haunches before me. I flinch as it reaches out, but it—he? I definitely get a male vibe—only lifts the wet cloth I discarded and tucks it into his belt. His gaze meets mine, and he tilts his head, studying me as much as I'm studying him.

As we stare at each other in silence, a door opens and a second creature stalks in. This one is a slightly smaller version of my captor, only with large bat-like wings draping down his back. I'm pretty sure it's a he because of the loincloth hanging between his legs.

"Tor, why did you bring that back here?" he asks, looking down at me in disgust. "We needed a high-ranking captive, not a pet."

"She belongs to the High Commander," the first Vgotha —Tor—answers. In the gloom of the ship, he looks even more like the Horned God, though his antlers look slightly smaller. Maybe they can grow at will. His teeth are long with canine-like incisors, and his ears are pointed. The second Vgotha also has elfin ears, along with the rippling muscles of a beast with fur tufted at the joints.

Of all the alien races who could kidnap me, I'm the captive of ones that look like elf-demons. Great. Just great.

The winged Vgotha cocks his head to the side, studying me in the same manner Tor is, a slight look of disbelief on his face. "She is the Tribute? But she is so small. Is she sentient?"

"I believe so. The Tsenturions have high standards."

The winged one laughs. I scowl at them, using anger to help cover my fear. Obviously, they don't think much of the Tsenturion standards.

"Welcome, Tribute, to the Vgotha ship," the winged Vgotha says mockingly, his leathery wings shifting with a sound like crackling paper.

I don't answer, pressing my lips together to keep my temper at bay. I have no idea what these creatures will do to me, but I don't think a spanking would be their first move. My heart pounds, but my fear feels muted. Maybe I'm getting used to being abducted.

"What now, Tor?" Mr. Demon Wings asks.

Tor studies me thoughtfully. "Let's see just what lengths the High Commander is willing to go to in order to save his little Tribute."

I shrink into my seat on the bed as the giant monster alien rises and stalks away, Mr. Demon giving me an assessing look before following. The door closes behind them, leaving me all alone. Which I should be happy about, but I'm not. I'm even more terrified than before.

I suck in a breath, trying not to panic. There's a little hum in my chest that tells me not to worry. A little voice in my head that says—*My mate is big and strong, and he will save me*. Talk about being brainwashed. I realize I'm stroking my collar, as if for reassurance, and immediately snatch my hand away.

Who am I kidding? Gavrill doesn't want *me*. He can just ring up the Jabol and order another Tribute. Brunette this time, or maybe a redhead. One who won't fight him so much. The Jabol can put together a catalogue, complete with swimsuit photos. Maybe even Bogdan will get on board. And me? I'll be trapped with new aliens whose only use for me is apparently to bargain with the Tsenturions.

So what's going to happen to me when they realize the Tsenturions don't think I'm worth bargaining for?

The yellow blob I'm sitting on quivers and hums a little, as if to reassure me. It sounds like it's alive. In fact, the whole ship feels like I've been swallowed by a living, breathing creature. That would explain the rainforest feel.

I gulp and push myself up. I already know there's going to be no white knight riding to my rescue. I don't mean enough to any of the Tsenturions. Heck, I doubt Bogdan would even think twice before blowing up a ship I'm on if it meant he got rid of all the Vgothas on it, too.

I'm not tied up, I'm not in a cell, I'm not even sure I'm guarded... and it's up to me to get myself out of this.

GAVRILL

"COMMANDER, we're picking up a frequency from a Vgotha ship," Sholtorin says, cutting through the panic that has gripped me ever since I knew Dawn was taken. We still don't know where or even how.

The camouflage on the small Vgotha hunter and raider ships is frustratingly sporadic, allowing them to wink in and out of existence on our scanners. Whatever technology they're using to hide is not perfect, but it is enough to keep us from knowing which one managed to board us and take Dawn.

"The warship?" I ask.

"I don't believe so, Commander, but I'm not sure which ship. It's definitely one of the Vgotha though."

"Put them through," I say with a growl.

The main screen flickers, and a Vgotha appears. Sickeningly gray-green skin, puny horns, and brown eyes stare back at me. Beside me, Bogdan growls at the sight of our enemy.

"You are the High Commander?" the Vgotha asks, looking at me.

"I am," I say, my armor flashing dangerously. The entire bridge is full of black armor now, ready for battle. "Who are you?"

"I am Tor, Chief of the Vgotha."

I want to demand to know where Dawn is, what they've done with her, but to do so would be to show weakness. Instead, I pretend that nothing is amiss.

"Why did you hail us?" I ask, keeping my voice level. "To surrender?"

Tor chuckles. "I infiltrated your hold and snatched something of yours right from under your nose. You can't even find our ships. Why should I surrender?"

"Because you're spreading yourself thin and dying in the scramble to find enough food and weapons to live through the next cycle. Surrender, and your deaths will be quick."

"Your pride will be your downfall, Commander. I have someone I'd like you to meet. Or perhaps you know her."

The screen flashes to Dawn, exploring a mossy looking room of wherever they're holding her. A sharp pang rips through my chest as I stare at her. Other than a bruise on the side of her face, she doesn't look as though she's been harmed. As I watch, she brushes her long fall of blonde hair back from her shoulder in a familiar motion, scratching at the tender spot that has been bothering her. Something clenches in my gut.

"Your Tribute has come for a visit." Tor returns to the screen. "As you can see, she has not been damaged."

"You will return her to us. Now." I can feel Bogdan looking at me from the corner of his eye, but I ignore him. I am not thinking, I am acting on my emotions, but I can't seem to help it. Just that small glimpse of my Dawn is enough to tear any logic I have to shreds.

"Or else what, Tsenturion?" Tor mocks. "My ships fly undetected past your sensors. I boarded your ship, infiltrated your personal quarters and took your prize. What's to stop me from disappearing and taking her with me?"

"What do you want?" I ask, clenching my fists. "If you think we will surrender, you are wrong. We will fight."

"With Jabol weapons, I know." Tor stares at me. "The time for fighting has passed. You, Commander, will come to my warship *alone*, within the next cycle, or you will not see your Tribute again."

The screen goes dark.

"Drakk," I shout as the visual of the Vgotha's ship disappears, along with Tor's hard-eyed gaze. Pacing, I smash a fist into a wall panel, and the warriors around me startle. My crew has never seen me like this. I'm a microcycle away from losing control. "Where are they? What do our sensors tell us? Report!"

"We're scanning the area, High Commander," Klaxeston says tightly, head down and eyes on his instruments. "They cannot have gone far."

I curse again, and Miths and Borodem twitch. Shouting at them will not help. Nor will ripping my chair from the floor and throwing it.

"Commander." The low voice at my elbow makes me whirl. Medik's eyes meet mine, full of understanding. "She wasn't hurt. She looked well. We will find her."

No, we won't. Because Tor is right. And even if we did somehow manage to locate the ship that she's on, it might be too late. I won't risk her that way.

"I'm going to the warship," I say grimly, turning toward the door to the bridge. I can see the crew jumping up, protests halfway out of their mouths, as Bogdan steps in front of me, barring my way.

"You cannot abandon your post."

"Do not," I growl, "tell me what to do."

"We need you here, in command," Bogdan barks. "With all due respect, you are not in possession of your senses."

"Is this mutiny?" I roar. "Get out of my way!" I'm taller, but my second has more bulk. He is a mean fighter, but I do not want to fight with him—that will take up precious time. I just want him out of my way. Red flashes from my suit and seems to leap to his. My anger reflects on his face.

"Stop it, both of you," Medik snaps. "We need to talk about this."

"We cannot throw away our chance to capture a Vgotha ship." Bogdan points to the side screen, where the abandoned ship still sits in empty space. "If we can cripple it, can bring it in for testing, we will have a chance to learn of their weapons and defenses. It could turn the tide of war to our favor. *That's* what we should be scanning for, what our goal should be."

"And what of my Tribute?" I grit out. I know what he's going to say, but I want to hear him actually voice it. If he dares.

"They are using her against us."

"You heard the Vgotha. I have a cycle to get to that warship. They will kill her."

"An unfortunate casualty of war," Bogdan says softly. To my surprise, he almost looks sorry, but he does not back down. "But she is not even one of us. There will be other Tributes, you can have whichever one of them you want."

I surge forward, ready to correct my second's arrogant opinion with my fists. Medik steps between us, keeping me from my target, and I shout over the older Tsenturion's shoulder at Bogdan.

"I don't want another Tribute. Dawn is *not* replaceable."

Shock is clear on Bogdan's face at my reaction.

"Commander," Medik murmurs. "I agree that we must retrieve the Tribute immediately. Their population has also been depleted in this war. If we take too long to enter into negotiations, they might decide to breed her."

"That's not possible." Klaxeston's suit flares bright green with horror. Even Bogdan looks ill at the thought.

"From the information the Jabol gave us on them, Vgotha anatomy is close to ours. She might be compatible," Medik says. "We must free her before they decide to find out."

I stare at the blank screen, willing Dawn's image to reappear.

"I will go," I repeat. "Bogdan, you are in command. If you want to find a way to capture the warship, you will have to do it while I am on it. You are correct, I am emotional, and I am no longer fit for duty. I am giving in to the Vgotha's demands, what happens next with them will be up to you."

The bridge is silent with shock.

Bogdan's eyes darken. "This is not what I want, brother."

"I know. But it is necessary." I would do anything to have Dawn back, safe in my arms.

"Commander—"

"Know this," I raise my voice so the entire deck hears, "Dawn is more than just a Tribute. She is my mate. I would give my life a thousand times to spare her any harm."

The men around me stare at the statement. At my side, Medik wears a sad smile. Bogdan slowly shakes his head.

"The bridge is yours," I say, stepping around both Medik and Bogdan as I begin to run towards the bowels of the ship, where the scout ships are docked. The sooner I reach the warship, the sooner Dawn will be safe.

If not, the universe will not contain my rage. I will hunt the Vgotha down and destroy them all.

17

D awn

I PACE THE SMALL ROOM, trying to figure out how I'm going to get out of here.

It's feels like it's been hours. There's still some wishful part of me that hopes help is coming... but I can't see it happening. Not when I'm so replaceable.

I pause in front of one of the walls of my prison where the Vgothas had exited. Once the door shut, the wall reformed as if the entryway never existed. Creepy, but kinda cool. The whole interior of the ship feels alive—in more than a vegetation sort of way. The air is moist and heavy like a rainforest, and I can't get over the feeling that I'm being watched.

I put my hand on the wall and press. It feels like damp moss, and I'm tempted to rip it off, but if it's living material, the Vgotha might be alerted that I'm trying to escape. The forest has eyes. Instead of yanking at anything, I start patting my hands over it, checking for weak spots. Maybe I can find the crack to the door. There's got to be a way out.

"Please let me out," I whisper, feeling kind of silly, but I can't shake the feeling that the ship can hear me. Understand me. I keep running my hands over the wall, moving to the next one beside where Tor and the other Vgotha left through. "I don't belong here, I don't want to be here... please... my name is Dawn, and I just want to go home... please..."

I keep moving my hands over the wall, pleading the whole time.

To my shock, the moss suddenly melts away, showing a small tunnel, just wide enough to fit a smaller sized being... like a human.

"Thank you." I don't feel so silly now. Maybe a little creeped out, but... I'm not throwing away my shot.

I duck inside and start crawling. Once I'm a few feet in, the wall behind me forms back in place. I take a moment to swallow my panic along with a slight dose of claustrophobia. Only one way to go—forward. I keep crawling. The light at the end of the tunnel seems to get further away—and at one point, the tunnel twists as if to stop my progress. I keep deep breathing and wait for the way to open up again. After a moment it does, as if the tunnel closing down was a test and I passed. At one point, I have to contort myself to twist around a particularly hard right turn. Good thing the Tsenturions healed my knee and that I've kept up with my yoga. I don't know if I could handle this tunnel if I couldn't contort with the best of them.

At last, the tunnel widens and light floods in. I pull myself to the edge and look out into a long, low-ceilinged room. No sign of a Vgotha, but there's a tiny pod, a lot like the one the Jabols used to deliver me to the Tsenturions a lifetime ago.

Not quite believing my luck, I wait a moment in the mouth of the tunnel. The walls around me contract with a slight murmur, pushing me forward, a lot like the bean bag pushing me to my feet. This is unreal, but if the ship is helping me escape, I'm not going to question it.

"Thank you," I whisper, drop to the floor, and rush to the pod. It's long and narrow, just large enough to fit one person. I press my hand to the panel beside it, and it lights up. The pod door opens upward. After a moment's hesitation, I climb in and lie down. The panel beside the pod beeps a few times, and the door closes with a sigh. I practice my deep breathing again, trying not to compare lying in the pod to lying in a coffin. A slight shudder, and the wall in front of the pod grows around a large dark spot, widening like an ink stain on the brown-green wall. Another shudder, a whooshing sound and the pod shoots forward. I scream as points of light rush over me, the air growing close and suffocating for a moment, and then the pod is floating in black space, faraway stars like little bright diamonds twinkling to guide the way.

I did it. I'm free. The Tsenturions won't believe I got away with only the help of a sentient ship. I bet the Vgotha have no idea I'm even gone. I can't imagine why the ship would let me go and then tell them. I guess the only thing I can rely on is the aliens underestimating me. Except for the ship. I frown trying to think through the ramifications of that, which is kind of hard when I'm so jittery.

The pod keeps floating smoothly along, fast enough that the starscape changes every few minutes or so. The panel beside my face has all sorts of buttons, but I'm afraid to touch it. I hope the Tsenturions are out looking for me and that I can figure out destination coordinates, otherwise I'll be lost in space. But one thing at a time.

Shadows crawl over the glass like clouds over a sky, interspersed with rays of light. The pod shoots past a sun—a giant burning ball bright enough that the glass seems to tint, and I still have to shield my eyes. Then we're past it and flying through dark space again, coming out to weave through a field of meteors. I don't know how I'm moving so fast and I'm still able to see the sights close up. Silt hits the pod like a spray of pebbles. A giant rock looms close, and I throw up my hands, afraid we're going to hit it. At the last second, the pod zooms around it. After a few close calls like that, I close my eyes until we hit darkness again. The pod knows what it's doing. I hope.

I don't really have a choice except to trust it.

A soft light warms my face, and I open my eyes to clouds of pinkish interstellar dust. Golden streaks swirl through the cloud. It's so beautiful, I forget to be afraid. A part of me wishes Gavrill were here. If I have eleven hundred years to live with him, we could take some great trips. Explore the universe. A visit to one of these nebulae would make a hell of a honeymoon.

Darkness encloses the pod again, and I realize I'm holding my breath whenever we hit these black patches. This time we're slow coming out. Flashes of light in the distance make me tense. It looks like lightning, a million miles away. My heartbeat picks up as the flashes grow closer. There's a storm in front of us, and we're heading right towards it.

I fucking hate storms.

"No, no, no." I press on the walls of the pod. I even risk hitting a few buttons on the panel. It chirps at me but doesn't alter course. Grey-brown dust billows around us, clouding my view. We hit another meteor belt, and tiny rocks pelt the pod like hail on a windshield. A few larger ones hit with enough force to make me yelp. The lightning in the distance is a lot closer, and the dust is now swirling like a tornado, sucking us forward.

Fuck. We're going right into the storm.

White light splits the mist of greyish particles swirling around the pod. I scream. Lightning racks the pod again and again while I cover my head, whimpering. The storm took everyone I loved—my mom, my grandma, my dad before I even knew him. It sucked me through a vortex into another galaxy, and now it's trying to wipe me out before I return to him.

"No," I scream, "No!" I kick the smooth glass top of the pod and punch the air. I will not go quietly into the night. Wet tracks down my cheeks, and I'm sobbing, my chest cracking into pieces to let the emotion out, but it doesn't feel like dying. It feels good. Few more lightning strikes, and the air around the pod shimmers. The violent clouds are fading in the distance, disappearing into the blissful darkness.

My shaky sniffles turn into a giggle. I've weathered the storm and come out the other side. Alive. As laughter bubbles in my chest, I raise my arms and whoop.

Stars sparkle on a clean velvet backdrop. The pod dives through rings of colored gas, then navigates past a planet, moving at record time. I resist the urge to flatten my face against the glass and study the gorgeous grey and blue orb. The temperature falls slightly, and I shiver. A rummaging study of the pod unearths a thick fur, and I pull it over me. It smells like a Vgotha, earthy and rainforest-y with a slight musk that reminds me of a shaggy dog. It's not unpleasant. I snuggle beneath the fur and resist to urge to laugh.

I was captured by Vgothas, and all I got was this lousy

fur robe. I still don't know how I managed it. I completely lucked out with this pod. Not only is the autopilot working like a dream, but the ship is regulated to my body temperature. Frllil told me human anatomy was similar to Tsenturions; that was why we were considered compatible mates. Maybe the Vgothas are the same?

The more I think about it, the less I think luck was involved and that the ship and this pod have to be sentient and decided to let me go for some reason. I mean, what are the chances the tunnel from my prison room would lead straight to an escape pod? That the coordinates would be set to get me as far away from the Vgotha ship as possible? Not that I have any hopes of doing much more than drift in space until someone finds me. I can only hope it's a Tsenturion ship.

Then I see it—shiny black and floating out from behind the frozen planet like a lesser moon. I know the shape from all the videos Frllil made me watch. It's Tsenturion, and not just any ship—the High Commander's.

"Hey," I shout, as if they can hear me hail them. I study the panel buttons, frantically looking for one that will let me open a communication channel, send up a flare, do the Hokey-Pokey... something to get them to notice me. Hell, I'll take off my shirt and wave it if that might help flag the guys down. Gavrill might not like me showing my body off... but Gavrill might have already written me off as lost. God, that hurts more than I want it to—like a knife in my heart. For a second, I struggle to breathe.

But I know it's probably true.

I grip the fur robe and stare at the huge Tsenturion ship, looming larger as it grows closer. Suddenly, I'm not in a rush to be rescued anymore. Homesickness, a longing for Earth, for *humans*, for thinking I have even a chance at love fills me. But that's not what I'm going back to.

Still, at least I'm alive. Think positive and all that. Besides, it's not like I have anywhere else I can go. Drifting off into space and dying alone in the blackness doesn't exactly appeal either.

A microcycle later, the pod jerks and a hum fills my ears. A whitish glow surrounds me, enveloping the whole pod. Beyond it, the stars blur. We're caught in a light beam of some sort, and it's pulling us towards the Tsenturion ship at high speed. I grab the fur with one hand and press the other to the wall for balance. This pod needs some 'oh shit!' handles. A panel on the side of the Tsenturion ship opens, revealing a loading bay. Thank God. I was afraid for a moment I was going to crash into the side of the ship or get blown to bits by the tractor beam like a mosquito caught by a bug zapper.

The approaching side of the ship fills my window, and then my pod is safely inside. The doors close, and Tsenturion soldiers pour onto the deck, weapons in hand to deal with my unidentified pod.

I throw the fur off my shoulders in case the Tsenturions think I'm an undersized Vgotha and blow me to bits. Gavrill has probably trained his men to be more discerning than that, but I bet a lot of them are pretty trigger-happy right now, and I'm in a Vgotha escape pod.

The pod opens, and I suck in air. It's over. I've done it. I'm back—for better or worse. I can't deny the relief I feel at the sight of so many Tsenturions as I look up from my seat. Judging from the light colors of their suits, they're glad to see me too.

"Commander, we found her!" one of the warrior cries. Relieved to be back on the familiar ship, I don't even protest at the mistruth. The Tsenturions didn't find me. I saved myself.

Before I can pull myself out of the pod, the group of soldiers parts and Gavrill emerges, rushing to my side with more urgency than I've ever seen before.

"Dawn. My Dawn. Are you hurt?" His voice is full of anxious worry, and his hands roam over me, searching my exposed skin, delving under the thick fur on my lap. With a growl, he rips the fur off and tosses it away. The colors on his armor are rippling, like a muddy rainbow, making it impossible to know how he's feeling.

"I'm fine," I say, trying to reassure him.

"Commander, keep your distance, they might have contaminated her in order to poison us—" Bogdan sounds serious and worried.

"They didn't," I say, but before I can finish my sentence, Gavrill is already picking me up, ignoring Bogdan's warning and shouting for the doctor.

"I'm fine, I'm fine," I repeat, even as I mold myself against his firm body, relaxing in his arms.

"Bogdan is right. They could've given you poison. Medik!" He calls out again, turning as he looks for the older Tsenturion. The rippling colors on his armor intensify, flashing so quickly it almost makes me nauseous to look at it, as close to out of control as I've ever seen him. "We need a medkit here, now!"

The crowd of warriors parts to make way for the stooped Tsenturion, who is hurrying forward as fast as he can. Gavrill moves to meet him, holding me out slightly in front of him like I'm an offering. Quick as a wink, Medik runs a scanner up and down my body.

Beside us, the Tsenturions examine the pod I came in.

"What is this technology?" one of the warriors breathes.

Another pokes it with his gun.

"Don't hurt it," I snap, then bite my tongue. I need to explain my theory of the ship being alive to Gavrill. Hopefully, he'll be interested enough to believe me and not harm it considering I wouldn't have been able to escape without it.

"Commander, I must protest, she may have been infected with their symbiote—" Bogdan starts again.

"She's clear," Medik says hurriedly as Gavrill's face twists with anger. "Just the rash that she acquired here."

"I'm taking her to my quarters," Gavrill barks at his second.

"We need to debrief her—"

"Stand down," Gavrill roars. The warriors snap to attention, even Bogdan. Ignoring all of them, Gavrill carries me between the saluting rows with ground-eating strides.

"I'm fine," I reassure him softly, patting his chest. I know he's more upset that his special tribute prize was taken and that this doesn't mean he actually cares about *me*, but it's still nice to pretend. Being held by him again, I feel protected, and I know that's true.

"You could've been killed." He practically growls the words, but I can also feel something else—anguish? Maybe. It's too faint to really know. Or maybe that's just wishful thinking on my part.

"Is Arkdhem okay?" I ask, since I don't see him.

Lips pressed together, Gavrill nods.

"It wasn't his fault. The Vgotha hit him with some sort of trance spell. It didn't seem to work as well on me."

"I know," Gavrill says, although his expression is still implacable. I huff. Hopefully, he isn't holding a grudge against Arkdhem, although I don't know what I can do if he is. It's not like Gavrill will listen to me.

18

Gavrill

I CARRY Dawn to my cabin, my hearts pounding inside my chest so noisily that I can barely hear my thoughts. I feel split in two. I was about to board a ship to rescue my Tribute, when the sensors picked up the advance of a Vgotha ship. I was ready to bring it on board and tear it apart myself and torture the occupants until they told me where to find Dawn. When the pod opened and revealed her pale face, I couldn't keep myself from touching her.

I've broken protocol in front of all of my warriors. Possibly even put them in danger. Fortunately, there was nothing wrong with her, but Bogdan's paranoia could have easily proven true.

I know he's also right that we need to debrief her. We need to know what she saw, what she heard, any information she can give us on the Vgothas and their ships. She's the only being we know of who has ever been on one and made it out alive.

But that duty wars with my personal need to check her over, to ensure she is unharmed, and to protect her. I want her safely tucked away from everyone, to have her completely for myself, just for a bit.

"Where are we going?" she asks.

"Our temporary quarters." Our old quarters need repairs after the infiltration. "I need to check you over."

"I'm *fine*," she says again, sounding exasperated. I know she's telling the truth, and yet I also know I won't be satisfied until I've examined every part of her with my own eyes. Possibly my hands too. Just having her in my arms is rousing my need to claim her irrevocably. "They didn't do anything to me except put me in a cell. They seemed to think I was a pet."

If I wasn't so out-of-sorts, I would have chuckled at the disgruntled note in her voice. "You might seem like a pet to them. I doubt they have ever seen a human before."

The cabin door opens before us as she lets out a little snort.

Gently setting her down on the bed, I begin to look her over, frowning when I come to the dark red spot on her neck. Medik had assured both her and me that it was just some kind of rash, but it looks as though it has gotten worse.

"Does this still itch?" I ask, my finger hovering over it.

Dawn shakes her head. "Not really. It just looks bad."

She blushes a little, her eyes slightly downcast as she looks away from me. I do not like that she will not meet my eyes. Before the Vgotha took her, she was sad, but now she doesn't seem so... if anything, the sense of her emotions that I get is determination.

"Anything else?" I ask, running my hands over her arms.

"No, I told you, I'm fine... look, stop, just stop touching me." Suddenly she jerks back, leaving me empty-handed and shocked.

A few semicycles ago, I would have pulled her over my knee and spanked her until she acknowledged my right to touch her however I pleased. Right now, though? Having her just returned to me, only for my touch to be rejected?

"What did they do to you? What did the Vgothas do that you don't want my touch?" I demand, rising and stepping back to give her the space she apparently needs.

"Nothing, I told you, they did nothing!" She stands too, her eyes now meeting mine, wide, blue, and filled with tears. "But I can't stand you touching me like you care, I can't sit here and pretend everything is fine between us when it's not."

"I do care—" I start to say, but she cuts me off.

"You care about *your Tribute*," she says, the sarcasm in her voice mocking the endearment I enjoy so much. "You care about me as your Tribute, but nothing more. Someone came and took your shiny toy, and you're happy to have me back, but you don't really care about me. You made that abundantly clear before I was taken, and I cannot deal with you acting like anything has changed just because I was taken away from you for a while."

I stare at her, my armor dulling to grey as I try to understand what she's saying to me. Of course I care about her, she is my Tribute. My future. My Dawn. I was willing to abandon my post to save her. I don't understand how she can think I wouldn't care about her. Her words don't make sense to me.

"What do you want from me?" My words are a baffled plea for instruction. None of her manuals covered anything quite like this. I thought I had earned my place as her Master, but...

I do not understand what is wrong, so I do not know how to make it right. Whatever it is, I will do it.

Big blue eyes look up at me, filled with tears.

"I want to go home," she whispers. "Back to Earth. I don't want to be your Tribute."

Something inside of me tears, ripping through me with a greater force than any weapon she could have used on me. I would give her anything but that.

But it is what she wants.

Not trusting my voice, I nod and turn away, retreating because I cannot think what else to do. The agony crawling up the inside of my chest is hauntingly familiar. I felt it the last time I lost everything.

~

Dawn

IT'S THE RIGHT DECISION.

That's what I tell myself, even as the expression on Gavrill's face, the sad grey of his armor, and my own needs make me want to call him back. Or chase after him.

My shoulder twinges, right where the red spot is, and I put my hand over it. It had spiked with pain when I told Gavrill I wanted to go back to Earth, and I'm starting to think that Medik is wrong about it being a harmless rash, but it doesn't really matter right now. I'm not sure anything matters.

Slowly, I sink back down onto the couch and curl up into a little ball.

I'd sworn to myself at the beginning of this that I would escape. That I would find a way back to Earth. That's what I was doing. I can't stay here, in love with an alien that sees me as nothing more than a possession.

Soon enough, he'll have another Tribute.

One who actually signs up for the experience, even if she thinks it's a joke when she does it.

It won't—can't—be me. I can't handle being in love with someone who just sees me as an incubator for his babies. Someone who is happy to fuck me into oblivion but pulls away from me just when it seems like his emotions are becoming involved.

The door swishes open, and I don't even look up. If my friggin' Tsenturion Master wants a little sub to greet him, he can replicate and program a sex robot. Maybe Frllil could make one for him.

"Tribute?" a soft voice calls from near the door. Not Gavrill—the doctor.

"Here," I raise a hand, too tired to ask him to call me Dawn again.

The older Tsenturion approaches me warily. "Are you feeling well?"

"I'm fine," I wrench myself up to prove it. "The Vgothas didn't do anything to me."

"The Commander wishes me to check and debrief you."

"Okay. Fine." I sit and let him scan me, turning my head and offering my wrist when prompted. I'm still thinking about calling Frllil and asking him to make Gavrill a sex doll, maybe one that can incubate Gavrill's sperm until they replicate a female Tsenturion ovum. Or better yet, Frllil could clone him. That's just what the universe needs, twenty million hard-jawed Gavrills, commanding ships and guarding every corner of the known universe.

"Dawn…" I realize that Medik has been calling my name for some time. I blink and focus on his frowning face. "Your vitals are normal, but there seem to be some lingering effects on your conscious state…"

"There was a gas. Or a spell or something—" I explain the way Tor seemed to hypnotize me with his voice.

"I have heard of a drug that can do this. It comes from a mushroom that an ancient civilization cultivated on their planet. If one ingests enough of the fungus, their skin emits a pheromone that makes the people around them susceptible to suggestion."

"That sounds about right."

"The mushroom was destroyed along with the planet. The Vgothas must have gotten a specimen and cultivated it."

"That would make sense," I say. "Their whole ship was like a garden." More like an indoor marijuana farm.

"The High Commander will want a full account of your experience, but he will question you later about it."

I nod. Of course he does. That way, he and Bogdan can get down to the business of destroying the Vgothas. No sense in importing more Tributes if your sworn enemy is just going to break all your pretty, pretty toys.

"I think perhaps it would be good for you to rest," Medik continues.

I shrug. "I can do it now, while the memory is fresh."

"I do not think that is wise. Physically you are healthy, but there seems to be a lingering malaise."

"No, I felt this way before the Vgothas took me. I just didn't have the courage to talk about it." The trip through the storm took care of that. After my family died, I hid in my grandmother's house and never made any close connections, as if by having no relationships I could avoid the pain.

I know better now. Life is brutal and dangerous. And it's

beautiful. I can shrink from it, or I can brace myself and enjoy the ride.

It only took a trip to another galaxy to teach me how to live on Earth.

"Is there anything I can do?" Medik asks.

I take a deep breath, ignoring the ache rising in my chest. "Yeah, actually. Can you start by taking this collar off me? Also, since you're so involved in the Tribute program, can you contact Frllil for me?"

He straightens. "The Jabol?"

"Yes." I clench my hands into fists to keep from rubbing my chest. "I just told Gavrill, I want to go back to Earth. I just need to talk to Frllil to see how we can make that happen."

"You wish to leave?" Medik seems shocked, stuck on that one point.

"I don't think there's any reason for me to stay," I say quietly, looking down at my fists where they rest in my lap. The pain in my chest is growing, an empty ache that causes tears to spring up in the back of my eyes. "All he really needs is a womb and a female willing to lend her genes. He doesn't need me... and I can't do this anymore. I just can't."

A pause. I keep my head down, not looking up because I know there will be disappointment on Medik's expression. After a long moment, he speaks again.

"I thought you and the Commander had started to bond."

I wince. Yeah, so had I, but that just shows what we both knew.

"I honestly don't think he's capable of it, and there's no way in hell I'm having kids with a man who treats me like an object. You'd have to strap me down and sedate me." I glower at Medik, just daring him to try. Although my birth control shot would keep that from happening for at least another month. Definitely not mentioning that, though.

He sighs. "That would not lead to healthy children."

"No, it won't." I clear my throat, feeling a bit sorry for the old alien. "I won't do it willingly, but I bet another woman would. I can work with Frllil, see if we can make contact and find someone else for Gavrill."

"You'd do that?" Medik's suit tints in surprise.

Do I want to? Hell no. But will I? Yes. I'm leaving. I... okay, I'm going to be honest, if only to myself—I love him. I want him to have everything I can't give to him. Will it suck the big one, choosing my replacement? Yes. I'll still do it.

"He deserves the life that he wants. A mate and children. I want him to have that." Jealousy nearly chokes me, but I push it away. There's no point in being jealous when this *is* my choice.

"If you really feel that way, I will see what I can do—"

"Thank you."

"—if you tell me why you want to go."

I sigh and rub my shoulder. It still aches, although at least it has dulled since the initial stabbing spike of pain.

"Look, this isn't working. I know you want me to be the Commander's bonded mate and all, but," I shrug to hide my roiling feelings. "I don't think it's possible."

Medik stays silent while I massage the sore patch of skin below my neck and try to think of how to explain it to him. *The sex is great, but he doesn't care about me. I can't go through a thousand years feeling like a casual hookup.*

"I thought about it when I was on the Vgotha ship. No, the Vgothas didn't say anything. To them I was just a bargaining chip—something they kept safe but didn't mess with at all. I might as well have been a piece of furniture." My throat and chest tighten, making my voice rasp a little.

"That's how Gavrill thinks of me, too. I'm fun and diverting and pretty to look at, but he doesn't care about me any more than... a prize on a shelf."

Beside me, Medik jolts as if he might say something but doesn't interrupt as I press on.

"I didn't even think he'd rescue me," I tell him, sadness welling all over again, the sense of abandonment stinging the backs of my eyes as tears threaten. "That's why I escaped. I didn't think he'd come for me. Why rescue me when he can just get another Tribute?" I clench and unclench my fists, trying to get some blood moving through them, not meeting Medik's eyes. "So that's what he should do. Replace me. I can't be with someone like that. I won't. Having children with him—forget it."

Would he even care for his children? Or would he see them as little soldiers ready to be trained to carry out the Tsenturion mission?

The silence descends heavily between us.

"He cares," Medik says after a long moment. His voice is soft but sincere. "He was very upset when you were taken."

"That's just because the Vgothas took something he thought belonged to him. It's simple one-up-man-ship. In a few cycles, he won't care about me again. Maybe he'll be grateful that I helped start the Tribute program." My shoulder twitches with a stab of pain, and I rub the marked skin. "There are probably plenty of women on Earth who would be happy to be his Tribute, even though he'll never love them. But not me." Just the thought of it makes me feel nauseous. I've lost too many people in my life. I'm ready to love again. I can't imagine sharing a life with someone who will never love me in return.

Somehow, I have to get my body back to normal and get myself back to Earth. If Medik won't help me get in touch with Frllil, then I'll probably have to ask Gavrill to. Just the thought makes me quail, but I will if I have to.

Medik and I sit in silence a while. I still can't meet his eyes. It feels like I'm bleeding inside, the jagged shards of pain like glass cutting through my chest.

When Medik finally speaks again, it's the last thing I expect him to say.

"If I could prove to you Gavrill cared for you? Then would you stay?"

I start to shake my head. "I don't... how would you prove it?" Stupid heart. Stupid hope blooming in my chest. Stupid me for asking.

"Let's just say I could. Do you care enough about him to stay?"

I blink a few times, but I can't stop a few tears leaking out.

"Yes," I whisper. "I would stay. I want him... but only if he wants me. *Me*. Dawn. Not just a Tribute, but me as myself."

Medik nods with a satisfied smile. "In that case, I have something to show you."

19

G avrill

ON THE BRIDGE, I stare at the picture of empty space where the Vgotha ship once sat and baited us. Around me, the warriors are running scans to try to find it again.

It's no use. The enemy has disappeared again, taking their scuttled ship. Maybe even that had been a ruse, maybe there had been nothing wrong with it in the first place. We've lost this skirmish, just as we failed to protect our flank and the most precious person on board. I should be angry, channeling all my energy into hunting the enemy down. Instead, I can hardly bring myself to focus on anything except Dawn's voice echoing in my head.

My Tribute. The thought is mournful. Wishful. Because she no longer wants to be mine.

She wants to leave. Even if she can't, she never wants to

see me again. *I didn't think you'd come for me.* Have I failed so much as her Master?

I rub at an itchy patch on my arm, which feels like it's throbbing in time with my heartbeat. The edges sting as the nanotech tries to heal the strange wound. Every so often, I feel a sharp pain, like needles pricking into it.

Kalexston's panel beeps as it finishes scanning. "No sign of the Vgotha, Commander," he reports.

"I knew it," Bogdan mutters. I barely notice him glancing at me, but I can't think of anything to say. Clearing his throat, he speaks louder. "What about the Vgotha pod the Tribute stole?"

"My crew is still running preliminary tests. It seems to be a living organism," Miths says. My interest is stirred, in a very distant kind of way.

"Sentient?" Kalexston asks, intrigued.

"Undetermined. It does seem to have some shielding capabilities that bypass our scanners," Miths continues. "Commander, permission to modify our scanners to sense this, ah, organism."

I wave a hand. To my left, Bogdan huffs. He's been cheated out of a battle, he's not going to get to destroy the pod, and he's upset. I should feel the same, but it's like I'm numb.

Perhaps I should step down and give command over to him, for the sake of the mission while I'm in this mindset, but... I can't bring myself to do so. Without Dawn, I will have nothing to live for but endless cycles of patrol.

Pain stabs through me like a shot to the chest, and I grimace. If I had known I would gain a Tribute just to lose her, I would never have agreed to the program.

No, that is a lie. Because any amount of pain is worth the few cycles I held Dawn in my arms.

"Commander, have you asked your Tribute about the Vgotha?" Bogdan turns to look at me. He almost looks regretful but also determined. I don't answer, but he can tell from my expression what the answer is. He sighs. "Permission to question her. Or perhaps Miths can, since his crew is working on the pod?"

"No," I order, my need to protect her rousing. "Leave her alone."

"Commander, I must protest, the Tribute—"

"I said no. I will question her myself. Later." Much later. When I can actually face being in her presence again while knowing she is no longer mine. My pain in my chest is growing, and my armor flashes before I can control my emotions.

Bogdan turns away, mumbling something that sounds like "grown too attached to a breeder."

"She is not a breeder. She is leaving the Tribute program and returning to her home planet," I announce to the bridge. I will have to tell them eventually, and I do not think I can feel any more pain than I currently do, so I might as well now.

"What?" Kalexston gasps, ugly streaks of yellow shooting through his grey suit.

"You allowed this?" Miths asks.

"It was her choice," I say above my crew's disturbed muttering.

"But what about—" Kalexston bites off his question, obviously wanting to ask whether the program will continue.

"You can't do that," Bogdan protests, an abrupt reversal of his previous position. I am so numb to emotions that I do not even feel shock, although the rest of the bridge is looking at him as though he's grown a second head. "The continuation of our race..."

A small rushing sound signals the arrival of the lift and the doors opening to allow someone to enter the bridge. I can't even find the energy to look and see if it's Corin, arriving for his shift.

"I thought you wanted us to focus on our duty," I say to him, my bitter words almost taunting. I didn't expect my second to look so shaken at the end of the Tribute program. "You thought Dawn was a distraction. You thought I should spend less time with her. You thought she didn't matter and that any female would be acceptable as my Tribute. You were wrong. Dawn gave me purpose. She made my life better, made me better, she is the only Tribute I want, ever... and I failed her."

My hand is over my arm, where the stinging patch of skin is under my armor, and it feels like the nanotech is finally working, because it is starting to feel warm and tingly rather than painful. I look around to see the warriors are all staring in the direction of the lift. Turning, shock slams into me as Dawn steps on to the bridge, a wide-eyed, intent expression on her face, Medik behind her on the lift.

~

Dawn

"Dawn?" Gavrill rises from his command chair. His face looks like it's carved from granite. If I hadn't heard his words with my own ears, I would have never known he'd just been talking about me. That he'd just been confirming everything I'd heard on the video. His expression flickers to something closer to alarm. "Is something wrong?"

"High Commander, I apologize," Medik calls from the

lift, sounding way too happy for anyone to think that he's serious about his apology. "I could not stop her—she demanded to come."

I take a step towards Gavrill, my eyes trained on him. No one else matters.

"You were going to trade yourself for me?" My voice is husky. I already know the answer, but it feels like a dream. I want to hear him say it, to *me*. Purposefully and meaning-fully. The words from the video the doctor showed me still ring in my head: *Dawn is more than just a Tribute.*

His suit glitters as he nods.

"Me. And not just any Tribute. You wanted me."

"Yes."

I would give my life a thousand times to spare her harm.

"I didn't think you cared for me," I croak. My face is wet. I swipe at my cheeks as I walk to Gavrill. The rest of the bridge has faded to nothing.

As I near him, Gavrill reaches for me, then checks himself. His hands hover between us, wanting, but not daring to touch.

"Dawn," his voice is husky, "I cannot... I will not live without you. There is nothing I wouldn't do for you. If I lose you... there will be no other."

She is my mate.

"You love me," I whisper. "Not just your Tribute. Me."

His brow wrinkles in confusion. "You are—were—my Tribute. I don't understand."

That, right there, is the crux of our miscommunication I realize. His voice practically caresses the words 'my Tribute', and he doesn't even realize that being called that makes me feel as though I'm not valued as an individual. To him, it's the most loving endearment he could call me.

I just didn't realize it.

"I love you, too," I choke out the words. "I want to stay and be your Tribute."

His eyes widen, his armor flashing to a pure, brilliant gold.

I gasp as the mark on my shoulder flares—the sensation is so intense that I can't tell if it's painful or pleasurable, and I cry out. I cover the spot with my hand as the pressure turns to heat, shudders wracking me. Facing me, Gavrill mirrors my movement, his large hand covering a spot on his forearm. I stare at him as the sorrow and tension of the past cycle melt away, leaving a warm, liquid pleasure flowing through my body. I lurch towards him, suddenly unwilling to go a second without his hands on me. He reaches out to catch me, my hands falling into his, and his armor slides back, up to his elbows. I stare down at the dark gold symbol on his forearm, darker than the rest of his skin. If he were human, it would be like he had gotten henna done or something.

"Dawn." Awe fills his voice. Awe, shock, and utter delight. I can practically feel it pulsing through me... no, no, I really *can* feel it—his emotions. They are separate from my own, utterly foreign to me, and yet somehow it feels right too. His hand slides to frame the marked spot on my shoulder, and I scrunch my neck to see. The itchy red mark is gone. In its place is a bright gold brand, a circle filled with delicate angles, like the cut of a jewel.

"What—" I let go of his hand to touch the symbol with a hesitant finger. It doesn't hurt or itch or anything anymore. The smooth design feels like it's been there forever, like an old tattoo. And Gavrill's forearm bears an identical one.

Gavrill reaches out to trace the gold circle on my shoulder, his touch raising goosebumps all over my body. Okay, when he touches it, it feels totally different, and a rush of pleasure spreads through my body.

"The bond," he says softly. My eyes widen; his meet mine. Suddenly, an emotion floods through me, a tidal wave stealing my breath. I hang on to Gavrill, shaking a little as I make sense of the feelings inside me. A curious lightness has replaced the stark ache. Instead of a hollow pain, there's a strong glow, pulsing like a heartbeat, leading straight to...

I stare up at Gavrill. He's there on the edge of my senses like a fifth limb, only more—bigger, stronger, and full of a warmth. The pain in my chest is gone, filled with a presence, a second heartbeat, a perfect peace.

"Holy hell." My voice is thick. "Does this mean what I think it does?"

"We share a mark." Gavrill strokes my shoulder with reverent fingers. His face reflects my own awe.

"It's a heli crystal," Medik breathes, "symbolizing eternal union." He and the rest of the officers on deck are all staring at us.

"The bond is complete," Gavrill murmurs and draws me close to him. I feel a thread of concern through his emotions. "You are sure now, you want to stay with me?"

"Yes." I press my fingertips against his chest, looking up at him so he can see the sincerity in my eyes, willing that he'll be able to feel me as easily as I can feel him. "I never wanted to go. I only wanted to be yours."

"You are mine," he says, smiling down at me. No one sighs, but I swear the entire bridge crew is practically humming with satisfaction at the romance of the moment, totally enthralled by the drama playing out between Gavrill and myself. "My captive. As I am yours. The bond binds me to you as much it does you to me."

"What about your duty?"

"You're my Tsenturion mate. We will figure it out. Together." The bond between us hums a little, filling my heart with happy music. I step back a moment, hand on my chest, as warmth rushes over me. Gavrill lets me go, as if he understands I need a moment to catch my breath. To find my footing in this awesome flood of love. The screen stretched over my head shows nothing but black, empty space. My heart beats against my palm as I find myself in the new current that flows between us. I am still me, and he is still himself, but if we give ourselves over, we are also one. It's enough to overcome a lifetime of loneliness.

I turn back to face Gavrill. My eyes meet his, and a new surge of warmth fills me. One prick, and it could pour out from my skin, filling the bridge, the ship, the black velvet expanse to the nearest star and beyond.

I open my mouth to tell him all this, but he already knows. Anything I say would sound maudlin. There aren't words to describe it.

Perhaps I will invent some. I have a thousand cycles to do it.

Around me, golden light flashes from the warriors' suits, making the bridge look as though we're bathed in golden sunlight. Everyone, even Bogdan's. The entire race benefits from knowing our bond is complete.

It's still a little embarrassing that such an intimate thing happened in front of everyone.

"I, uh, interrupted your shift." I blush and start to edge away as everyone's eyes on me starts to make me feel a little shy.

"Yes," Gavrill matches my bland tone. "But the interruption had merit."

"I'm not in trouble for coming onto the bridge without permission?"

Mischief glimmers in his eyes, and he steps towards me. Aw crap. I don't need to be in tune with his emotions to know what his intentions are.

"I didn't say that. After all," he continues in a louder tone, "we warriors cannot allow our Tributes to trample over protocol. When we return to the room, you will be chastised."

I raise my chin, about to say something defiant, when the lift swooshes open behind me. I turn to see if Medik has left, but no, he is standing beside the door. Corin is disembarking from the lift. Uh oh.

"Fortunately," Gavrill says as I whip my head back around to look at him. "I am officially off duty now." The wicked smile he gives me makes me press my thighs together even as my hands move behind me to cover my bottom. Pointing to a spot in front of him, Gavrill commands softly, "Come here."

I hesitate, my head turning back towards the door and the lift...

"Dawn," Gavrill warns. A second before I decide to dash, he strides forward, dipping at the last moment to plant his shoulder in my belly. He lifts me easily in a fireman's hold as I squawk.

"Corin, you have command, as my Tribute requires my attention," he announces. Cheers erupt around the bridge, along with several ribald suggestions that make me blush furiously. One hand grips the cheek of my ass, holding me in place as he points to Bogdan.

"You're next," Garvill tells him, and I get the satisfaction of seeing the surly warrior's suit whiten. Balancing on

Gavrill's hard shoulder, I laugh. He claps his hand against my bottom, and I yelp.

"I am not finished with you, naughty one," the High Commander growls as he carries me to the lift, his hard fingers firmly pressing into the soft cheek of my ass. "It is time you learned to respect your Master."

My muscles clench in eager anticipation.

∾

GAVRILL

The door to our quarters barely slides shut before I toss Dawn on the bed. Catching the hem of her dress, I rip it from her body, directly up the middle as I direct the nanotech of her belt to recede, baring her body to me. My cock stands at a stiff angle from my body, my *seela* quivering and waving in the air, reaching for her. Instead of grasping Dawn's hips and plunging inside her primed body, I stretch out over her, my body atop hers but not inside of her yet.

"You belong to me," I say, bracing myself on my forearms and tracing the golden edge of her mark. A true, full Tsenturion bonding. I can feel her inside of my head—happy, warm, loving... She fills a void that I hadn't even known was there. Sharing my emotions with her is strange, but it also feels right.

"Yes," she breathes, lifting her face for a kiss. I bow my head to claim her lips but stop just short, brushing mine against hers as I reach up to pinch her nipple. She squeals at the little burst of pain, but I can also feel her excitement and arousal despite the noise of protest she makes.

"Yes, what?"

"Yes, Master," she giggles. I roll us both and rise to settle her over my broad thighs, her bottom turned up for my palm.

Smack! Smack! Smack!

The sound reverberates from the walls, interspersed with her breathy cries. I paint her cheeks pink with my hard hand, spanking her quickly but not harshly. The excitement I feel pulsing off her is growing, and my cock is aching to be inside of her. I pause long enough to command her Trainer to trickle down the crease between her cheeks and fill her bottom hole.

Shifting her further forward on her lap, my *seela* brush against her clit and wet folds, teasing her sensitive bits as I begin to spank her again. This time my hand comes down harder, on already pink cheeks.

Smack!

"Gavrill! Please!"

Smack!

She shudders as my *prime seela* circles her clit, even as my hand smacks against her tender bottom. The sight of her trainer bisecting her red cheeks, burrowing into her ass, urges me on to greater heights.

Smack!

Dawn

"Master, *please.... I need you!*"

I feel like I'm about to explode from all the sensations filling me. The pain, the pleasure... my desire, his passion...

Smack!

"*Master!*" A sob rises in my throat. My ass clenches around the trainer as it thickens inside of me, buzzing slightly like a vibrator.

When he suddenly picks me up, putting me back on my back, I cry out as the trainer feels like it's pushing even deeper while my sore bottom flares with the impact of my weight on the bed. Then he's on top of me, his cock thrusting inside of me, his hands pushing mine above my head and pinning them there as his mouth lowers to mine.

Thigh to thigh, hip to hip, chest to chest. Mark to mark. Pleasure pulses from my mark to his.

He thrusts hard, fast. My legs wrap around him as his tongue slides against mine. I can feel him inside of me, stretching me, filling me. The nanotech in my ass buzzes faster, swelling larger as I clench around his cock. My clit pulses against his *prime seela* as it strokes me each time he sheathes himself.

I arch, my breasts rubbing against his chest as his hands tighten around my wrists. As our passion rises, I feel his *seela* latch on to my pussy. The tendrils pull us closer, sealing us together as we both cry out in ecstasy. The rise and fall of our shared orgasm crests and flows between us, pleasure upon pleasure, his and mine together until the intensity amplifies a hundred, a thousand times.

I don't see stars… I see galaxies.

But slowly we return to the ship, to each other. Our breath slows. The ecstasy ebbs. I pant for air, nestling my head against his shoulder. I feel quivery all over.

"Dawn. My Dawn. My Tribute." His lips move over my temples, and I can feel the complete love, the awe, the happiness that infuses each word.

Now I understand that it doesn't matter whether he's calling me by my name or by my title. Both mean the same thing to him—*his love.*

"My Gavrill," I whisper back, tilting my lips up to kiss the underside of his square chin. "My Master."

My love.

Against all the odds, we've found our happily-ever-after... and I no longer feel so bad about the Tribute program. Every woman should have the chance to find the same happiness.

EPILOGUE

Pareena

BEEP. Beep. Beep. I never thought the hum of hospital machines would become the soundtrack to my life. But the sound, along with the rattle of breath in my chest, tells me I'm alive. The sound is sweet because I won't hear it for much longer.

Hospitals are never quiet. A never-ending stream of doctors, nurses, and food service workers, coming in, checking charts, dropping off food trays and picking them up. The doctors frown. The nurses murmur "how ya doing, honey" and force smiles as they plump my pillows and check my vitals. The food service people don't comment as they pick up the food trays with most of my meal uneaten. I can only manage a few bites a day, another sign that I can measure the rest of my life in minutes and hours versus weeks and years.

I used to be so busy. Used to be one of the white-coat workers hustling past patient's doors. I used to hate being late, hate waiting, hate making small talk. I had so much time, I had the luxury of complaining that I had none.

Now my seconds are measured by the drip, drip, drip of my IV. I have nothing to do but doze or watch silly sitcoms on the tiny TV suspended in the corner of my room. Both early and late to my death, I'm happy to wait. I have nothing left to do but die.

My fingers crawl to the edge of the bed and find the smooth surface of my new best friend—a glossy black e-reader. I don't know who left it on my hospital bed but it's full of stories I'd never let myself read before. The ones I'd avoided at the library—the ones with strong-jawed, shirtless guys on the cover, with bulging muscles, and another bulge straining the front of their tight pants. I was always tempted to read them, but too embarrassed. I was such an elitist coward. I missed so much.

The Tribute rises from the Jabolian pod. Her body is lithe and strong, all the scars from her past are gone. Her skin glows and her hair falls in shining waves past her waist.

Now that's a fantasy. I haven't had hair in a long time. The chemo took everything, including my eyebrows.

Her Tsenturion master stands on the receiving deck to greet her. His suit molds his strong frame, a glittering grey color that reflects his impatience. As his female tribute approaches, the suit glimmers with a silvery sheen. By the time she has walked the long path to stand before him, the silver has turned to gold.

She is a worthy Tribute.

I finish the story and sigh. Becoming a Tsenturion bride sounds great right about now. Fix all my imperfections and heal my disease. Replace the cancer cells with healthy ones.

Throw in a pair of eyebrows, and it'd be worth getting abducted.

I click back to the beginning of the story, ready to read it again, but as I swipe to the first chapter, the e-reader blinks a few times. A new screen appears.

Initiate questioning phase.

New words form onscreen: *Are you Doctor Pareena Singh?*

I jolt awake and glance around the empty hospital room. How did the device learn my name?

The e-reader gives a little chirp as if reminding me to answer the question. *Are you Doctor Pareena Singh?*

I click "Affirm identity" and type in my full name and title as prompted. I haven't referred to myself by my title since I stopped working as a psychologist, after the first round of chemo failed. The staff around here don't know I have my doctorate.

It feels good to be recognized. I turn the e-reader over, checking for signs that someone has tampered with it. Whoever sent it to me must have programmed it with my name.

Another question appears on screen. *Do you have children?*

What the hell? That's invasive. I should throw the thing aside in protest. Instead, I hit "No" in a huff. I must be really bored.

Another question pops on the screen. It keeps chirping, so I keep answering.

Over an hour later, I lay back on the pillows, exhausted. I've answered over a hundred questions. They just kept coming—asking about my family, my career, even whether or not I had a cat. It reminded me of a dating site one of my friends got me to join—answer all the questions and they'd match you with your true love. After my diagnosis, I stopped dating. I didn't want to find my true love only to tell him I had a few years to live.

I close my eyes for a moment until the device beeps impatiently. New words swim across the screen.

<Swipe right for abduction>

That's new. The text blinks at me, green.

<Swipe right for abduction>

This has got to be the weirdest computer game ever invented.

<Swipe right for abduction>

Well, what can it hurt? I touch the screen with a finger, pressing lightly to steady it. My hands are bony with veins standing out. They look like they belong to a much older woman.

<Doctor Pareena Singh> My name scrolls across the screen once again. <Swipe right for abduction>

What the hell. I'm stuck in this hospital bed, dying of Stage IV cancer. My e-reader wants me to swipe right to play a stupid game?

I have nothing to lose.

I place a trembling finger on the screen. The e-reader gives an encouraging chirp as I slowly slide my finger to the right. The screen starts to glow.

Is something happening to my eyes now? The doctors didn't say anything about my eyes possibly being affected, but I'm not sure that means anything. They don't tell me a lot of things these days if they don't think I need to know.

I can't tear my eyes away to find the call button for the nurse though... it's like the screen is fracturing into rainbows, filling my vision... and it's beautiful. Something tugs at me, pulling at my body.

Am I finally dying? Is this the light that I'm supposed to go toward?

I open my mouth to call for help—I'm not ready!—but there's no air and suddenly it feels like there are tight bands around my chest, pulling me towards the light. Tears slide down my cheeks in despair. I'd hoped to come to accept my death but now I have no choice.

Rings of light burst ahead of me as the darkness closes in. Pain, which thankfully feels distant because of the morphine, swirls as I shatter apart.

My last thought is mournful.

I'm not ready.

ONE CLICK ALIEN TRIBUTE, book 2 in the Tsenturion Masters series!

ALIEN TRIBUTE

~Swipe right for abduction~

Two minutes ago I was lying in my hospital bed, waiting to die of cancer, reading an awesome sci fi romance on a mysteriously delivered e-reader.

Now I'm in another galaxy, cancer free. The aliens abducted me because they want me to be a bride for one of their warriors. Weird. The whole thing sounds a lot like the story I was just reading...

Except the surly warrior who's supposed to claim me **doesn't want a mate.**

Disclaimer: The authors are not responsible for any actual alien abductions that may result as a consequence of your purchase of this book.

~

"Okay," I say. "So I'm a Tribute... so now what?"
Frllil is watching me with an air of anxious wariness, and I'm

kind of getting used to his odd appearance, but it's still creepy when he smiles widely. It's so close to approximating a real, human smile, but the fact that it's so close somehow make it more unsettling rather than less. It's the Uncanny Valley effect, but knowing that doesn't make it less strange.

"I must say, you're taking this a lot better than the last Tribute," he says, sounding very relieved.

"Is there any way to escape?" I ask, because it seems like he expects me to say something.

Frllil shakes his head. His expression doesn't change - he isn't sorry. If anything, he looks pleased. "There is no way for you to access the wormhole you came through, and a return trip would be inadvisable, even with the improvements I've made to your physical form."

I shrug. "Then resistance is futile. So what comes next?"

"Now we begin your training."

Read Alien Tribute, Bogdan and Pareena's story.

AUTHOR'S NOTE

Once upon a time, in a coffeeshop far, far away, two authors met to talk about reading books, writing books, publishing books, cosplay and more books. Naturally the conversation turned to giant alien cocks.

Okay, maybe that's not how it happened, but over soup and salad, we started playing with the seed of a story. The seed took root and now you have this book. If you like it, please let us know —we have plans to continue the series, starting with Bodgan's book. If you nag us, you might get it sooner...

Love to our editor Miranda, our author friends and supportive family, the Goddesses and Angel Legion on Facebook. And to you, who read this book all the way to the end.

XOXO
    Golden & Lee

ABOUT LEE SAVINO

Lee Savino is a USA today bestselling author, mom and choco-holic.

Warning: Do not read her Berserker series, or you will be addicted to the huge, dominant warriors who will stop at nothing to claim their mates.

I repeat: Do. Not. Read. The Berserker Saga. Especially not the hot excerpt on the next page...

Download a free book from www.leesavino.com (don't read that, either. Too much hot sexy lovin').

EXCERPT: SOLD TO THE BERSERKERS

A MÉNAGE SHIFTER ROMANCE

By Lee Savino

I woke tied to a tree.

The light was lower, heralding dusk. I struggled silently, frantic gasps escaping from my scarred throat. My stepfather stepped into view and I felt a second of relief at a familiar face, before remembering the evil this man had wrought on my body. Whatever he was planning, it would bode ill for me, and my younger sisters. If I didn't survive, they would eventually share the same fate as mine.

"You're awake," he said. "Just in time for the sale."

I strained but my bonds held fast. As my stepfather approached, I realized that the scarf that I wrapped around my neck to hide my scars had fallen, exposing them. Out of habit, I twitched my head to the side, tucking my bad side towards my shoulder.

My stepfather smirked.

"So ugly," he sneered. "I could never find a husband for you, but I found someone to take you. A group of warriors passing through who saw you, and want to slake their lust on your body. Who knows, if you please them, they may let you live. But I doubt you'll survive these men. They're foreigners, mercenaries, come to fight for the king. Berserkers. If you're lucky your death will be swift when they tear you apart."

I'd heard the tales of berserker warriors, fearsome warriors of old. Ageless, timeless, they'd sailed over the seas to the land, plundering, killing, taking slaves, they fought for our kings, and their own. Nothing could stand in their path when they went into a killing rage.

I fought to keep my fear off my face. Berserker's were a myth, so my stepfather had probably sold me to a band of passing soldiers who would take their pleasure from my flesh before leaving me for dead, or selling me on.

"I could've sold you long ago, if I stripped you bare and put a bag over you head to hide those scars."

His hands pawed at me, and I shied away from his disgusting breath. He slapped me, then tore at my braid, letting my hair spill over my face and shoulders.

Bound as I was, I still could glare at him. I could do nothing to stop the sale, but I hoped my fierce expression told him I'd fight to the death if he tried to force himself on me.

His hand started to wander down towards my breast when a shadow moved on the edge of the clearing. It caught my eye and I startled. My stepfather stepped back as the warriors poured from the trees.

My first thought was that they were not men, but beasts. They prowled forward, dark shapes almost one with the shadows. A few wore animal pelts and held back, lurking on the edge of the woods. Two came forward, wearing the garb of warriors, bristling with weapons. One had dark hair, and the other long, dirty blond with a beard to match.

Their eyes glowed with a terrifying light.

As they approached, the smell of raw meat and blood wafted over us, and my stomach twisted. I was glad my stepfather hadn't fed me all day, or I would've emptied my guts on the ground.

My stepfather's face and tone took on the wheedling expression I'd seen when he was selling in the market.

"Good evening, sirs," he cringed before the largest, the blond with hair streaming down his chest.

They were perfectly silent, but the blond approached, fixing me with strange golden eyes.

Their faces were fair enough, but their hulking forms and the quick, light way they moved made me catch my breath. I had never seen such massive men. Beside them, my stepfather looked like an ugly dwarf.

"This is the one you wanted," my stepfather continued. "She's healthy and strong. She will be a good slave for you."

My body would've shaken with terror, if I were not bound so tightly.

A dark haired warrior stepped up beside the blond and the two exchanged a look.

"You asked for the one with scars." My stepfather took my hair and jerked my head back, exposing the horrible, silvery mass. I shut my eyes, tears squeezing out at the sudden pain and humiliation.

The next thing I knew, my stepfather's grip loosened. A grunt, and I opened my eyes to see the dark haired warrior standing at my side. My stepfather sprawled on the ground as if he'd been pushed.

The blond leader prodded a boot into my stepfather's side.

"Get up," the blond said, in a voice that was more a

growl than a human sound. It curdled my blood. My stepfather scrambled to his feet.

The black haired man cut away the last of my bonds, and I sagged forward. I would've fallen but he caught me easily and set me on my feet, keeping his arms around me. I was not the smallest woman, but he was a giant. Muscles bulged in his arms and chest, but he held me carefully. I stared at him, taking in his raven dark hair and strange gold eyes.

He tucked me closer to his muscled body.

Meanwhile, my stepfather whined. "I just wanted to show you the scars—"

Again that frightening growl from the blond. "You don't touch what is ours."

"I don't want to touch her." My stepfather spat.

Despite myself, I cowered against the man who held me. A stranger I had never met, he was still a safer haven than my stepfather.

"I only wish to make sure you are satisfied, milords. Do you want to sample her?" my stepfather asked in an evil tone. He wanted to see me torn apart.

A growl rumbled under my ear and I lifted my head. Who were these men, these great warriors who had bought and paid for me? The arms around my body were strong and solid, inescapable, but the gold eyes looking down at me were kind. The warrior ran his thumb across the pad of my lips, and his fingers were gentle for such a large, violent looking warrior. Under the scent of blood, he smelled of snow and sharp cold, a clean scent.

He pressed his face against my head, breathing in a deep breath.

The blond was looking at us.

"It's her," the black haired man growled, his voice so guttural. "This is the one."

One of his hands came to cover the side of my face and throat, holding my face to his chest in a protective gesture.

I closed my eyes, relaxing in the solid warmth of the warrior's body.

A clink of gold, and the deed was done. I'd been sold.

SOLD TO THE BERSERKERS

When Brenna's father sells her to a band of passing warriors, her only thought is to survive. She doesn't expect to be claimed by the two fearsome warriors who lead the Berserker clan. Kept in captivity, she is coddled and cared for, treated more like a savior than a slave. Can captivity lead to love? And when she discovers the truth behind the myth of the fearsome warriors, can she accept her place as the Berserkers' true mate?

∾

Sold to the Berserkers is a standalone, short, MFM ménage romance starring two huge, dominant warriors who make it all about the woman. Click to read now

ALSO BY LEE SAVINO

Sci Fi Romance

Draekons (Dragons in Exile) with Lili Zander (menage alien dragons)

Crashed spaceship. Prison planet. Two big, hulking, bronzed aliens who turn into dragons. The best part? The dragons insist I'm their mate.

Paranormal romance

The Berserker Saga and Berserker Brides (menage werewolves)

These fierce warriors will stop at nothing to claim their mates.

Bad Boy Alphas with Renee Rose (bad boy werewolves)

Never ever date a werewolf.

Contemporary Romance

Royal Bad Boy

I'm not falling in love with my arrogant, annoying, sex god boss. Nope. No way.

Royally Fake Fiancé

The Duke of New Arcadia has an image problem only a fiancé can fix. And I'm the lucky lady he's chosen to play Cinderella.

Beauty & The Lumberjacks

After this logging season, I'm giving up sex. For...reasons.

Her Marine Daddy

My hot Marine hero wants me to call him daddy...

Her Dueling Daddies

Two daddies are better than one.

Innocence: dark mafia romance with Stasia Black

I'm the king of the criminal underworld. I always get what I want. And she is my obsession.

Beauty's Beast: a dark romance with Stasia Black

Years ago, Daphne's father stole from me. Now it's time for her to pay her family's debt...with her body.

ABOUT GOLDEN ANGEL

Angel is an international best-selling BDSM and interracial romance author and self-described bibliophile with a "kinky" bent who loves to write stories for the characters in her head. If she didn't get them out, she's pretty sure she'd go just a little crazy.

She is happily married, old enough to know better but still too young to care, and a big fan of happily-ever-afters, strong heroes and heroines, and sizzling chemistry.

She believes the world is a better place when there's a little magic in it.

Sign up for the Angel Legion newsletter here - smarturl.it/ AngelNewsletter - and grab several FREE sexy stories immediately in a welcome message!

Read on for an excerpt from her alien romance, Mated on Hades...

EXCERPT: MATED ON HADES

"Welcome to your new home for the next four twenty-cycles," he said, stepping aside so she could enter the cabin behind him, his tone dryly sarcastic. "As you can see, you would have been better off with my parents."

Rather than telling him that the room was about the size of her entire living space back on Earth—and unlike her home there, this room wasn't crammed with equipment—Jules just looked around as she walked past him. Sparsely furnished, the massive bed on the far wall dominated the whole area. It was even bigger than the bed in her room at Tobik and Sirilla's, and she'd thought *that* was huge.

Turning around, she enjoyed the disgruntled look on Tarrik's face as he set her bag down next to the open closet door. Since his clothing seemed to consist mostly of pants and a kind of tunic vest that she'd seen on a lot of winged Hadesians, there was plenty of space for her meager belongings.

"This looks great," she said. "As long as you keep to your side of the bed."

Now his expression was almost infuriated. "Of course I will. I'm not the one who can't keep her hands to herself."

"Excuse me?" Jules' hands slammed onto her hips as she glared back at him. "Since when have I not kept my hands to myself?"

"Uh, that would be last night when you kissed me."

She gaped. "You kissed me!"

"I sure as hell did not," he snapped back. "I'm not even attracted to you."

"Is that why your cock was digging a hole in my stomach last night when *you kissed me*?"

"Look, just stay on whichever side of the bed you pick, keep your hands to yourself, and this trip will be over before you know it."

Jules was still sputtering and trying to find a good retort as he swept out of the room. *Jerk!* She couldn't believe she'd let him have the last word.

"Stupid butt monkey," she muttered, flopping back onto the bed just to see how it felt. It was ridiculously comfortable of course. Which only made her more irritated with him for some reason, even though he had nothing to do with it.

He'd definitely kissed her first.

At the very least, they'd kissed each other.

Her lips pursed as a wicked idea occurred to her. It would be playing with fire a little bit... but on the other hand, he definitely deserved it. And it would be even more amusing than keeping his ship grounded until her say so.

Just as that thought flickered through her mind, she felt the reverberations of the ship as it began to blast off. Excitement surged. She, Jules, who had never even thought she would see planet other than Earth, was now on her second spaceship this week and off to see a whole *bunch* of planets.

While part of her couldn't help but wonder what was happening back on Earth, if anyone was helping those in need, another part of her was thrilled to be on an adventure. New places, new beings, new things to see and do... If this was how traveling made Tarrik feel, no wonder he didn't want to give it up.

As soon as she thought it, she scowled. She didn't want to feel sympathy for him dammit.

Pushing any thoughts of the alien male aside, Jules made herself get up from the bed and start unpacking. The sooner she was done, the sooner she could explore the ship.

THE SYSTEMS WERE RUNNING PERFECTLY, the entire crew was happy, and Tarrik was feeling a lot better than he'd expected. The only thing that would make this trip better was if Juliette wasn't on board.

Not that she was in the way. No, she was entirely helpful, going out of her way to make herself useful.

Tarrik told himself he wasn't jealous over the way she and Mrik had obviously bonded. They definitely weren't behaving as though they were sexually attracted to each other—Tarrik knew that Mrik would never move on Tarrik's female regardless—but he still got a gnawing feeling in his stomach when he saw them laughing together. It might be more envy than jealousy though... she definitely didn't smile at him that way or laugh with him...

Not that he'd given her any reason to.

Because I don't want to, he reminded himself for the umpteenth time. The problem was that saying it wasn't making it true.

She was beautiful when she smiled. Engaging when she

laughed. The rest of the crew definitely liked her, she'd already made fast friends with his maintenance engineers, Lessys and Sasslys, who were both Vloss and mated to each other. When they asked if Juliette had ever seen anything like them before, she said they looked like miniature Godzillas, without the back plates. The whole crew found this hysterical when Myrik looked up what she was speaking of.

So he wasn't in the best mood by bedtime.

His mood got a hell of a lot worse when he laid down and Juliette announced she was going to take a shower.

"Great," he said. And then nearly choked when she started undressing right in the middle of the bedroom. She pulled her shirt over her head, revealing tanned skin, soft mounds of her breasts filling out her feminine support, a gently rounded stomach that he suddenly ached to draw his tongue over... When she began tugging down her pants, he finally managed to find his voice again even if it did sound like he was being strangled when he spoke. "What the gark are you doing?"

Juliette glanced at him and he bit back a groan as her pants slid to the ground, revealing muscled legs and tight-fitting panties. The white underwear wasn't the sexiest he'd ever seen, it was more utilitarian than anything else, and yet he found he couldn't look away. The temperature in the room seemed to have risen by a few degrees and his tail was lashing back and forth furiously as his cock started to swell.

"I'm taking a shower," she said, blinking at him like he'd said something incomprehensible.

"The shower is in there." Pointing to the facilities, he shifted slightly to hopefully cover up his growing erection.

"Why do you care?" she asked, pulling off her support garment. Tarrik almost whimpered as her rounded, full breasts were revealed, perfectly sized to fit in his palm, with tightly ruched brown nipples just begging for attention. His erection swelled to fullness and his tail had taken on a mind of its own—any attempt to control it was useless. "You're not attracted to me, remember?"

Turning, she bent at the waist to pull her undergarments down, giving him a glorious view of her ass before she sauntered into the bathroom.

Closing his eyes didn't help in the least. The image of her naked body was burned into his retinas. Gark it, he didn't even *want* to forget.

When he heard the water turn on, he did groan, because now all he could think about was the hot water sluicing over her body, caressing her skin the way he wanted to.

Garking...

Laying back in the bed, Tarrik jerked off the tunic he was going to sleep in out of respect for her. Immediately he fisted his hand around his shaft and groaned as he began to pump, closing his eyes and picturing her rounded bottom and the little smirk on her lips... the way the water would slide over her breasts and stomach and down between her legs... he hadn't gotten nearly as close a look of *that* as he'd wanted to.

He'd seen images of nude human females though, and his feverish brain extrapolated for him.

Wet flesh, ripe and ready for him.

He pumped his cock harder, faster as he imagined her bent over for him, the way she had taken off her underwear, his hand slapping against her ass as he pounded into her from behind, his tail twining around her breasts...

He wanted her *bad.*

Pleasure surged and his *jimen* spurted, sticky and hot onto his stomach, leaving him only slightly less wound up.

WAS HE... WAS HE MASTURBATING? JULES' paused as she washed her hair, her body flushing as she heard another low masculine groan, just barely audible to her. Yeah, so much for not being attracted to her.

Of course, she was very much in the same boat. Just stripping down in front of him had given her a little thrill. She'd never known she had a little bit of exhibitionist in her, but she'd definitely gotten turned on feeling his eyes sliding over her naked skin with every article of clothing she'd peeled off. It had made her feel freaking sexy.

Knowing he was out there jerking off after the little show she'd put on...

Well that just made her feel even sexier.

It didn't help that she hadn't gotten laid in... geez, it had been months since her last encounter with the male kind. So she also had a lot of pent-up sexual energy to work off.

Her hands moved over her body, slick and soapy, touching her hard nipples and massaging her breasts before moving down her stomach. Leaning back against the cool wall, she kept one hand on her breast while the other slipped between her pussy lips. Biting her lip to keep her own moans quiet, she closed her eyes and pictured him coming into the bathroom, watching her touch herself...

Then he wouldn't be able to stay back. He'd step in, crowding her in the shower, his body hot and hard against hers as he lifted her up, and she'd wrap her legs around his waist as she slid down his body and right onto his hard cock.

Shuddering, Jules managed to keep her noises to heavy breathing as she rubbed out a hard, fast orgasm that took the edge off but didn't completely satisfy her. She didn't want to take too long in the shower though; she definitely didn't want him to think she was in here getting off to him... the same way she was pretty sure he was getting off to her.

Stepping out of the shower, Jules quickly dried off and went into the main cabin. The lights were already dim and Tarrik was on his side of the bed, the sheets pulled up to his waist and he'd built a wall of cushions down the center of the bed. His muscled chest and arms were clearly visible— he'd taken off his tunic and it lay in a crumpled heap on the floor. Had he been wearing anything else? Or was he naked under the sheet?

Don't think about that!

In the dark, her body thrumming with sexual frustration, Jules was no closer to sleep than she had been when the lights had been turned on. Despite the wall of cushions between them, she was far, far too aware of the insanely sexy alien on the bed with her, less than a foot of distance separating them. How much body heat did a Hadesian emanate? Because she swore she could feel him.

Then she really did feel something, touching her ankle between the sheets, and she shrieked, kicking.

"Sorry, sorry!" Tarrik's deep voice actually sounded sincere. "That was my tail, sorry."

Jules' heart pounded so hard it felt like it was going to go right out of her chest as her fear of the unknown settled.

"Well get your tail under control," she hissed at him, pulling her legs up slightly, closer to her body and telling herself that she definitely was not going to think about the possibilities of a tail that had a mind of its own.

"It's not exactly easy," he hissed back. "I can *smell* your arousal. So don't bother lying and telling me that you aren't."

Heat flushed her cheeks and she was very glad the room was dark enough that he wouldn't be able to see her blush.

"That's just a physical response—and you were the one who started jerking off while I was in the shower!"

"You stripped down in front of me!"

"*You* said you weren't attracted to me!"

"I lied, alright?!" There was a strange ominous red glow in the darkness and suddenly cushions went flying. Tarrik loomed over her, wings spread slightly in his agitation. Holy fracking radiation. He freaking glowed in the dark. "I'm attracted to you, okay? That doesn't mean I want to mate you."

"I don't want to mate you either, you overgrown ignoramus."

"But you want to *fuck* me, right?" From the way he said 'fuck', she could tell he'd looked up the human word at some point but that it wasn't terminology he was used to. The glow of his skin brightened a little more, illuminating her body as he taunted her, his own sexual frustration clear on his face. It was eerie and sexy all at the same time and this time when his tail curled around her ankle, the heat of his flesh warming her skin, she didn't jump or kick.

"Oh shut up and do something useful with your mouth," she snarled back, reaching up to grab his face and pull his lips down to meet hers.

MATED ON HADES

The Celestial Mates agency always knows what - or who - you need.

TARRIK WOULD DO anything to avoid breaking his mother's heart, so he begrudgingly signs up for Celestial Mates and agrees to come home and settle down once the agency finds his match. There's just one catch: he's not ready to give up his free and easy life traveling the galaxy. And he's doing exactly as his mother asked, so what will it hurt if he makes himself as unappealing as possible on his mate application?

JULIETTE IS a woman on the run. Her attitude, and more importantly her hacking skills, have pissed off all the wrong people. Now the target of a contract hit, she's decided the solution to her problems is to leave the planet as fast as she can. The Celestial Mates program is exactly what she needs. By the time her "mate" realizes she's impossible to live with, hopefully it will be safe for her to return to earth. She wasn't counting on a seriously hot alien who looked like the devil and could do the most sinful things with his tail...

THE SPARKS FLY at first meeting when their chemistry ignites. But they can barely stand to be in the same room with each other.

THEY SHOULDN'T WORK AT ALL.

BUT CELESTIAL MATES always knows best.

ALSO BY GOLDEN ANGEL

Free stories on her website

Stronghold Doms and Venus Rising (Contemporary Bdsm)

Bridal Discipline and the Domestic Discipline Quartet
(Victorian Domestic Discipline- this is Lee Savino's favorite!!!!! :)

Big Bad Bunnies (paranormal romance)

Dark erotic romance under the pen name Sinistre Ange

Standalone novels - including a sci fi romance involving an alien who has a naughty tail...